LOVING THE MOVIE STAR

JENNIFER YOUNGBLOOD

ARBOR
HOUSE

YOUR FREE BOOK AWAITS

Get Beastly Charm: A Contemporary retelling of beauty & the beast as a welcome gift when you sign up for my newsletter. You'll get information on my new releases, book recommendations, discounts, and other freebies.

Get the book at:

http://bit.ly/freebookjenniferyoungblood

1

The cool water was soothing against Blade's tight shoulders as he sliced through the water in smooth, rhythmic strokes. Twenty minutes later, when he stepped out of the lap pool and dried off, he felt a little better. He was grateful the hotel had a private pool for VIP guests, because he much preferred swimming to exercising in the workout room. As he walked back to his suite, the jitters returned. The day after tomorrow, Christian Ross was arriving on set and they'd spend the next few days filming together. Acting alongside the great Christian Ross was more than a little intimidating. The man was Hollywood royalty, after all. Blade still found it hard to believe he'd gotten this chance to star in a heavy-hitting action movie. *Hostile Territory* would be Christian's last movie as the famed Jase Scott, rogue CIA operative. This movie was a step in grooming Blade to take over the series. Christian would pass the torch, along with the keys to the kingdom. Now all Blade had to do was keep from blowing it.

He offered a perfunctory nod to the burly bodyguard standing outside the door of his hotel suite.

"How ya doing, Mr. Sloan?" the man said in a sing-song, island tone.

"Good, thank you." He tried to recall the guy's name. It was Tal ... from Tonga? Or was it Samoa? Blade stepped into the spacious suite, decked out in what his personal assistant termed Hollywood Regency —fitting considering he was here making a movie. Although, Blade didn't have a clue about interior design. All he knew was that the suite was ultra-fancy with the lavishly curved furniture and shiny metal accents, like something out of an old Hollywood movie. He strode over to the mini-fridge in the corner and grabbed a water. He guzzled down the entire bottle in a few swigs, then crushed the empty plastic with one hand and tossed it into the trash like he was scoring a basket. "Two points."

He sighed, not looking forward to the long afternoon and evening stretching before him—too much time to think about everything that could wrong the day after tomorrow. He sighed, pushing aside the negative thoughts. He needed to resume the mental exercises his acting coach had taught him. He forced his mind to run through the litany of events for the evening. He'd eat dinner with his older brother Doug, who was about as conversational as a fence post, in the hotel restaurant. Then he'd meander through the hotel lobby to the back terrace and make his way to the beach for a walk at sunset. And, of course, his bodyguard would linger nearby like an ominous shadow, reminding him that his life was forever changed. He was no longer Blake Stevens but Blade Sloan, a rising star. There were scores of people who'd give anything to be in his shoes, so he shouldn't complain. He was grateful for this opportunity, but his climb to the top was starting to feel lonely. He was tempted to go out and enjoy the nightlife to blow off some steam, even if his bodyguard insisted on tagging along. But Doug would have a coronary at the mere mention of the idea. Doug was a rule follower to the nth degree, always warning Blade about the importance of keeping up a good appearance so the studio officials would consider him easy to work with. Until Blade became a household name, things were tenuous. At least that's what Doug kept shoving down his throat. Blade scowled, then felt a twinge of guilt for mentally throwing his older brother under the bus. Somewhere, hidden deep within Doug's iron-clad exterior was a good guy—Blade was sure of it. Thanks to Doug, Blade had gotten his start, so it seemed only fair to bring Doug on as his manager. When they started filming *Hostile Territory*, the director took one look at Doug and cast him as Blade's body double, which was a perk for Doug who loved acting. From a distance, Blade and Doug looked similar. Both were just over six feet tall with a lean, muscular build. Both had dark brown hair and rugged features. Were it not for the difference in their eye color, they might've passed for twins. Doug's eyes were greenish-brown whereas Blade's were blue. Doug's features were a little harsher than Blade's, his face slightly thinner. And he looked older, but not much.

It was good to have family around, even though Doug drove him crazy. Deep down, however, Blade knew Doug was right. He had to remain focused to be able to give his all on set. And he couldn't do that by staying out half the night at some nightclub, not when the bulk of his day tomorrow would be spent running through his lines so he'd be in top condition to act alongside Christian Ross the next day. Blade missed his friends in LA and toyed with the idea of either going there or home to Denver for Christmas. Filming for the movie went right up until the day before Christmas Eve and then resumed after the first of the year. It might be nice to get off the island for a week. He was enjoying Oahu, loved the beach, but it was hard to get in the Christmas spirit when everything was bright and sunny. He missed the snow and the Christmas traditions of decorating a tree and snuggling by a fire with a steaming cup of hot chocolate. Christmas had always been a big deal in his home growing up. His mother insisted on drenching the house in decorations and started playing Christmas music around-the-clock the day after Thanksgiving. A pang shot through him as he thought of his mother who'd passed away. Even though it was eleven years ago, he still missed her every day. What he would give to be able to talk to her again, put his arms around her to tell her how much he loved and appreciated her. She always knew the right thing to say when he asked for advice. She would know how to help him navigate through this stressful time. From the outside looking in, an actor's life seemed like a never-ending thrill ride; but in reality, it was often mundane with countless hours spent on set—repeating takes of the same scene until the director finally captured the perfect shot.

Briefly, he thought about calling his co-star Eden to help ease the loneliness, but it wouldn't be fair to give her the wrong idea. He chuckled, knowing it usually only took about five minutes before Eden started getting on his nerves. Besides that, he had a strict rule of not dating other actors. He didn't want to be one of those actors who "fell in love" with every female co-star. Plus, if Doug even thought he was entertaining the idea of going out with Eden, he'd put together some elaborate PR campaign to generate hype around a budding romance. No, Blade certainly didn't want that. He didn't want to draw any more attention to his personal life than there was already.

Blade went down the hall to his room and tossed his towel over the back of a chair. He'd just come out of the shower, and thrown on a pair of shorts and t-shirt from the day before, when he spotted the box of chocolate-covered macadamia nuts in the center of the bed. Natalie his personal assistant, was the motherly type, always going the extra mile to make him feel comfortable. She knew how much he loved these things and must've gotten him a box. "Thank you, Natalie," he said aloud as he picked up the box and lifted off the lid. His heart lurched when he saw what was inside—the one thing he hoped he'd never see again. He dropped the box like a hot coal, causing the single white rose to fall on the bed. The edges of the petals were tipped with blood that splattered across the white bedspread. There was a note—the same style as before.

His mind whirled. Had the stalker followed him to Hawaii? It seemed impossible ... ridiculous. And yet, the evidence was right in front of him, plain as day. Beads of sweat lined his brow as he took in a ragged breath. Somehow, the person got past hotel security and his private security team before coming into his suite, to his bedroom. He glanced around, goose bumps lifting over his flesh. Had the stalker gone through his things? Was she lurking around the hotel, watching him? The thoughts made his stomach roil.

Things had been quiet the past month since he'd come to Hawaii to film. So much so that he'd begun to hope the ordeal was finally over. He'd felt safe and protected here, like nothing bad could touch him. He barked out a cynical laugh as he stumbled back and slumped down in a nearby chair. He should've known better. Stalkers didn't give up so easily. That's what the detective in LA had told him when he first started receiving random gifts and notes at the studio. At first, the gifts had been harmless—a teddy bear, bouquet of flowers, box of chocolates. Then he started finding items on the doorstep of his condo with notes attached—*I saw you today on set. Why do you keep ignoring me?*

The month before Blade left for Hawaii, the roses had started arriving. They were left in private areas where only Blade or his security team could go—his dressing room at the studio, his trailer on location, the bedroom of his condo. Each white rose was tinged with blood and had a note with it. The notes were made with words cut from magazines and newspapers. There were never any fingerprints or other distinguishing features that could point to the sender. He'd learned from lab tests by the police department that the blood came from small animals. Each note seemed to grow more desperate and menacing. Detectives investigated his case for six long months, turning up nothing. Who was this deranged person who got her jollies out of sending him random gifts and notes? Blade assumed it was a woman, but who the heck knew? A morbid curiosity propelled him to stand and read the note, making sure not to touch anything. *Did you think I wouldn't find you? You're stabbing a stake through my heart! I need you.*

His throat grew thick with fear as he swallowed and sat back down, trying to determine his best course of action. There was a single knock before the door burst open. Blade looked up as Doug stepped in. Doug took one look at Blade's face and knew something was wrong. "What up?" he demanded, the corners of his jaws twitching.

Blade motioned with his eyes to the bed. Doug's eyes popped as he flinched. "When did this come?"

"It was on the bed when I got back from taking a swim."

He swore. "How in the heck did someone manage to get past security?"

"I don't know." The stricken look on Doug's face mirrored Blade's own feelings. Why was this happening to him? It wasn't as if he was a megastar. Granted, if this movie went as well as his agent was predicting, he'd become a superstar. But up to this point, his acting résumé was limited to being regular on a long-running soap opera and the star of an independent film with a scant audience.

Doug stuck his head out the door and yelled. "Natalie, get in here. You too, Tal," he snapped.

A moment later, Tal hesitantly stepped into the bedroom. His jaw went slack when he saw the rose and splattered blood. "W-what's this?"

Doug eyed him. "That's exactly what I want to know."

Natalie came rushing in. She took one look at the bed and gasped, her hands going to her mouth. "Oh, no. When did this come?"

"I went to the pool to swim a few laps. It was here when I got back." Even as he spoke the words, the scope of the situation hit home. The walls seemed to be closing in around Blade, making it hard to get a good breath.

A wild look came into Natalie's eyes as she turned to Doug. "What're we going to do?"

Doug glared at Tal. "Did you see anyone enter the suite?"

Tal spread his hands. "No, I didn't see nobody."

Blade could feel the large man's anxiety, noticed he was starting to sweat.

Doug stepped up to him, his voice heavy with accusation. "Were you standing in front of the door the whole time?"

"Um, yeah," Tal said, but his head seemed to shrink into his thick neck as he broke eye contact with Doug and looked down at the floor.

"Tell me the truth," Doug's voice rose, his face going flush.

Tal drew back. "I mean, I was there the whole time ... except for the time when I went to the bathroom."

"What?" Doug raged. "I hired you to watch the suite, not hang out in the bathroom."

"A man's gotta relieve himself," Tal mumbled.

Doug got up in his face. "What was that?"

The whites of Tal's eyes popped as he blinked rapidly. "I had to go to the bathroom. I tried to call you, but you didn't pick up. Maybe you should've hired two bodyguards instead of one. I was only gone for a couple of minutes."

A murderous look came over Doug and for a split second, Blade thought he was going to lose it and throw a punch at Tal, which wouldn't have ended well considering Tal was solid muscle and outweighed Doug by at least a hundred pounds. Doug balled his fists, his face squeezing with anger, but then he seemed to regain his control. "You're fired," he barked.

"What?" Tal frowned.

"You heard me," Doug hurled through clenched teeth.

Blade jumped to his feet. "Hey, Doug, take it down a notch. It's not Tal's fault. He's right. We should've hired two bodyguards per shift instead of one."

Tal looked surprised, then vindicated.

Doug spun around, eyes flashing. "And just whose idea was it to scale down?"

The hair on Blade's neck rose. He hated it when Doug got all high and mighty and started bullying everyone. "Mine," he said evenly.

"That's right, little brother, you made that decision despite my better judgment." He jabbed a finger into Blade's chest. "And look what happened." He shook his head, giving Blade a withering look. "When're you gonna learn to listen to me?"

The condescension in Doug's voice was the last straw. Blade felt the urge to punch something. "Stop talking down to me like I'm ten."

Doug smirked. "I'll make a deal with you, little brother, you start acting like a grown-up and I'll treat you like one."

Blade looked Doug in the eye, not backing down an inch. "Don't forget who pays the bills, brother." He caught the momentary flicker of uncertainty in Doug's eyes and knew he had him. Doug could get on his high-horse and act like he called the shots, but Blade was the one holding all the cards. He turned to Tal. "You're not fired. You got that?"

Tal looked relieved, Doug furious.

Doug gave him a steely look. "You can stand here and act like the big man on campus all day, but if you don't start improving your performance, we'll all be out on our ears."

"What're you talking about?" He hated the smug expression on Doug's face. Hated the unease that trickled down his spine. Hated how Doug took every opportunity to prove his superiority.

Doug straightened to his full height so they were standing eye to eye. "The director pulled me aside and expressed concern about your lackluster performance this week. He said if you have a prayer of making it in the big league, you're gonna have to make some drastic improvements. You're coming across stiff in front of the camera."

"You're lying. If Matt had a problem, he'd come to me." His voice sounded desperate in his ears.

"You sure about that, bro? Matt came to me because he's afraid you're too fragile to hear the truth."

Blade rocked back, not sure what to make of this. Sure, he'd been a little off lately, but that happened to everybody. It was hard to be a hundred percent all the time. "I'm not fragile," he grumbled. Hearing that Matt had gone behind his back was a kick in the pants.

Doug sighed heavily. "Look, bro, I don't have to tell you what an amazing opportunity this is. Christian Ross is coming Thursday." His voice took on an urgent note. "You've got to deliver. If you don't, someone else will."

No one could ruffle Blade's feathers faster than Doug. The comment sliced through him like a knife as he balled his fists. "Like you? Is that what you mean?" His voice rose. "Go ahead and say it because I know you're thinking it. It should be you starring in the movie. You're the one who's been dreaming of making it big your entire life. I'm just your kid brother who happened to be on set at the right time ... got the whole thing dumped in my lap." He was tired of carrying guilt over something beyond his control. It wasn't his fault the casting director had picked him for the soap opera role. And he'd worked his butt off ever since, trying to prove himself.

Doug chuckled as he shook his head. "You should heed your own advice and take it down a notch, bro. Those are your issues, not mine."

"Don't patronize me." Blade saw the uncomfortable looks on Natalie and Tal's faces. They looked embarrassed to be caught in the middle of the argument.

"Go ahead, throw your little tantrum and then be done with it, because you've got a job to do." Doug motioned toward the bed. "And I've got a mess to clean up." He retrieved his phone from his pocket.

Blade tensed. "What're you doing?"

He rolled his eyes like Blade was a moron for asking. "For starters, I'm calling the hotel security to get them to check the surveillance footage, then I'm calling the cops."

"No," Blade blurted.

"What do you mean *no*? We don't have another option. The stalker followed you to Hawaii. This is more serious than we thought."

Blade knew Doug was right. It was serious, and calling the cops was the sensible thing to do, but Blade couldn't stand the thought of everything starting up again—the heightened security with people following him 24/7. Everyone on eggshells, waiting for something bad to happen. "I can't handle it right now." He hated to admit that out loud, but it was true. He was sucking wind as it was. The pressure was getting to him. Somehow, he had to push the stress aside and focus on his craft. He needed space to prove he could be an A list actor. "If what you said about Matt is true, then I need to up my game. I can't do that with the police breathing down my neck." For a fraction of a moment, Blade felt like he might be getting through to Doug, until he shook his head.

"Sorry, bro. I understand where you're coming from. But above all else, my job is to keep you safe. We have to notify the police, and we have to boost security—make sure there are people with you at all times."

An invisible noose tightened around Blade's neck. "No."

"You have to be reasonable, bro."

His head was on fire. "I refuse to go back to the way things were in LA. I couldn't even take a leak without someone looking over my shoulder." He had to get out of here, away from Doug, so he could think clearly. He pushed past Doug.

"Where are you going?" Doug yelled.

"Out!"

"Should I follow him?" Tal said.

Blade spun around, pointing. "If you want to keep your job, you'll stay put!"

Tal glanced at Doug like he was unsure what to do.

Doug blew out a heavy breath. "Do as he says and give him some space." He shot Blade a death glare. "If anything happens to him, it'll be his own stupid fault."

Blade stormed out of the suite. Adrenaline pumped through his veins as he half-jogged down the hall of the hotel. He didn't know where he was going, but it would be outside the reach of Doug's all-seeing eye.

2

Dani managed to sit down in a seat before the bus rolled forward. She reached in her purse, grabbed her phone, and put her earbuds in. Then she turned the music up full blast to drown out the noise from the people around her. She'd done it this time! Let her temper get the best of her. But it wasn't her fault that her jerk boss—ex-boss—was so anal. Her thoughts raced back to the events that had taken place earlier. Rena, Mr. Hadler's regular assistant, took the day off, so Dani was left doing double duty, manning the reception desk and helping Mr. Hadler with whatever he needed. From the minute Mr. Hadler stepped through the door that morning, Dani could tell he was in a foul mood. "Good morning," she'd said pleasantly as he entered. He didn't acknowledge her greeting, frowning as he walked right past her. Things went downhill from there. He barked orders at her all day—never satisfied with anything she did. The coffee she brought him was too watery. The next batch she brewed was too strong. And, according to him, she was taking too long to find the files he requested. Everything came to a head when he asked her to draft a letter, welcoming a new tenant. Mr. Hadler and his daughter Jane managed a large industrial complex near the airport where they leased commercial space to tenants. Dani tried to explain that she'd never written this type of letter before and wasn't sure how to do it. Mr. Hadler told her to use her best judgment, so she did. She Googled it and thought she did a pretty good job. But when she took the letter into his office and showed him, his face turned blood red. Then he tore the letter in half and tossed it in the garbage. She just stood there gaping while he fished the letter out of the garbage and taped it back together so he could point out the one word he didn't like. Stewing over the situation, she took it back to her desk and corrected it. Just because he was the boss didn't give him the right to treat his employees like dirt. Mr. Hadler was known for being cranky, most people tried to stay out of his way. Dani was ashamed of herself for remaining silent while he humiliated her. But the situation had taken her completely off guard. When she placed the corrected letter on his desk, she assumed the matter was closed. Instead, he declared, "The ending paragraph is all wrong." He wadded it up and tossed it at the garbage, but it landed on the floor instead.

Dani's hand flew to her hip, her eyes flashing. "Well, why didn't you tell me that earlier, when you changed that one word?"

His forehead wrinkled and his head turned red, emphasizing his baldness. "Are you questioning me?"

Dani's first instinct was to run as far away from Mr. Hadler as she could. But she straightened her shoulders instead. "I'm simply suggesting that if you'd told me earlier, it would've saved us both a whole lot of time ... and paper," she added, making a point of looking at the crumpled ball on the floor.

"What kind of nitwit did the agency send me? This is intolerable." He pounded his fist, then let out a string of curses that would've made a rapper blush.

Dani flinched like she'd been slapped. Had he really just called her a nitwit? An incredulous laugh bubbled in her throat. Her face burned like a dozen sunburns. Mr. Hadler was referring to the temp agency that originally hired Dani and sent her to work here before she came on as a permanent employee. It took every ounce of control Dani could muster to keep her voice even as she looked him in the eye. "Mr. Hadler, I'm sorry you're not happy with the letter, but I don't appreciate your insults, or your foul language."

His eyes widened, then narrowed. "If you don't like it, then maybe you should improve your quality of work," he blustered.

That's all it took for her to lose it. She leaned forward, the palms of her hands resting on his desk. "Mr. Hadler, you are a mean, spiteful old man. Do you ever wonder what your employees whisper behind your back?" Her voice rose. "Do you?"

He jerked, lips vanishing into a tight line.

"They can't stand the sight of you. And after working here for a month, I can see why. You're a bully." She shook her head in disgust. "And all the money in the world won't be enough to save you in the end. I pity you."

He stood. "You're fired," he roared. "Get out!"

"Gladly," she shot back, then turned on her heel and marched out. It wasn't until she reached the reception desk that she realized what she'd done. *Crap!* Another job down the tubes. And she actually liked this one. Well, she liked it, except for having to deal with that creep. With shaky hands, she grabbed her purse, unable to keep tears from pooling in her eyes. She blinked, forcing them away. She'd be darned if she'd let that old man see her cry.

Jim Baker the personnel manager came running after her in the parking lot. He waved his arms. "Hey, what happened in there?"

She offered a rubbery smile. "Didn't you hear? I thought the whole office heard. Mr. Hadler fired me." The words cut leaving her mouth.

He brought his hands to his head, fingers clutching his hair. "There must be some mistake. You can't go. We need you. You're the sixth receptionist we've had this year."

She let out a humorless laugh. "That's because no one can work for that man. He's intolerable."

He blew out a long breath. "Mr. Hadler's old and cantankerous, but the man's made more money than you and I'll see in our lifetimes."

"As if that gives him an excuse to belittle his employees," she snapped.

"I know, you're right." He rubbed a hand across his forehead. "Look, it's almost Christmas. I'll be hard-pressed to find anyone else to fill your position. Why don't you come back inside, and let's see if we can get this worked out? I'm sure if you'll apologize—"

She belted out a hard laugh. "Me apologize? I don't think so. Jim, I'm sorry my leaving puts you in a hard position, but there's no way I'm apologizing to Mr. Hadler. Not when I didn't do anything wrong."

"But if you don't, I can't fix this." His voice had a whiny edge to it.

"The only way you could fix it is if you put your foot down and stop letting Mr. Hadler ridicule his employees."

He gave her a nervous laugh. "You know I can't do that, he's the boss."

She lifted her chin. "Yep, that about sums it up." Jim would spend the rest of his career cowering to Mr. Hadler at the expense of the other employees. "It was nice knowing you Jim," she said, walking away.

The bus stopped and more people got on. Dani surfaced from her thoughts and realized how crowded the bus had become. Her eye caught on a guy about her age sitting a few seats away. Wow, he was really good-looking with chiseled features and crystal blue eyes. His hair was messy, and he had that bad-boy edge Dani found so irresistible. The old Dani might've finagled a way to sit next to him and strike up a conversation. Maybe she'd flirt a little, perhaps go on a couple of dates before he left the island and returned to his regular life. But she was turning over a new leaf—trying to be responsible for once, which is why she'd taken the job as a receptionist and made the long trek into town each day. She couldn't live in Samantha and Finn's guesthouse forever. She was passionate about her food blog and hoped it would, eventually, make enough money to sustain her. Until then, she'd have to find something else. She tore her eyes away from the guy and looked out the window at the craggy shoreline and foamy waves, spraying mist into the salty air. No matter how long she lived here, she never grew tired of the beauty of the island. Her mother kept trying to talk her into moving home to Sacramento to help with her boutique, but Hawaii had gotten into Dani's blood, and she didn't want to leave.

She glanced at the guy again. There was something compelling about him that made him hard to ignore—the kind of guy who commanded an audience wherever he went. If he'd looked her way, she would've smiled, but he seemed distracted. Oh, well. It was better this way. She needed to focus on getting another job, not getting caught up in some tourist. They'd go out and share a few laughs before he went back to the mainland. He'd promise to keep in touch, and they'd never see each other again. Such was the nature of life on an island. She'd been through the drill more times than she could count.

At the next bus stop, even more people piled on. All the seats were taken, leaving people no other option but to crowd into the aisles. Dani was surprised and impressed when the guy stood and let a woman with a small child take his seat. He moved up toward her, trying to find a good place to stand. Pretty soon, he was standing right in front of her. Now that he was closer, she noticed that he looked a little green around the gills. *Poor guy.* No wonder he kept staring straight ahead. It probably helped to maintain eye contact with the road.

———

CONCENTRATE ON THE ROAD, Blade commanded himself as he clutched the bar that went from floor to ceiling. After rushing out of the hotel, he hopped on the first bus that came along. In retrospect that probably wasn't the smartest idea. Blade was prone to carsickness, and being crammed in a stuffy bus on a winding road wasn't helping matters. His stomach lurched with every turn. He'd given up his seat to the woman and child, partly out of kindness and partly because he thought it might help to stand.

It wasn't.

He was getting sicker by the minute. Someone touched his arm.

"Are you okay?"

He looked sideways at the girl sitting in the seat to his right. She was around his age and very pretty. He managed a tight smile. "I'm okay. Thanks." Big mistake taking his eyes off the road, however. Nausea rolled over him like a tidal wave, followed by vomit. He gurgled trying to hold it back, but it exploded like a stink bomb all over him and the girl. Shock registered in her eyes as she jumped, then winced.

People around him gasped and shrank back, glaring at him like he had the plague. A few even started cursing. "I'm so sorry," he uttered.

The girl looked as mortified as he felt.

"Ew, it reeks! What's that smell?" This came from the teenager one seat in front of where he stood.

A woman pointed as if identifying a criminal from a lineup. "It's him. He vomited."

Blade wanted to shrivel up and die, but there was nothing he could do but stand there, enduring the humiliation. His shirt was wet and sticky, chunks clinging to it. The stench hit him full force, making him want to vomit again. The people around him were averting their noses. A body builder type wearing a wife beater shirt was standing beside him. From the sneer on his face, Blade thought he might attack him any minute.

Blade held up a hand. "Sorry, man. It was an accident."

The man's eyes narrowed to slits as he called Blade a couple of not-so-nice names.

Suddenly, the situation struck Blade as funny, as a disbelieving laugh bubbled in his throat. If only Doug could see him now. It was a good thing he wasn't yet an A-list actor, easily recognized. Otherwise, the press would have a heyday. He sniggered and then the laughter grew until he could no longer contain it. He had to admit, it felt good to release the tension, even though he looked ridiculous.

The muscle man bunched his thick eyebrows. "Why're you laughing?" When Blade didn't answer, he clenched his fist. "I asked you a question."

The girl jumped up, eyes blazing as she turned on the muscle man. "Give the guy a break, Hulk Hogan. *Geez.* Can't you see he's sick?"

Muscle man's eyes bulged. "Hey, lady, don't blame me." He pointed at Blade. "This bozo comes on the bus and vomits everywhere, more particularly on you, and now you're defending him? Unbelievable!"

"It was an accident," she countered. "It's obvious the poor guy's been through the wringer. Look at him. He's pathetic."

All eyes turned to Blade. He glanced down at his shirt. Yep, he did look pathetic. He'd run out without his phone or wallet. When the bus driver demanded payment, he'd pulled out a five-dollar-bill—the only cash he had—and shoved it at her. She tried to give him change and a transfer pass, but he'd pushed past her and sat down. It wasn't until about a half hour later that Blade realized his predicament. Then the sickness hit.

"Show a little compassion, people," the girl said, reaching over to yank the cord along the ceiling. A second later, the bus screeched to a halt.

"Come on," she said, slipping in front of him. Her expression held the tenacity of a thousand warriors facing down the approaching enemy. It went through Blade's mind that this was the kind of girl he'd like to have in his corner. "These people wouldn't know the definition of compassion if it hit them in the face," she grumbled. She threw a glance over her shoulder at Blade. "We've gotta get off." She threaded through the crowd, Blade following closely behind.

When they stepped off the bus, people cheered.

"Morons," she yelled, shaking her fist as the bus rolled away.

Blade turned to his defender, realizing he didn't even know her name. Then he glanced at her pink sundress, which had taken the full brunt of the vomit.

She looked down, wrinkling her nose in disgust.

"I'm sorry," he offered again, feeling like a louse.

She sighed. "I guess it's par for the day I've had."

"You too, huh?"

"Yep," she clipped matter-of-factly.

"What you did back there was awesome, by the way."

She pushed her purse strap higher up on her shoulder. "Thanks," she said offhandedly. Then she flicked her wrists like she was itching to do something about her clothes, but what could she do? Not much at the moment.

"I don't even know your name." On the bus, he'd found her attractive even though he was about to barf. But looking at her now, he realized she was gorgeous with soulful cocoa-colored eyes, high cheekbones, and a generous mouth. Plus, her thick mane of curly hair was the stuff of dreams. She was tall—about 5'10" and thin, but not fragile. This girl could hold her own ... obviously.

Amusement lit her eyes, turning them a warm caramel. "Maybe we should save the introductions for later, when we're not standing on the side of the road, drenched in vomit."

He chuckled. "Uh, yeah, I suppose you're right." The sting of embarrassment hit him full force. He'd put them in this position.

"Mokoli'i Park's just around the bend. They have outside showers where we can get cleaned up."

"Moko what?" he said dubiously. "That's a mouthful."

She laughed. "It's Hawaiian, but the park's also known as Chinaman's Hat."

"That's easier to remember than the Moko—whatever. Why's it called Chinaman's Hat?"

A smile curved her lips. "You ask a lot of questions, throw-up boy."

His jaw went slack, heat creeping up his neck. "Did you really just call me *throw-up boy*?"

She shrugged. "If the shoe fits ..." She motioned with her head. "Come on, I'm starting to get crusty."

3

When Dani got up this morning and took the bus into work, she never imagined she'd get fired from her job and end up in this crazy circumstance with some guy who up-chucked all over her. She'd just been thinking how her life was getting a little mundane and that she needed to step outside herself, get out more. Well, she'd done that—just not in the way she expected. She chuckled inwardly, wondering what her older sister Samantha would say about this. Samantha was always teasing Dani, saying how she had a knack for finding trouble. Well, she'd certainly found something ... but what exactly she'd found had yet to be determined.

Dani looked across the shower at him (she didn't even know his name). He was certainly dreamy with those arresting blue eyes as clear as the water at Sunset Beach on a cloudless, summer day. He'd removed his shirt and was holding it underneath the spray of water. She couldn't help but gawk mentally at his well-defined pecs and sculpted abs. It was obvious the guy knew his way around a gym. He was tan, but not surfer tan. Hmm ... what was his story? Was he a tourist? She'd not seen him remove a wallet or phone from his shorts before he stepped underneath the shower.

It felt good to wash off the gunk. She held up her hair, letting the water run over her shoulders and down her dress. She'd wondered if her dress would be ruined, but it seemed to be coming clean. Now she was left with another predicament—how to dry off. She squeegeed herself off the best she could with her hands. At least it was sunny today, unusual during the rainy season on the North Shore. Maybe it wouldn't take too long to air dry. The wind picked up. She rubbed her arms, warding off the chill.

He walked over to her with long, fluid strides. She wondered if he might put his shirt back on, but he held it in his hand instead. Okay, she needed to make a mental note to focus on his face. A sheepish grin stole over his lips, causing crinkles to appear around his eyes. "You look better."

Keep your eyes trained on his face. "So do you."

"I know I keep saying this, but I really am sorry for putting you in this predicament."

She felt herself smile. "It's okay."

He looked hopeful as he gave her a searching look. "I can almost believe you mean that."

A large smile broke over her face. "I do." The relief that washed over him was endearing. Dani had seen a lot of good-looking guys in her lifetime, but it was rare to find someone easy on the eyes with a good personality. Her sister found a great guy when she least expected it, and they were marvelously happy together with two sons. Dani always teased Samantha that with Finn taken, there was no hope for the rest of the female population. Looking at this gorgeous guy, Dani was reminded of how untrue that was. Well, as far as looks and first appearances went, anyway. But she knew from sad experience that first appearances could be deceptive. The old Dani might be tempted to get all starry-eyed and fall head-over-heels for this guy, but the new and improved Dani was trying hard to be responsible. She'd done a good deed—helped the poor guy out, but that's all. She wasn't naïve enough to believe this guy might play a part in her future.

He looked toward the island. "Chinaman's Hat. I get it now. It looks just like a hat someone left floating in the water."

"Yes, it does."

"Do you mind if we get a closer look?"

"Not at all."

They walked to the edge of the shore and sat down on a rock wall.

"It looks so close ... like we could just hop over there."

"Some people wade over during low tide, but most people either take paddle boards or kayaks. It's not as close as it looks. It's about four football-field lengths away."

"That's crazy. I'd like to go sometime."

"You should."

"Maybe we could go together."

She jerked slightly at the inference. "Maybe," she said evasively.

He cast a sidelong glance at her, a hint of teasing lighting his eyes. "So, do I get the pleasure of knowing the name of the wonderful woman who stood up for me?"

"Danielle Fairchild, but my friends call me Dani."

He held out his hand. She paused a fraction of a second before placing her hand in his. A tingle ran through her when their skin touched. *Interesting.* He clasped his fingers around hers. "It's nice to meet you, Dani. I'm Blake Stevens."

"Nice to meet you, Blake." It was then that she realized he was still holding her hand. She gave him a questioning look. He only chuckled and released it. "So, are you here on vacation?" She asked the question, knowing he probably was. He'd respond that he'd been here for a week already and was leaving tomorrow. That was just her luck. Then again, he'd said he'd like to go to Chinaman's Hat some-time in the future, so maybe ...

"No, for work."

She cocked her head, hope springing in her breast. "Really? You live on the island?"

"No, just here temporarily."

"Oh." She crashed back to earth. Just as she thought, he was only passing through. Over the past five years she'd gotten used to people coming and going, such was life in Hawaii. But she'd learned, and made a rule of not getting too attached. "What type of work do you do?" She caught the tightening of his jaw, could tell he was trying to figure out how to answer. Her curiosity was piqued as she turned, studying him.

"My brother's a body double in a movie being filmed here."

"That's exciting."

"Yeah, I suppose."

"You don't like the movie industry?"

"I guess you could say I have a love/hate relationship with the hoopla. But my brother lives for it. He's wanted to be an actor for as long as I can remember."

"What movie is it?"

He shifted, and then made a zipping motion over his lips. "Sorry, I'm not at liberty to discuss it ... you know, nondisclosure agreements. Yada, yada, yada. Stuff like that."

She laughed. "Yep, I understand all about stuff."

"How about you? What's your story? Are you here on vacation?"

"No, I live here."

"Wow, that's neat. Do you like it?"

"It's great."

He motioned at the splendid sight before them. "Life on an island sounds like a dream come true."

"Sometimes, although living in Hawaii's a lot different from vacationing in Hawaii."

"Yeah, I can see that." He grinned. "I'm mean it's not every day you get thrown-up on, right?"

"Definitely a first."

"Are you from here?"

"No, from Sacramento." When he remained quiet, she knew he was waiting for her to expound. "My sister and her husband live here. They have two boys. I live with them ... in their guesthouse."

"Guesthouse, huh? Sounds posh."

"It's okay," she said casually. Samantha and Finn didn't like broadcasting their wealth. "Lots of houses here have attached apartments and guesthouses. The cost of living is so high that people take on renters to help offset their mortgage payments."

"I see." His blue eyes appraised her, shooting a jolt of energy through her. There was something magnetic about him. Not that he was trying to draw attention to himself, but some innate trait that came as easy to him as breathing. She'd been drawn to him on the bus, but now that it was just the two of them the connection was even stronger. With his rugged features, messy hair, and piercing eyes, he could pass for a movie star. If his brother looked anything like Blake, she could see how he would do well with acting. "Your brother's here for an acting job. What do you do?"

"Well, to hear my brother tell it, I don't do anything well."

Underneath the sarcasm, she caught a trace of hurt. But then he flashed a disarming smile. "Sorry, I don't mean to drag you into my family drama."

"No worries." She got the impression he did that a lot, used a smile to deflect his true feelings. If she had a smile like that, she'd use it too.

He waved a hand. "Enough about me, tell me about you."

She pursed her lips together. "Hmm ... that's the second time you've sidestepped my question."

"What do you mean?"

"You don't wanna tell me what it is that you do."

"I'd tell you, but then I'd have to kill you," he said straight-faced, then couldn't stop from smiling as warm laughter rumbled in his throat.

Dani rolled her eyes. "Okay, wise guy." She pinned him with a look. "What is it that you're hiding?" It was kind of fun going rounds with him. She couldn't remember the last time she'd been intellectually stimulated by a guy she found attractive. "Are you some high-level spy?"

His eyes seemed to catch the glimmer from the sunlight sparkling on the ocean. "How did you guess?" He tsked his tongue. "Whoops. Now my cover's blown."

She tsked her tongue. "And here I was thinking you were some bedraggled tourist who got carsick at the drop of a hat."

He pulled a face. "Yeah, that too ... at least the motion sickness part, I should've known better than to get on a bus." He frowned. "I think the bus driver was determined to torture me with every turn."

"Indeed," she laughed. "And Hulk Hogan probably would've pummeled you if I hadn't intervened."

He leaned forward, sending shivers circling down her spine as an awareness of him wafted over her. "I guess I owe you one," he said softly.

The tension between them was electric, making her wonder for one wild second if he'd kiss her. "Yes, you do. And don't you forget it," she quipped. "Now tell me who you are."

He grew thoughtful. "Let's see ... who am I? Is this some philosophical question—meaning-of-life kind of thing?"

She arched an eyebrow, waiting. Not giving him an out.

"You don't wanna hear about me," he drawled. "It would put you to sleep before the end of the first paragraph."

"Try me."

"I wanna hear about you," he countered.

Okay, he wasn't going to be forthcoming. Never one to let things lie, Dani's gut reaction was to pepper him with questions until she got an answer. But then again, what did it matter? She'd probably never see Blake again after today. She assessed him, her finger going to her chin. "Where are you from?"

"Denver, Colorado."

He'd given that information freely enough. "Let's see ... what do you do for a living?"

Amusement filled his eyes. "Okay, I'll play along. You get three guesses. If you guess correctly, I'll own up to it." He held up three fingers in a salute. "Scout's honor."

She wrinkled her nose. "Don't tell me ... you're an executive in the Scouting program."

"Is that your first guess?"

She scoffed. "Not on your life." She folded her arms. "Are you a surfer?" He certainly had the body for it—lithe and muscular. But there was the tan thing. Surfers got super dark.

He laughed in surprise. "What?"

"A surfer," she repeated.

"No."

She cocked an eyebrow. "An artist?"

He grinned. "Couldn't draw a straight line if my life depended on it."

She couldn't help but smile. "That's good."

"You don't like artists?"

"Nope. I've sworn off artists and surfers, so it's a good thing you're neither of those."

He swiped his forehead. "Whew, that was touch-and-go."

She shoved him. "You're funny."

"So, do I get to hear the stories behind the surfers and artists?"

"I see how it is. You wanna know my life history, when you won't even tell me something simple like what you do for a living."

"Touché." His eyebrow lifted in a challenge. "You have one guess left."

"We've ruled out a spy, surfer, and artist." She paused, thinking. "A doctor?"

He straightened and spoke in a distinguished, professional tone. "I'm sorry to have to inform you, ma'am, but your son has sustained a comminuted fracture of his right femur. I'm afraid it will require surgery."

"Ha!" She pointed. "I knew it. What type of doctor? Let's see … broken bones … that's orthopedic, right?"

He rewarded her with a large smile. "Yep."

She assessed him. "You're a doctor. That's neat." Then she thought of something. "It's good that you could take time off to come here with your brother."

He cleared his throat. "Okay, enough about me. Let's talk about you. What do you do?"

She frowned. "Well, up until a few hours ago, my day job was receptionist at an industrial park."

"What happened?"

Everything came rushing back, leaving a sour taste in her mouth. "I got fired," she muttered. The surprised look on his face reminded her how crappy the whole thing was. She dreaded telling Samantha. Her sister had been so proud of Dani for getting a real, grown-up job that had potential to develop into something more. She'd be sorely disappointed. Heck, Dani was disappointed too.

Blake put a hand on her arm, the warmth from his fingers spreading through her like a comforting blanket. Then she saw compassion simmering in his eyes. A lump formed in her throat, which she swallowed back down. "Well, for starters, my boss was a big fat jerk," she spat.

His eyes rounded, then he burst out laughing. "You certainly have a knack for telling it like it is."

"Tell me about it," she said dryly. "That's why I got fired."

"What happened?"

After she told him, he shook his head. "I'm sorry. It sounds like the guy had it coming."

"Oh, he did." Fresh anger welled in her breast. "Everyone in the office tiptoed around him, like he was a king." She shook her head. "Just because Mr. Hadler was wealthy, that didn't give him license to treat his employees like dirt."

"Amen to that. It sounds like you'll be better off away from that place."

She sighed. "Yeah, I suppose. But now I have to find another job."

"What do you like doing?"

"Cooking."

He looked impressed. "Really? What type of cooking?"

"Healthy recipes, mostly. I like developing recipes that don't require pretentious ingredients."

"Oh, wow. You come up with your own recipes?"

She nodded. "I have a food blog."

"There you go. That's your future."

"Yeah, I hope so. But unfortunately, it's just getting off the ground and doesn't pay the bills, know what I mean?"

"Gotcha."

Dani's phone buzzed. She retrieved it from her purse. It was a text from Samantha wondering where she was. "Shoot! I forgot. It's my nephew's birthday. We're having a dinner and cake for Jax. He's four years old." She stood. "I need to hop on the next bus to get home."

Blake also stood. "Sorry I kept you."

"No worries." She tucked a strand of hair behind her ear. "It was nice meeting you, despite the circumstance."

He reached for his shirt that he'd laid out to dry. "I guess I should put this back on," he said, slipping it over his head.

She hated to rush off, but was late already. She held out her hand to shake, but he hugged her instead. She grunted in surprise, feeling his muscles move against her.

A second later, he pulled away and broke the connection. "Thanks again. I don't know what I would've done if you hadn't been there." He shifted, suddenly looking unsure of himself. "I'd like to see you again."

Yes, she wanted that, but there was no future in it. He'd be here a few more days, then head back to Denver. And she didn't do long-distance relationships. It was too painful.

He looked crestfallen. "You don't want to see me again," he said flatly. "I guess I can't blame you."

"It's not that," she said gently. "How about this?" The hopeful look in his eyes shot a dart through her heart. Was she turning her back on something wonderful? Walking away before it had the chance to bloom? "Let's let fate decide."

A furrow appeared between his brows. "What do you mean?"

"If we happen to meet again, then we'll go on a date." She shrugged. "If not, we'll know it wasn't meant to be."

He looked like he might argue, but nodded instead. "Okay, we'll leave it up to fate," he said glumly. His eyes held hers. "It was nice meeting you, Dani."

"Nice to meet you too, Blake."

An inexplicable wave of sadness washed over Dani as she turned to walk away. She glanced back over her shoulder and waved. He smiled and waved back. Then it hit her. He was just standing there, looking lost. He'd not removed his wallet from his shorts, probably because he had no wallet on him. She turned to face him. "Do you even have a way to get back to your hotel?"

He looked sheepish. "I'm afraid not. I forgot to bring anything with me when I left."

She sighed. "That's what I thought. A bit irresponsible for a doctor, huh?"

He pushed a hand through his hair. "Yeah, afraid so."

"I can give you money to catch a bus back." The horrified look on his face caused her to chuckle. "Scratch that. You don't wanna have another vomit episode. The next one might not end so well." A hint of teasing came into her voice. "And I wouldn't be there to protect you."

His eyes held hers. "Pity," he murmured, sending a wave of attraction through Dani.

She swallowed. *Hold it together, Dani.* "I could get you an Uber."

"That would be better." He hesitated. "But I hate to put you out. You've been so kind already."

"No worries. I have the app on my phone."

"I really appreciate it. I can pay for it when I get back to the hotel."

She nodded. "Okay, I'll take care of it. Then, I have to take off."

A few minutes later, after everything was arranged, Dani flashed an apologetic smile. "Sorry I can't wait with you, but my sister will kill me if I miss my nephew's party."

He waved a hand in a cavalier motion. "You go. I'll be fine. You told the driver where I am."

Her heart lurched. She really didn't want to say goodbye, but it was better to do it now ... before her feelings got all tangled up in some guy whose life was in Colorado. "It was nice to meet you, Blake Stevens."

"You too, Dani Fairchild." A crooked smile stole over his lips. "Hopefully fate will smile down on us and we'll meet again."

She shrugged. "Maybe, time will tell."

And with that, she was off.

4

"I think I made a mistake." Dani looked at Samantha who had her knees drawn up to her waist, her arms folded around them. They were sitting on Samantha's back deck, listening to the soothing sound of the waves rolling into the shore.

Samantha tipped her head, her expression attentive. "What do you mean?" Not only was Samantha Dani's older sister but also her best friend and confidant. Ever since their father had died suddenly of a heart attack, the two had been nearly inseparable. In many ways, Samantha was like a second mom with her temperate personality and practical advice.

Dani let out a long sigh. "I met someone today."

"Wow, you got fired and met someone. You've had an eventful day."

"Oh, you don't know the half of it," Dani chuckled. When Dani made it home from the bus and rushed in the door, Samantha was putting dinner on the table. They'd had Jaxson's favorite—spaghetti with meatballs and then cake and ice cream. After Jaxson opened his presents, Samantha put two-year-old Mason to bed while Finn took Jaxson out hunting for crabs on the beach. Dani and Samantha found their way outside to their favorite spot—the back deck. She'd told Samantha about her job right away, because she knew if she didn't, she might lose her nerve. Samantha had taken it better than Dani expected.

"Tell me everything that happened today," Samantha said, interrupting her thoughts.

"I left work and was on the bus."

Samantha frowned. "I thought you were getting your car back from the mechanic today."

"I was supposed to, but he called and said the part didn't come in." The original plan had been to take the bus from work to the mechanic's shop, but when she realized her car wouldn't be ready, she rode the bus home. Dani looked out at the darkening sky, streaked with fiery orange and pink ribbons from the setting sun.

Samantha nudged her. "Okay, I want to hear the rest," she said impatiently.

"I was on the bus, sitting down, and this guy was standing in the aisle, right beside me."

"Oh, so you met him on the bus," Samantha sounded unimpressed.

Dani held up a hand. "Wait. It gets better. I could tell he wasn't feeling well so I asked if he was okay. He told me he was fine." She paused, knowing Samantha was hanging on every word.

"And?"

"He threw up all over me."

Samantha gagged. "Are you serious?"

"Absolutely." She laughed, remembering.

"That's disgusting."

"Totally. It went all down my dress."

Samantha went bug-eyed. "The dress you're wearing right now?"

"Yep."

"I'm surprised you didn't change when you got home."

Dani caught the reproof in Samantha's voice. "I would have, but I was already so late. You were putting dinner on the table. Jax was chomping at the bit to start the birthday celebration. And besides, I got it all out. You didn't notice."

"I'm glad I didn't get close enough to smell you," Samantha countered.

Dani lifted the material and sniffed it. "I don't smell anything. Then again, maybe I'm immune to the smell."

"Gross."

She twirled her hand. "Hush. Let me tell you the rest. Everyone was ticked. There was this Hulk Hogan-looking dude who was about to pummel Blake, but I came to his defense." She felt a burst of pride as she announced this. "We got off the bus and walked to Mokoli'i Park and showered off. And then we just sat and talked."

Samantha's eyes lit with interest as she sat up in her seat. "Tell me about him."

"Well, gorgeous doesn't even begin to describe him. He's tall and thin, but really fit with an incredible six-pack."

It took all of a second for the mother hen in Samantha to come out full force, hands on her hips. "And just how do you know that?"

"Down girl," Dani chuckled. "He barfed on his shirt, so he had to take it off."

Her brows scrunched together. "Well, that's convenient."

Dani cut her eyes at Samantha. "Hey now, don't act like a prude. It's not like you haven't gawked over Finn's six-pack."

Samantha gurgled like she was choking as she rubbed her neck. "W-what?"

"It's me, remember. I was there when you threw poor Anthony aside for the hunky surfer. Not that Napoleon deserves any pity," she added when she saw the dark look on Samantha's face. She'd dubbed Samantha's former fiancé Napoleon. He was the biggest jerk on the planet. The only reason Samantha got engaged to him in the first place was because she was trying to save the family from financial ruin after their father died and left a mountain of debt. Samantha fell in love with Finn, thinking he was a simple surfer, not realizing he was a software billionaire. "I don't fault you for thinking Finn's hot. Heck, anyone with eyes can see that."

"Really, Dani, you always say the craziest things." Samantha pulled at her shirt, color creeping into her cheeks.

Dani laughed. "No, not the craziest things. Just the truth." She waved a hand. "Anyway, needless to say Blake looks good. He's got these killer blue eyes that can see into your soul."

"You've always had a thing for blue eyes."

"Remember when I used to try to talk you into trading eyes with me?" Samantha had beautiful blue eyes, and Dani always felt like hers were a boring brown.

"How could I forget?" Samantha shook her head. "You didn't understand why I couldn't just trade. You thought I was so mean."

"I know. Dad had to sit me down and explain the situation." Tenderness welled inside her as she thought of her departed dad. "I miss him."

Samantha's eyes grew moist as she reached for Dani's hand, squeezing it. "Me too."

Dani drew in a breath, clearing the emotion. "How's Mom?"

"Great. Running crazy with the boutique. You know how busy it gets this time of the year."

"I'll bet she's excited you and the boys are going home for Christmas."

"She is, but not as excited as Jax. He keeps asking when we're going to fly on the airplane." She made a face. "I dread taking Mason on the plane. I hope he does okay."

"Yeah, I don't blame you. It could be rough," Dani admitted. Flying with a two-year-old was not for the faint-hearted. "At least Finn will be with you."

"At least," Samantha said, then opened the conversation they'd had at least a dozen times already. Samantha and her family were going to Sacramento for Christmas to spend time with their mom and Finn's family. "I wish you'd come with us." She brightened. "Now you can't use your job as an excuse."

Did Samantha have to bring this up again? She shot Samantha a sour look. "Admit it. You're just afraid I'll get into trouble if I'm alone for two long weeks."

"That's not it."

Dani eyed her, knowing that was exactly it.

Samantha let out a long sigh, then pinned her with a steely look only an older sister could perfect. "You have a knack for finding trouble. I mean, who else meets a guy because he barfs on her?"

"Hey, I was just sitting there. I can't help it if Blake got motion sickness." She couldn't even say it without laughing. "Okay, you're right. I do get myself into messes, but I promise, I'll keep my nose clean. Honest."

"It's not just that. We'll miss you."

"I'll miss you too, but I'm looking forward to spending Christmas on the island. Every year, we go back to Sacramento. I'd like to do something different this year. Plus, I have lots of stuff scheduled with friends." She didn't dare tell Samantha exactly what she had planned. Better to keep that to herself. Samantha and family were leaving tomorrow afternoon, and her event was the following day. If things went well, it could be a big boost for her cooking blog. She was keeping her fingers crossed. "Besides," she continued, "all Mom cares about is seeing her grandsons. She'll get tired of me after a few minutes."

"True."

"Hey," Dani countered, nudging her. "You didn't have to admit it."

Samantha shrugged. "The only reason Mom's tolerating me and Finn is because we're bringing the boys. We'll just have to make sure it's not too much for her. I'll have to plan enough activities to keep the boys busy and give Mom a break."

Their mother had a heart condition, so they had to make sure she didn't overdo it. They'd feared the worst when their father Elliott suddenly passed, but Katia seemed to be holding her own and was normally fine, so long as she didn't get too tired or stressed.

Samantha cocked her head. "Oh, I almost forgot. What mistake did you make?"

"Huh?"

"You said earlier that you were afraid you made a big mistake. What was it?"

"Oh, yeah. Blake wanted to plan another time for us to meet, but I told him we should just let fate decide. If we ran into each other again, we'd know it was right." Her voice trailed off when she saw the disbelieving look on Samantha's face.

Samantha burst out laughing. "Why in the heck did you say that?"

Seeing Samantha's reaction made Dani realize how stupid she was. "I don't know." She groaned. "It seemed like a good idea at the time. I didn't want to start a relationship with someone who was just passing through."

"Wow, you are making some big strides. That's smart. Long distance relationships are never a good idea."

"Exactly." If she'd made the right decision, then why did it feel so wrong? She could feel Samantha assessing her with those keen eyes. "Blake is so dang hot. And he has a great personality. I'm telling you, you should've seen his abs." She made a show of fanning herself.

Samantha shook her head, chuckling. "Only you." She spread her hands and chirped, "Well, I guess it's up to fate now."

Dani put a finger to her chin. "Hmm ... let's see ...I could Google him. He's a doctor in Denver, Colorado."

"A doctor? Wow. Impressive." She gave Dani an appraising look. "I'm glad to see you branching outside of your usual—surfers."

Dani scowled. "I'm done with surfers," she muttered darkly. "Never again will I play second fiddle to the ocean." She thought of something. "I called Blake an Uber. I can find out where he's staying on my app."

"That's a good idea."

Dani sat up, the notion sparking hope. "It shouldn't be hard to find him. All I have to do is call the hotel and ask for Blake Stevens. Heck, I can even stop by there. It's not like I don't have plenty of time now."

Samantha gave her a long look. "I'm really sorry about your job."

She let out a breath, the events from earlier in the day turning her stomach sour. "Me too. I guess I should learn to keep my big, fat mouth shut."

Laughter bubbled in Samantha's eyes. "Yeah, it might take more than losing a job to bring that about."

"Hey, now, you don't have to kick a girl when she's down."

A contrite smile touched Samantha's lips. "Sorry." She held up a finger. "Oh, I meant to tell you. Whatever happens with Blake—" her eyes twinkled "—regardless if fate smiles on you or not, everything's arranged with Gibson."

Just hearing Gibson's name made Dani feel like she was being squeezed into a straitjacket. She thrust out her lower lip. "Do I have to go out with him?"

"Yes, you do." Samantha gave her a steely look. "You promised."

She groaned. "I know. Okay, I'll go already. *Geez.* When does he get here?"

"Next Thursday."

Dani's eyes widened. "But that's the day before Christmas Eve." The stern look on Samantha's face left no room for argument. They'd been discussing this for over a month. Samantha knew Dani was ready to settle down and set about trying to find her a respectable guy. Considering Dani's track record, she couldn't blame her sister for stepping in to help. Samantha had stopped bringing it up, but Dani knew she was still disappointed that Dani had jilted Liam Barclay at the altar. Even though she'd never openly admit it, Dani sometimes questioned her own judgment regarding that decision. If she'd married Liam, she would've had a cushy life, probably have a couple of kids by now. But she'd fallen for a surfer and thrown caution to the wind. She frowned. Those days were past. Dani was turning over a new leaf, trying to make something of herself. But just because she wanted to find a good guy didn't mean she had to settle for someone boring. Gibson was a programmer who worked for Finn's company. He was moving to Hawaii and needed someone to help him get acclimated. Of course Samantha nominated Dani for the position. Gibson seemed like a nice enough guy, but every time Samantha droned on about his qualities—how responsible he was, how he'd studied chemistry before going into programming, how he spoke several languages—

all Dani could picture was this computer geek that seemed like one long yawn.

"Gibson has your contact information. He's expecting you to pick him up at the airport Thursday afternoon and take him to his hotel. I suggest you go the extra mile. Show him around the island." Samantha flashed a hopeful smile. "You never know. The two of you may just hit it off."

"And I may suddenly sprout wings and fly to the moon," Dani quipped, and then saw Samantha's face fall. She let out a sigh as she gathered her hair in a ponytail with one hand and fanned her neck with the other. "Okay, I'll be a good little hostess and show Gibson around the island," she said sweetly.

"Thank you. I appreciate it." Samantha's eyes grew tender. "I just want you to find the same happiness I've found with Finn."

"I know, sis. I want that too. Truly." But Dani was pretty sure that wouldn't be with Gibson, the Geek. She'd appease Samantha and go out with Gibson when the time came. And in the meantime, she was gonna search high and low for Blake Stevens, even if she had to turn this blasted island inside out.

Voices drifted up from below, Jax's high-pitched, exuberant tone followed by the baritone undertones of Finn.

"Mommy, are you up there?"

Samantha stood and leaned over the handrail. "Hey there."

"We got crabs. Lots of them!"

"That's fantastic, honey."

"Come on down, and we'll show you our catch," Finn said.

"Okay, be right there." Samantha turned back to Dani. "I'm glad we had our talk." She offered a comforting smile. "You're gonna be okay, sis. It'll all work out."

"Eventually," Dani muttered. She could tell Samantha was caught between wanting to rush down to Finn and Jax and making sure she was okay. She forced a smile. "I'm good. Go." She made a shooing motion with her hands.

Samantha's features softened. "Love you, sis."

"Love you too."

As Samantha bounded down the steps, Dani hugged her arms and looked out at the ocean. The vivid colors of sunset had faded to a fathomless blue. The cool of the evening sank into her pores, giving her a feeling of tranquility. She loved living on the ocean where the forces of nature were so prevalent. She let herself get lost in the melodic sound of the crashing waves, her mind going back to Blake Stevens. No, she wouldn't go searching for him, despite her desire. There was no future with Blake. His presence here was fleeting. She'd heard once that the definition of insanity was doing the same thing over and over and expecting a different result. She'd been down this road before, knew how it ended. The fact that she was even entertaining the idea of Blake Stevens let her know she still had a long way to go toward becoming responsible. Leaving things in the hands of fate was a wise decision. If she happened to run into Blake again, she'd take that as a sign that they could move forward. Otherwise, he'd become a distant memory.

Her phone buzzed, vibrating against the glass tabletop. She picked it up and answered. It was her co-worker and friend. Rena was Mr. Hadler's assistant and had taken the day off, which is how Dani got in a pickle to begin with. Of course, that wasn't Rena's fault. Rena probably heard the news about Dani getting fired and was freaking out.

"Hello."

"Is it true?"

The distress in Rena's voice caused her to gulp. "I'm afraid so."

"What happened?"

She told her about the blowup with Mr. Hadler.

Rena swore. "That old fart's losing it. I'm sorry. If I hadn't taken the day off, this wouldn't have happened."

"It's not your fault. I shouldn't have lost my temper." She noticed that Rena didn't say anything, probably because she agreed.

"What will you do now?"

"I'm not sure." With Christmas coming up, it would be hard to find a job. Samantha and Finn didn't charge Dani rent, but she tried to pay them a little something anyway, just so she didn't feel like she was mooching off them. She had enough saved to tide her over for a few weeks, and if push came to shove, she could go a couple of months without paying rent and catch up when she got a job.

"I'm sure you'll find something," Rena assured her. "This is changing the subject, but are we still on for Thursday?"

She hesitated, dragging a hand through her hair. "Yeah, I'd like to go ... but do you think it's a good idea? I don't want to get your friend into trouble."

"We won't."

She frowned. "What if we get caught?" Considering her luck of late that was highly probable.

"What's the worst that could happen? They throw us out?"

"Yeah, I guess."

"I promised my niece I'd go, but you don't have to, if you're worried about it."

Dani twisted a lock of hair around her finger, mulling it over. "It would help my blog if I could make a connection with Chef Ray."

"Yes, it would," Rena agreed.

She chewed on her inner cheek. "Okay, I'll go."

"Fantastic! Let's just meet in the parking lot outside. Let's see. Ten o'clock?"

"Works for me." Dani thought of something. "You're having to take off work again for this. Is Mr. Hadler gonna freak? Now that there's no receptionist to fill in?"

Slight pause, she could hear the hesitation in Rena's voice as she spoke. "They brought someone in from a temp agency to fill in until a permanent employee is hired."

"Oh, okay." *Geez.* It had taken them all of a few hours to replace her. Talk about expendable. "Well, I'm glad you won't have any problem taking off," she said, trying to sound cheerful. "See you Thursday."

"What's going on Thursday?"

Dani jumped as Samantha came up the steps. "Oh, nothing. Just getting together with Rena for lunch."

"Oh, good. I'm glad you're staying busy while we're gone."

"Yep, don't worry about me, sis. I've got plenty to do. I'll use this time to get caught up on my blog and start looking for a new job." There was no way she was telling Samantha what she was really doing on Thursday. Better to keep that to herself and hope all went okay.

5

B lade had learned that in these types of situations it was better to keep his mouth shut and let Doug spew.

"You can't just keep disappearing on me. I had no idea where you'd gone, and you didn't even take your phone. I had no way of getting in touch with you and no way of knowing if you were okay."

"I'm a big boy. I can take care of myself."

Doug shook his head. "The detectives wanted to talk to you about the rose." He spread his hands in defeat. "But you were nowhere to be found."

"So you called the cops." Blade didn't try to hide the accusation in his voice as he glared at Doug, who was sitting in the chair across from him. It was starting all over again. His stomach went queasy.

"I had to, this isn't some game, Blade. This is serious stuff."

"Trust me. I know it's not a game." The all-too-familiar frustration rose within him, causing his chest to tighten. It was crazy that he had to deal with a stalker considering what happened to their mother.

"The stalker's nearby, bro. Got close enough to leave something in your room. For all we know the stalker could've followed you on your escapade today."

A chill slithered down Blade's spine. Had he been followed today?

Had the person witnessed all that happened on the bus? He hated feeling so vulnerable, like his private life was on display for some psycho.

Doug glowered at him. "Where were you anyway?"

"Nowhere important." He turned his attention to a soccer game playing on the TV. Better to pretend to watch it than be put through the third degree with Doug.

"Where were you?" Doug pressed.

"I jumped on a bus and rode around the island."

The look of horror on Doug's face was almost comical. "What?"

"Yeah, it was low key. I just kind of ... vegged."

Doug reached for the remote and turned off the TV.

Blade sat up. "Hey, I was watching that."

"Did anyone recognize you?"

"I don't think so." He shook his head. "No, they didn't," he said decisively, to put Doug at ease. If Doug knew what actually happened, he'd flip his gourd. Dani had consumed his thoughts all afternoon. It only took getting a few miles away from her to realize there was no way he was leaving seeing her again up to fate. He kept thinking about how Dani's eyes lit up when she flashed that mischievous smile, how her soft, toffee-colored curls tumbled over her shoulders. Dani was a breath of fresh air, and he wanted to see her again— get to know her better. He couldn't remember the last time he'd felt so free—like the world was his oyster. He kept seeing the stubborn set of her jaw as Dani jumped to his defense on the bus. He still couldn't believe she'd called him *throw-up boy*.

"What's so funny?"

He jerked, wiping the smile off his face. "Nothing."

Doug's eyebrows shot up, carving deep lines across his forehead. "Are you even listening to me?"

"Of course." He fumbled to recall what Doug had said.

Doug folded his arms, assessing him. "Do you want to be here?" He motioned. "All of this is for you. And you don't even give a crap."

"If I didn't give a crap, I wouldn't get up every day and work my butt off, brother." He met Doug's glare. *So it was on.* With Doug, there was no dancing around the subject. You had to confront it head-on. "I have enough stress on me without you breathing down my neck every minute." The veins in Doug's neck roped, and Blade could tell he was trying to keep his temper in check. When he spoke, his voice was controlled.

"You're right."

"What?" Blade barked reflexively, and then realized what Doug said. He shook his head. "I'm sorry, what did you say?"

"I said, you're right. I've been too hard on you, and I apologize."

Blade was at a loss for words. He just sat there, his mouth hanging open. Had Doug really apologized? This was new.

"We've got a lot riding on this. I'm stressed, and I've been taking it out on you. That's my bad."

Blade wasn't sure what to make of this. "Thanks," he uttered, feeling himself soften. He often wondered if things would've been different between Doug and him, if their parents had stayed together. Growing up, whenever Blade found himself in difficult situations, he'd fantasize about what it would be like to have an older brother to protect him and fix things. Then when their mom passed away so suddenly in a snow skiing accident and he went to live with Doug and his dad, things were strained. Blade was a stranger to them. Aside from the occasional Christmas or other holidays, they'd not spent any time together. The idea of having a big brother was vastly different from the reality. Even so, Blade and Doug managed to co-exist and develop a semblance of a relationship. Then Doug moved to LA to pursue his dream of acting. After Blade graduated from high school, he found himself adrift, not sure what to do with his life. It was their dad who first suggested Blade go live with Doug in LA. Doug reluctantly agreed when their dad offered to pay a portion of the rent on Blade's behalf. Blade spent the first year waiting tables at a restaurant. Then Doug got him a job as an errand boy on the set of the soap opera where Doug had landed a small part. Blade was goofing off, laughing and cutting up with his co-workers when he caught the eye of the casting director, who felt he'd be perfect for the part of a young doctor. He auditioned, got the part, and the die was cast. Neither Blade nor Doug had any idea the temporary role would turn into a full-time position, eventually catapulting him to stardom. Blade had a knack for acting, but talent only took a person so far. Over time, Blade also developed a love for acting and knew he had to perfect his craft. He hired an acting coach and got an agent who suggested that Blade Sloan had a nice ring to it, much better than mundane Blake Stevens. So, Blade Sloan he became. Blade knew it was hard for Doug to see his younger brother getting all the accolades. But just because Blade didn't start out with grand ambitions to become an actor didn't mean he didn't want it now. He'd worked hard to get where he was, and was tired of Doug treating him like his kid brother, who didn't have enough sense to blow up a balloon.

"Look, I'm tired of us fighting all the time."

Blade's eyes widened. "Yeah, me too."

A brief smile touched Doug's lips. "Truce?"

"Sounds good to me."

"I'll back off on the micromanaging."

It was Blade's turn to offer something. "Uh, I'll try not to be so defensive and do a better job of keeping you informed of my whereabouts." He held up a finger. "But I can't handle having a bodyguard on my tail 24/7."

"Not even Tal? You seem to have a good rapport with him."

"Because I didn't want him fired?" His voice escalated. How easy it was to fall back into old habits.

"Like I said, I don't wanna fight," Doug said, a warning tone in his voice.

"Yeah, me neither."

"You gotta give me something, bro."

He caught the desperation in Doug's voice. At the end of the day, Doug was only trying to protect him. "All right, I'll agree to Tal trailing along ... some of the time. But, only Tal."

"Okay, we'll have to pay him extra to work overtime."

"We can afford it."

Doug nodded. "And I want you to talk to the detectives when they stop by."

"I told you, I don't want anything to do with that."

"You have to. Look, I don't like this stalker thing any more than you do, but it's staring us in the face, and we have to deal with it. Just talk to the detectives and be done."

Blade's shoulders were tight to the point of aching. "Fine."

"Good, and you have to promise that you'll be at the top of your game when Christian Ross comes on Thursday."

"I'll do my best," he shot back. A long beat stretched between them as they looked at each other.

"I know you will," Doug finally said. He forced a smile that looked more like a grimace. "You'll do great. You're a natural."

"Thanks." For some reason the compliment felt more like an insult. Then again, maybe he was just ultra-sensitive where Doug was concerned.

Doug pulled out his phone and glanced at the time. "You hungry?"

"I could eat. Is Natalie coming with us?"

"No, she's resting in her room, probably gonna order room service."

A knock sounded at the door. Doug got up to answer it but only got partway before it opened.

"Hello." Eden's cheery voice filled the room as she flashed a toothy smile in Blade's direction. "Hey."

"Hey." Blade stood. He caught a whiff of her sophisticated perfume as she hugged him, strands of her long blonde hair tickling his cheek. An image of Dani flashed through his mind accompanied by an unexpected longing.

Eden looked at him, adoration on her beautiful face. "What're you doing for dinner?"

"Doug and I were just about to grab something."

Her light eyes clouded. "Oh, I was hoping we could go out."

"You can," Doug inserted. "I'm tired. I think I'll just hang out here in the suite."

Eden's face brightened as she put a hand on Blade's arm. "Good. There's this sushi restaurant everyone keeps raving about."

Blade winced. "Yeah, thanks for the offer, but I'm not a big sushi fan."

"What're you talking about? You love sushi," Doug boomed. He waved a hand. "Go, have fun."

Blade wanted to wrap his hands around his brother's traitorous neck and squeeze that snide smile off his face for pushing him into this. Sure, Eden was gorgeous and an accomplished actress, but aside from his rule about not dating co-stars, she wasn't his type. All he could think about was a certain sharp-tongued brunette with eyes the color of rich cocoa and a captivating smile. He wanted nothing more than to get dinner over, so he could come back here and research Dani's food blog in hopes of finding her.

Eden laughed as she linked her arm through Blade's. "Come on tough guy, you'll enjoy it." She winked and tossed her golden hair. "Promise."

The more Blade tried to avoid Eden, the harder she pursued him. Maybe it was because Eden was used to being the one chased after and liked having the tables turned for once. Or maybe she was just a sucker for punishment. He really didn't get it. "Okay, I'll go."

Doug plopped down on the couch in the same spot where Blade had been, and propped his feet on the coffee table. He reached for the remote and flipped on the TV.

Sly dog. He probably wanted to get Blade out of the room so he could have it all to himself. Or maybe, he really did view a romance with Eden as a promotional opportunity. Doug always had some type of angle. Blade shot him a dark look, to which Doug laughed. "Don't forget your phone this time, little brother."

"I've got it," he said dryly.

Eden tightened her hold on his arm. "Good, then we're all set. The limousine's waiting."

"You called a limo? To take us to dinner?" Blade didn't go in for the pomp and circumstance that went along with acting.

She gave him a funny look. "Of course, I've been using the same service since we got to Hawaii."

"Sure beats the bus," Doug hooted, laughing at his own joke.

Blade wasn't amused.

"Loosen up," Eden said, tugging on his arm. "You act like you're going to the guillotine rather than dinner."

That should be your first clue, Blade wanted to say, but didn't want to hurt Eden's feelings. He forced a smile instead.

"Have him home by midnight," Doug called, as they went out the door. "Otherwise he'll turn into a pumpkin."

6

"Of all the crazy things I've done, this tops them all," Dani muttered, glancing around at the security guards buzzing around the hotel lobby like stormtroopers.

Rena cocked an eyebrow. "You mean aside from the time you went out with that surfer you'd only just met and almost got kidnapped into human trafficking?"

Dani jerked. She'd forgotten about telling Rena that. When would she ever learn to keep her mouth shut?

"Or was it the time you jilted the billionaire on your wedding day?"

She popped Rena on the arm.

Rena yelped. "Ouch! What was that for?"

"For being a brat."

Rena just laughed. "Whatever."

Since it first opened, Dani had been hearing how fabulous the Windsurf Hotel was, but hadn't had the chance to check it out. Her gaze swept over the enormous twin chandeliers, glittering like balls of diamonds. The furniture screamed luxury with bold patterns and dramatic curves. A black and white checkered floor set everything off to perfection. Dani didn't watch many home shows, but even she was familiar with Trevor and Kat Spencer and their Hawaii makeover show.

There were certainly lots of security guards. It was dang intimidating. "Is this all for the chef competition?"

Rena gave her a funny look. "No, I thought I told you—a Jase Scott movie's being filmed here ... at least a portion of it anyway."

"W—what?" she sputtered. "No, you didn't tell me that!"

She shrugged. "Sorry. I thought I mentioned it."

Anticipation thrummed through Dani. Blake's brother was in a movie. Was it possible it was this one? She looked around, hoping she might see him. Her hands went sweaty, her heartbeat cranking up a notch.

"You never know. We may even get to see Christian Ross."

Dani's eyes widened. "That would be nice." She put two and two together. "Kat Spencer is Christian Ross's sister. Do you think that's why the movie's being filmed here?"

"Probably. It would make sense."

"Where's the chef competition being held?"

Rena pointed. "Out back by the pool."

The host of the hit show *Premiere Chef* was holding a competition between three local chefs vying for a slot on next season's show. Rena knew how much Dani wanted to make her food blog a success and getting an endorsement from any of the chefs would do wonders. But there was one chef in particular Dani hoped to meet. Chef Ray from Creative Culinary was a local celebrity specializing in adding a unique flair to island food. Like Dani, Chef Ray used everyday ingredients in unexpected ways, and he steered toward healthy dishes. Dani wasn't sure how to approach him. She only knew that she wanted to meet him.

Rena, on the other hand, was here to meet Aiden Anderson, the hunky host of *Premiere Chef,* in hopes of getting his autograph for her niece Kelly. Dani and Rena talked about the event for weeks and how awesome it would be to go, but tickets weren't being sold to the public. Then Rena concocted a plan for the two of them to get into the hotel. It seemed brilliant at the time; but now that they were here,

Dani was having serious reservations. She felt intensely conspicuous, like everything about her and Rena screamed they didn't belong here. She had no idea how she'd respond if one of the security personnel approached and demanded to know why they were here.

"Try to act natural," Rena whispered, as if reading her thoughts.

Rena's friend, a security guard, had met them at the front entrance and gotten them in. Then he had to go back to his post, leaving them to fend for themselves.

"Come on," Rena said, tugging on her arm.

Dani drew in a breath, trying to calm her nerves. She'd been apprehensive enough about going up to a chef cold turkey, introducing herself and trying to get an endorsement for her blog. But now that she realized the possibility of running into Blake, her nerves were sparking like a live wire cut loose from the pole. *I can do this*, she kept repeating. If she didn't have confidence in herself and her blog, how was anyone else supposed to?

"Dang it!"

Dani nearly jumped out of her skin. "What?" For one terrible second she feared they'd been found out, but then realized Rena was looking at her phone.

"Mr. Hadler ... again. This is the third time he's called. It's my day off, man," she groaned. "The man can't wipe his nose without my help." Her phone buzzed. "Now I'm getting a text from Jim Baker asking me to call Mr. Hadler." She sighed. "I'd better take this. You go on out. I'll join you in a few minutes."

"You're not coming with me?" She didn't want to go out there alone. "I'll wait for you."

"No, it may take me a while. You know what Mr. Hadler is like."

"Unfortunately, I do," Dani muttered. She straightened her shoulders as she looked through the breezeway area leading to the pool and the expanse of the sparkling ocean beyond. "Okay, I'll see you in a few minutes."

BLADE LOOKED at his reflection in the mirror, trying to psyche himself up for all that was ahead of him. Today was the day he was meeting the great Christian Ross. They'd go through a preliminary warm-up session this afternoon where they'd run lines together, then they'd reconvene tomorrow morning for a day-long shoot. From what Blade gathered, Christian was reserved and polite off camera. A seasoned actor, he came ready to get the job done so he could go home to his family. The movie was primarily being filmed in Hawaii to make it more convenient for Christian to come and go as he pleased. "Don't blow it, man," Blade muttered, scowling at his reflection. He'd prayed all morning that he could keep the stress from eating at him and remain loose. His thoughts kept vacillating between all that was at stake and Dani Fairchild. He couldn't seem to get her off his mind. A part of him hoped she'd somehow find him. But that would be nearly impossible seeing as how he'd given her his real name and led her to believe he was a doctor. As soon as he'd walked in the door from dinner with Eden the night before, he went straight to his bedroom and Googled Dani. Her blog was the first thing that came up. He spent an hour reading her posts and looking at snapshots of her, as she posed, displaying various dishes. Dani was exotic looking and stunningly beautiful, but she was down-to-earth and carefree. He loved her open smile and how zany she was. He got the feeling that life with Dani would be the ultimate thrill ride. What he would give to spend a few days with her—away from the demands of his job.

"Hello," a female voice chimed.

He jumped slightly. It was Eden. Maybe it was time to set a few ground rules. Eden's suite was adjacent to his, and she'd gotten in the habit lately of just barging in. Tal was on duty today, just outside the door. Blade made a mental note to tell him not to allow Eden to come in at will.

"Good morning, handsome." She looked him up and down, not trying in the least to hide her attraction to him. Then she pulled him into a hug and lifted her mouth to kiss him full on the lips. He averted his face, so her lips grazed his cheek instead.

"Good morning," he mumbled, heat creeping up his neck as he stepped back.

Eden laughed. "Come on, Blade," she teased in a sultry voice, a naughty sparkle in her light eyes. "You had no problem kissing me a couple of days ago."

"That was business."

"Uh-huh, you keep telling yourself that," she purred, trailing her index finger down his cheek before giving it a pat.

They'd done a few kissing scenes together for the movie and still had a few to go. It was always awkward to kiss someone you weren't attracted to for the sole purpose of getting it on film. But after working on a soap opera for several years, Blade learned to deal with it by drawing a clear line between his co-workers and love interests. But Eden wasn't having that. She was determined to act like they were a couple.

He picked up his phone and wallet from the nightstand and placed them in his pocket. From now on, he'd be more careful about making sure he had those important items before leaving the room.

Eden brought her hands together. "The lobby's buzzing with people. You ready to shine, tough guy?"

Every time Eden called him that, it grated on his nerves, mostly because of the intimate way she said it. He pasted on a polite smile. "Let's do it." The studio execs arranged a chef competition, and Blade and Eden were kicking it off with a meet-and-greet with the press. These types of events came with the territory. Most of the time, Blade didn't mind going with the flow. Today, however, he was ready to get this event over with so he could focus on meeting Christian.

As they stepped through the door of his suite, Eden linked her arm through his. Blade stiffened and tried to pull away, but she held him fast. He gave her a questioning look and was about tell her for the umpteenth time that there could never be anything between them.

"Relax, it's just for show." She patted his arm. "Doug thinks it'll help generate more hype if the press speculates that we might be a couple."

Was that why Eden was pursuing him so heavily? In a strange way, the thought helped put him at ease. Maybe after filming was over, she'd lose interest in him.

Tal offered a curt nod. "Good morning, Mr. Sloan."

"Good morning," Blade replied. He still felt a little ashamed for running out the way he had the day before, and for arguing with Doug in front of Tal. He'd have to find a time to apologize. Doug told him that Tal had agreed to take the primary role as his bodyguard, which was reassuring. Blade appreciated Tal's quiet strength and how he stayed out of his business.

"We're headed down," Tal said, craning his neck sideways to speak into his earpiece. "All clear," he announced, a second later. "They're waiting for you in the lobby." He motioned. "After you, Mr. Sloan and Miss Howard."

Blade offered a nod of appreciation. "Thanks, Tal. And it's Blade, if you don't mind."

Tal's eyes widened a fraction as he nodded. "Yes, sir."

Eden grinned. "This is gonna be fun."

I can hardly wait, Blade added mentally, but only smiled.

THE CHEFS WERE BUSY, getting their stations ready. From what Dani understood, they'd all be given the same ingredients and a certain amount of time to create three appetizers, which would be judged by a panel of food critics. Watching them work, Dani felt their anxiety. She hated to interrupt Chef Ray, but this was why she'd come. If she didn't approach him now while no one else was around, there probably wouldn't be another chance. She straightened her shoulders, her heart hammering in her chest, as she propelled her feet forward.

"Chef Ray, it's so nice to meet you," she said, her voice sounding unnaturally high in her ears. A smile strained overtook her face as she thrust out her hand. "My name is Dani Fairchild. I'm a big fan."

He looked at her hand like it was a foreign object, and for a second she feared he might not shake it, but finally, he did. His grasp was limp as he dropped her hand the instant their skin made contact. At five feet ten, Dani was used to being tall, but she felt like she was towering over Chef Ray. In his early sixties, Chef Ray was small-boned, with dark, thinning hair and a pencil-thin mustache. He was of Asian descent and had grown up on Oahu.

"I'm sorry. Do I know you?"

His voice was soft with a lilt.

"No, we've never met, but you catered a wedding for my friend Julie Wilson. The food was divine."

Dani could tell from Chef Ray's blank expression that he didn't remember Julie, which was no surprise. He'd probably lost count of the many weddings and events he catered.

"I'm glad you enjoyed it," he said in a cool, polite tone then turned his attention back to his cooking utensils.

It was clear that Dani had been dismissed. A rivulet of sweat rolled between her shoulder blades. Should she walk away, or did she dare bring up her blog? *Better to walk away,* the angel on her shoulder advised. Chef Ray had no interest in talking to her. *You've come too far to give up now,* the devil on her other shoulder argued. *Just mention the blog. What have you got to lose?*

Chef Ray looked up, surprised to find her still there. Annoyance flickered over his features. "Was there something else you wanted?"

She moistened her dry lips. This was proving to be more difficult than she'd thought. The words gushed out. "Like I said earlier, I really respect you because our styles are so similar."

He cocked his head. "I'm sorry?"

"Our cooking styles. I author a healthy cooking blog, so I've wanted to meet you for some time." She cringed at the wariness that seeped into his eyes. But she was past the point of no return. Her heart was clawing out of her chest. In another second, it would leap through her mouth and splatter onto the cement. She felt shaky, but barreled forward, her eye fixed on the goal. "I was wondering if maybe we could network together ... I mean, if you would be willing to give me an endorsement. I'd be happy to return the favor. Feature your blog on mine." Even as she spoke the words, she realized how ridiculous they sounded. She was a nobody. Chef Ray had no reason, except for kindness, to associate with her. "Any exposure helps, right?"

He grunted out a laugh. "What do you have? All of ten followers?"

The hair on the back of her neck stood. "Excuse me?"

"I'm afraid I don't have time to do endorsements," he said crisply.

A raw heat blistered over her as she eyed the little man she'd admired for so long. She assumed he would at least be kind, even if he wasn't willing to help. "No worries." She flashed a saccharine smile. "My mistake, I just thought you wouldn't mind giving a fellow chef a helping hand, seeing as we all start at the bottom and work our way up. I can see that I was wrong."

He straightened himself up, his face tightening. "Are you affiliated with *Premiere Chef* or the hotel?"

"No, I'm a private citizen—a fan ... former fan," she corrected.

His face flushed as he shuffled around the utensils in jerky movements. "This is a private event. I don't appreciate you hassling me, getting me all ruffled before the competition." He looked past her, probably searching for an official to turn her in.

She swallowed. "I wasn't trying to hassle you."

He glared at her. "Yes, you were." He raised a hand. "I need some help over here."

Crap! She'd done it again! Let her temper get the best of her. She held up her hands, backing away. "I'm sorry to have troubled you."

"Over here," Chef Ray called.

Dani took another step back, intent on getting away as fast as she could. But to her horror, there was only air where the cement should've been. She clawed the empty space as she fell back. When she hit the water, her mind processed what was happening. She'd fallen into the pool. She choked, spewing water as she stood. Her purse, still on her shoulder felt like a ten-pound weight, the strap digging into her flesh. Tears welled in her eyes, mixing with the water, as she looked at the stunned faces around her. Humiliation burned through her veins as she looked down at her clothes, clinging to her. Everything in her purse was most likely ruined, including her cell phone, and she was sure she had streaks of mascara trailing down her cheeks. Then she saw Chef Ray, talking furiously to a security guard and pointing at her. The man nodded and stepped forward.

"Ma'am, I need you to come with me."

She nodded glumly, pushing through the water to get to the side. As she climbed out, she heard laughter, saw a few scornful expressions. She felt like a circus animal on display. This was like something out of a nightmare. How in the heck had things escalated to this? If only Samantha could see her now. No, it was a good thing she couldn't see her, or she'd high-tail it back to Hawaii. The guard clasped her wrist in an iron grip like she was a criminal.

"Come with me," he ordered.

She jerked her wrist out of his hand, her anger giving her courage. "Don't worry, I'm coming. It's not necessary to manhandle me."

The guard didn't try to touch her again, but stayed glued to her side like he thought she might try to sprint away any second. A hysterical laugh bubbled in her throat as she gulped it down, trying to hold onto what little shred of dignity she had left.

They were almost to the hotel lobby when she saw him. She stopped in her tracks. "Blake." She attempted a rubbery smile, but it came across as pathetic. "Hey," she squeaked.

To say he was shocked to see her would've been the understatement of the decade. She felt like a ragamuffin as he looked her up and down. Blake looked as fantastic as she looked awful in black slacks and a blue t-shirt that made his eyes pop. My, how the tables had turned.

He shook his head, a furrow appearing between his brows. "What happened?"

"I fell into the pool," she explained unnecessarily, like he couldn't see she was a drowned rat.

"I heard the splash, but wasn't sure what was going on."

"It's a long story."

A beautiful blonde rushed to Blake's side and placed a territorial hand on his arm. She looked Dani up and down, scowling. "Who's this?"

Dani was unprepared for the jolt of jealousy that ran through her. She should've known Blake would have a girlfriend. He was walking eye candy. She may've been drenched, but her eyes were working just fine. Wowser, he looked good!

"This is my friend Dani," Blake answered. Dani noticed that he moved his arm away from the girl. Maybe they weren't together. Hope sprang in her chest.

She hugged her arms, feeling chilled.

"We need to get you a towel." Blake looked at the security guard. "Would you please get her one?"

The man stood frozen, unsure how to respond.

"Right now," Blake commanded.

"Yes sir, Mr. Sloan."

Dani gave Blake a questioning look. Something wasn't adding up. He had an entourage around him. And the guard had jumped into action at his command. And he'd called Blake by a different last name. She shot Blake a questioning look. "Sloan?"

He shifted, rocking forward on the balls of his feet. "Yeah ... about that."

A man strode up to them. He bore a striking resemblance to Blake, but was older and not nearly as handsome. His eyes were muddy green, while Blake's were piercing blue. She knew right away this was Blake's older brother. He looked Dani over with disdain like she was scum before turning his attention to Blake. "What's this about? Do you know this woman?"

Dani glanced at Blake to see how he would react. To his credit, he looked the guy in the eye. "Yes, I do."

"Blade, the competition's about to start," the blonde whined, reaching for his arm again.

Confusion swirled in Dani's head. "Blade?" Then it hit her. He'd given her a fake name. His name wasn't Blake Stevens, but Blade Sloan. The ground seemed to give way beneath her for a second before she regained her balance. She didn't know what game he was playing, but didn't want to be a part of it. She had rotten taste in men, always attracted to the bad boys. Hurt splattered over her as she looked him in the eye. "You're not Blake Stevens, are you?"

"Of course he's not Blake Stevens," the blonde sniffed, rolling her eyes. "Duh."

"Actually, I am," Blade countered.

The blonde blinked rapidly. "W-what?"

"My real name is Blake Stevens, but my stage name's Blade Sloan."

"Oh," the blonde chuckled nervously. "I didn't think about that."

"You're not a doctor," Dani said flatly, a bitter disappointment steamrolling over her. She gulped out a humorless laugh. "Figures."

"What's that supposed to mean?" Blade demanded.

The blonde cackled like Dani had said something insanely funny as she turned to Blade. "You? A doctor? That's hilarious." She cast a smug look at Dani. "Do you not realize who he is?"

"Obviously, not the man I thought he was." She shot daggers at Blake or Blade, whatever the heck his name was.

Blade's brother brought his hands together. "Okay, enough fooling around. We need to get this woman out of here before the press arrives." He lowered his voice as he turned to Blade. "I don't have to tell you how disastrous it would be if the press saw you with her."

This time, Dani couldn't hold back the laugh. It came out sounding as bitter as she felt. "Yes, that would be tragic."

"Get her out of here," the brother ordered the guard.

Dani held up a hand. "No worries. I'm leaving." She moved to push past them.

"Wait!" Blade jerked away from the blonde and grabbed her arm.

Dani spun around. "What?"

Blade's eyes widened. "You can't leave."

"Watch me," she growled. "Now let go of my arm!"

"You're making a scene," Blade's brother said in a low tone. For a split second, Dani thought he was talking to her and almost gave him a piece of her mind, but then realized the comment was directed at Blade. "Let her go," he commanded.

Blade clenched his jaw. "No, I can't."

Dani wasn't sure how to react. What did he mean by that?

The brother gave him an incredulous look. "You're not making any sense. You don't even know this woman."

"Yes, I do." He looked at Dani. "She's my ..." he cleared his throat and began again "... she's my massage therapist."

For a split second, Dani thought she hadn't heard him correctly. She arched an eyebrow. "Your what?"

"My massage therapist," Blade said smoothly, still maintaining his hold on her arm. His eyes held hers, and she could tell he was silently pleading with her to go along with it. She was just about to tell Blade Sloan to stick it when she saw the mortified look on the blonde's face. Dani had half a mind to go along with Blade's cocka-mamie story just to thwart this snooty debutante. "Right?" Blade pressed. She sensed his desperation radiating out and circling around her like a lasso, impossible to escape. It was crazy how strong the pull to him was.

All eyes turned to her as she tried to decide how to answer. "O-kay ... yeah."

The brother scoffed. "This is ludicrous! You've never even met this woman before today."

"Actually, that's not true. We met yesterday, when Dani was kind enough to come to my aid." An intimate smile curved his lips as Blade's eyes captured hers.

Dani couldn't help but smile, remembering. "Someone had to," she said softly.

"I offered Dani the job yesterday, but she needed a day to think about it. She came here to let me know that she'd accepted my offer, but had an unfortunate accident ..." Blade motioned "... as you can see. In fact, we should be offering Dani dry clothes, instead of giving her the third degree."

Blade was so convincing that Dani could almost make herself believe the story he'd concocted.

The brother looked thoughtful like he was also considering it, and then shook his head. "No, I'm not buying it."

Blade frowned. "Which part?"

Dani couldn't help but chuckle, which seemed to infuriate the brother. It got worse when Blade started laughing.

The brother threw up his hands. "What's going on with you? You know what's at stake here. You need to be a hundred percent when Christian arrives," he said quietly.

Blade straightened his shoulders, his laughter vanishing faster than tourists on the beach during a thunderstorm. "I'm well aware of the stakes, bro. Which is why I need Dani. She's here to help me get loose, so I can perform to the best of my ability."

Dani ran the sentence through her head. *Perform ... ability.* Suddenly, it all made sense as she went bug-eyed. "You're the actor instead of your brother."

"Not just any actor, honey, the star of the whole show," the blonde retorted.

Dani went a little dizzy as the truth settled in. Blade was starring in a hit series with Christian Ross. And he wanted to pass her off as his massage therapist. She was in over her head, and it was getting deeper by the minute.

Blade motioned to a thickset Polynesian man standing nearby. "Tal, could you escort Miss Fairchild to my suite?"

"Sure thing, Mr. Sloan ... um, Blade."

Blade looked at her. "I'll have my assistant bring you some dry clothes to change into, and I'll meet you there shortly to discuss the terms of our agreement."

"Whatever. Your funeral," the brother smirked as he stalked away.

Terms of their agreement? Really? This whole thing was getting crazier by the minute. "Okay," Dani finally said, then leaned forward, lowering her voice as she pointed a finger at Blade's chest. "But you'd better come prepared to do some explaining. You understand what I'm saying, throw-up boy?"

The blonde gawked. "What did she just say to you?"

Dani wrinkled her nose. "Nothing you should worry your pretty little head about. You don't wanna waste all your brain cells on a single dilemma."

The blonde's eyes bulged as her face turned fuchsia.

Blade choked back a laugh, bringing a fist to his mouth and coughing. Then he straightened his shoulders and cleared his throat. "Okay, see you in a few." He flashed a dazzling smile, presumably to reduce Dani to a puddle of mush, as he turned on his heel and strode toward the chefs, the blonde scurrying to catch up to him.

Tal touched her arm. "You ready?"

Dani nodded. "Yep, lead the way."

7

A *few* was turning out to be an hour and a half. This was getting ridiculous! Dani was getting tired of waiting for Blade to return to his suite. Her phone was ruined, so she couldn't even call Rena to tell her what happened. Natalie, Blade's personal assistant, offered to let Dani make a call from the hotel phone or use her cell phone, but Dani didn't have Rena's number memorized.

The door opened. Dani sprang up from the chair, thinking it was Blade, but it was only Natalie. She plopped back down with a loud sigh.

"Are you doing okay?" Natalie asked.

"When is Blade coming back?"

Natalie offered a reassuring smile. "It won't be much longer. Blade sent me up to tell you he'll be up in about fifteen minutes."

"About time," Dani muttered. Right before Natalie came in she'd decided that if Blade didn't get here in the next few minutes, she was leaving. "Thanks," she added with a tight smile, not wanting to project her frustration on Natalie who'd been nothing but kind. In her mid-thirties, Natalie was petite and wiry with short, brown hair and square glasses. She'd purchased Dani a blouse and pair of shorts from the boutique in the lobby. And surprisingly, they fit so well Dani would've thought she'd picked them out herself. Kudos to Natalie, for correctly ascertaining her size. Dani towel-dried her hair and reapplied her eyeliner, mascara, and lipstick. Luckily, she carried a makeup bag in her purse. Everything was water-logged, but the makeup was okay. The only casualty was her phone. She'd have to remember to email Samantha tonight to let her know what was happening. Otherwise, Samantha would freak out when she couldn't get in touch with Dani. Like most households, Samantha and Finn didn't have a landline but used their cell phones instead. There was no phone at the house.

Natalie sat down in the chair across from Dani. "So, tell me about yourself. Dani ... is that short for Danielle?"

"Yes"

"Are you from Hawaii?"

"No, I moved here a few years ago from Sacramento. How about you? Where are you from?"

"Southern Cal, the Santa Ana area."

"How long have you been working for Blade?"

Natalie grew thoughtful. "Let's see ... about four years. I started about a year after Blade was on *Hope for Tomorrow*."

"*Hope for Tomorrow*? Is that a movie?"

"A soap opera."

"Oh, what part did Blade play?"

"A doctor."

Dani's eyes shot open wide as she started laughing.

Natalie shook her head. "I don't understand."

"Something Blade told me yesterday just clicked." She waved a hand. "Nothing important."

"How long have you been doing massage therapy?"

Dani jerked. *Crap!* How in the heck was she supposed to answer that? She could wring Blade's neck for getting her into this! "A couple of years," she said, guilt rolling over her. She hated lying to this nice woman.

"My sister specializes in deep tissue massage. How about you?"

"Uh, I do the overall massage."

"The Swedish?"

"Yes, that's it."

"Do you also do hot stone and shiatsu?"

Heat crawled up Dani's neck as she shifted. The door opened. This time, it was Blade. *Thank goodness.*

Natalie also stood. "I was just keeping Dani company 'til you got here."

"Thank you," Blade said, striding toward them. "Sorry, it took so long."

Dani gave him a hard look. "I was about to leave until Natalie told me you were on your way."

He nodded in understanding.

"I've got work to do, so I'll leave you to it," Natalie said, bringing her hands together. "Dani, it was nice meeting you. I'm sure we'll see each other again." She looked to Blade for affirmation as she spoke.

"Absolutely," Blade said.

Dani arched an eyebrow. "Really?"

"I sincerely hope so," he said softly, as Natalie left the room. He motioned. "Have a seat."

She sat back down as he followed suit, sitting where Natalie had been. "So," he drawled, crossing his legs. "It seems fate worked in my favor." A cheesy grin spilled over his lips, making him look adorable. "We meet again. I suppose that means you owe me a date."

Be strong, Dani, she commanded herself. *Don't think about his baby blues or the way his muscles move underneath his t-shirt. And certainly don't think about the way he fills up the room, charm oozing from every pore.* "Yes, Blake ... or Blade."

"About that." He held up a hand. "I can explain."

She crossed her arms over her chest, tapping her fingers on her arms. "You've got two minutes, mister, before I'm out of here. Why did you lie to me about your name?"

He squirmed like a worm on a hook as he rubbed his eyebrow. "Yeah... Whenever I go out, I make a practice of giving my real name."

She just looked at him.

He spread his hands. "I didn't want anyone to know who I was, okay? I mean, I made a complete idiot of myself."

"Yes, you did."

His eyebrows shot up in surprise. "Hey, now, you know it was an accident. You said so yourself."

"That's when I thought you were a nice, average guy who needed defending. Not some trumped-up movie star."

He frowned. "I take offense to that comment. There's nothing wrong with being an actor."

"No, not when you own up to it." She shot him an accusing look. "You should've trusted me enough to tell me the truth." *There. That was telling him.*

"But we'd only just met."

"So? I defended you. You owed me that much."

He let out a long breath. "You're right. I'm sorry."

She felt herself soften. He was so darn cute, sitting there all contrite. But she couldn't just melt like butter against hot toast. She had to stand her ground. "Thank you," she said solemnly. "I appreciate that."

He relaxed. "Good."

She leveled him a look. "Now tell me about the blonde."

His eyes rounded. "Eden?"

"The one hanging all over you," she snipped.

Amusement sparked in his eyes as he grinned. "Not jealous, are you?"

"Not hardly, throw-up boy."

"I wish you'd quit calling me that," he winced.

She chuckled. "If the shoe fits."

He wagged a finger. "You don't have any room to talk, pool girl."

That caught Dani off guard. "What?"

He laughed. "You made quite a splash earlier."

Heat stung her cheeks as she rolled her eyes. "Whatever."

Suddenly, he stood and closed the distance between them with two steps.

"What?" She leaned back, eyeing him.

"Let's sit on the couch." A mischievous grin curved his lips. "You're too far away." He reached for her hand, sending a jolt of electricity through her. Her mouth went dry as she gulped. *Sheesh.* It was hard to remain neutral where Blade was concerned. She allowed him to pull her to her feet. Her heart sped up as they moved to the couch. He sat down right next to her, resting his arm on the back of the couch, dangerously close to her shoulders. His eyes roved over her, causing a slow burn in her stomach. "You look fantastic," he murmured.

"Thanks." Her heart hammered furiously in her chest as she traced the outline of his lips with her eyes. If he kissed her right now, she wouldn't object.

"So, Dani."

She loved the husky edge to his voice, the way he spoke her name. "Yes?"

"I have a proposition for you."

She went stiff. "What?" Heat coursed through her veins. Surely he didn't think she was that kind of girl.

He laughed. "Not *that* kind of proposition," he clarified, as if reading her mind.

A dull relief thudded over her, making her feel a little embarrassed. "Oh."

"I have a deal for you. You need a job, and I need a distraction."

She didn't like the sound of this. Not at all. "A distraction?" What was she? Some bimbo?

"Things have been super tense around here lately, due to some things that have been happening."

"What kind of things?"

He shook his head. "That's not important."

She cocked an eyebrow. "If the two of us have any hope of having any kind of relationship, you've got to level with me. Understand?" She leaned forward, giving him a penetrating glare so he'd know she was serious.

"You're right. Someone is stalking me."

A laugh bubbled in her throat. "W-what? I thought that only

happened to women." When his face tightened, she knew she'd said the wrong thing. She touched his arm. "I'm sorry." She shook her head. "It just seems so silly that a guy like you would have to worry about a stalker."

He scowled. "Don't rub it in. I hate the whole thing."

She tilted her head, studying him. The frustration in his eyes sent a wave of compassion over her. "You're serious, aren't you?"

His lips drew into a tight line. "I'm afraid so."

"What's going on?"

He told her how it started in LA and was now happening here. "Yesterday, someone left a blood-tipped rose on my bed. My brother Doug and I had an argument. I rushed out, got on the bus—"

"And ran into me," Dani finished for him.

He nodded.

She took in a breath, processing it all. "You don't have any idea who's sending you things?"

"No, Doug called the police. They're coming around later to question me."

"I'm sorry."

"Thanks. Anyway, back to what I was saying. I've got a lot riding on this movie, but I've been too keyed up to perform."

"Understandably so." Dani's thoughts went back to that horrible night when she'd gone to a nightclub in Waikiki to meet Jett Barnes a local surfer she'd met on the beach. She'd had a school-girl crush on Jett, had been super naïve back then. Jett slipped a date-rape drug in her drink and was leading her out to his car when Samantha and Liam saved her. It took her a long time to get over the fear of that experience. She kept torturing herself, thinking about what would've happened if they'd not shown up in the nick of time. Jett had ties to a human trafficking ring and he'd most likely intended to kidnap her for that. She couldn't imagine what it must be like to know someone was out there, watching your every move—intent on doing you harm. She shuddered.

Blade looked concerned. "Are you cold?"

"No, I was just thinking about the stalker. I'm sorry you're going through this."

A slight smile tipped one side of his lips. "Thank you."

She shook her head. "I'm getting you off track. What were you saying about a distraction?" Speaking of a distraction, that's exactly what Blade was to her. He peered into her eyes, causing her to lose her train of thought. They were such a fascinating blue, almost turquoise like the purest water, she could dive in and lose herself.

"Yesterday, when I was with you, was the first time I didn't think about the stalker."

"Really?"

"Really." He caressed a strand of her hair, his fingers lingering there.

Her breath caught, her pulse pounded like a jackhammer in her ears.

"I felt free ... like I could accomplish anything." He crooked a smile. "You're my defender. My muse."

A feeling of gratitude washed over her. Was she really those things to him? The thought sent her soaring. "But we've only just met."

"I know." He moved his hand away from her face. "I know, and I'm not trying to make you uncomfortable."

"You didn't."

He smiled. "Are you always this direct?"

"Do you really want me to answer that?" She'd lost count of the many times her renegade tongue had gotten her in a jam.

"Your candor is what makes you a breath of fresh air."

She pulled a face. "Try telling my sister that. Or my ex-boss. Or the little weasel that caused me to fall into the pool."

"Speaking of which, what was that all about?" He clucked his tongue. "And to think, I thought you'd come to find me."

"Not hardly." She sighed. "If you must know, I was trying to get Chef Ray to put in a good word for my blog, and he freaked." She scrunched her eyebrows. "You'd think I'd asked him to give me his right kidney, rather than a simple endorsement."

Blade belted out a hearty laugh. "Are you serious?"

"Yeah, unfortunately." She didn't see what was so funny.

"You really are something," he said, admiration coating his voice. "By the way, I looked up your blog last night."

She was impressed. "Really?"

"Yeah, it's good."

"Thanks." A shot of warmth went through her as she allowed herself a minute to revel in his praise.

He gave her a speculative look, his light eyes twinkling. "So, you wanna be my massage therapist? I'll pay you a good salary, much more that you could make as a receptionist."

She arched an eyebrow. "But you don't know how much I was making, Mr. Money Bags."

"Whatever it was, I'll top it." He leaned so close she could feel his warm breath on her face. "Whaddaya say, Dani Fairchild? You know you wanna say, yes. The adventure is calling to you. I can see it in your eyes."

A tantalizing shiver circled down her spine, unleashing a legion of butterflies in her stomach. If she leaned forward a mere inch, she could kiss him. She wanted to kiss him! To throw caution to the wind and satisfy this tremendous craving rising like a tidal wave inside her. *Adventure.* Was she that transparent? She'd never been one to turn away an adventure. But could her heart risk it? She was already losing ground where Blade was concerned and it had only been a day. She didn't want to fall in love with someone who would leave. And a movie star, to boot. "I dunno. It would only be temporary, right?"

He rubbed his eyebrow. That was the second time he'd done that, probably an unconscious nervous gesture. "Well, yeah, until filming is over."

"When is that?"

"The end of January."

It would be nice to have the money ... and to not have to look for a job during the holidays. Plus, associating with a movie star could only help her blog. *Say yes,* her impulsive side screamed. Then her rational side took over. Was she one of these pathetic creatures that kept reliving her past mistakes over and over? She didn't want to leave Hawaii. It had become her home, but Blade couldn't stay here forever, not with an acting career. "It's a kind offer, but I don't think it'll work," she heard herself say. She moved to stand, but he caught her arm.

"I really wish you'd consider it." A smile played on his lips. "Think of all the fun we'd have together."

The challenge in his eyes made her want to meet it full force. *Stupid, stupid girl!* "I don't know the first thing about massage therapy," she hissed in a low tone. "Before you came in, Natalie was talking to me about it, and I had to make up a bunch of crap. I don't like lying to people."

"I hear you. I don't like lying either."

Her brows shot up in a challenge. "Like you lied to me about your name?"

"I told you I was sorry. I thought under the circumstance, you'd understand."

She shook her head. "I do. Sort of." He was a good negotiator. *Too good.* "Look, the two of us hanging out, me being your muse—it's a nice idea, but it won't work. I've got my own life to live. I can't tag along with yours."

His eyes met hers for one long moment. "That's not how I see it. I'm sorry you feel that way." He gave her a wistful smile. "For what it's worth ... thanks for yesterday."

"You're welcome. And thanks for coming to my aid as well." She let out a half laugh. "That idiotic security guard would've tarred and feathered me if you hadn't been there."

She stood. "Goodbye, Blade Sloan." Was she making a huge mistake? She was trying so hard to be responsible, but it was a real drag.

He also stood and tipped his head in a farewell gesture.

Doug burst through the door. "Christian Ross is here." He buried his hands in his hair as he began pacing back and forth. "You need to hightail it down to the banquet room ASAP. You don't keep a man like that waiting."

The first thought that ran through Dani's mind was that Doug was a stress case, sucking all the energy out of the room. It would drive her nuts to be around him all the time. She glanced at Blade to get his reaction and was shocked at the swift change that came over him. His face drained as he nodded. She felt anxiety radiating off him. "Are you okay?"

He set his mouth in a grim line as he nodded.

Doug halted in his tracks and pointed. "Don't mess this up, little bro. Remember, when you go in there, you need to be confident and loose. And for heaven's sake, don't forget your lines like you did the other day, or you'll look like a snot-nosed rookie. Christian doesn't like to do multiple takes. This is a one-shot-deal."

Blade tensed. "Got it."

"Words are cheap, brother. It's all about action."

The hair on Dani's neck bristled. "Maybe he could relax, if you'd shut your trap," she muttered under her breath.

Blade jerked, then sniggered.

Doug's eyes bulged like he was choking on his own tongue. "What did you say?" he sputtered.

"Only that I'm sure your little bro appreciates your super-duper, detailed instructions. But I have to say, it probably took less information to get a man to the moon. Know what I mean?" She wrinkled her nose, then flashed a gargantuan smile. She looked sideways at Blade who seemed more relaxed than he had a moment ago. The one thing Dani hated was a bully and Doug was one from the word *go*. Maybe he thought the tough-love approach would get the job done, but all it was doing was ripping Blade to shreds. She'd never been able to resist standing up for the underdog, and there was no way she could stand by and watch Blade flounder. Her hands went to her hips as she planted her feet on the floor. "You know what? I think I will take you up on your offer."

A relieved smile split Blade's lips. "That's fantastic."

She clapped her hands. "Come on, let's go. The great Christian Ross awaits."

"You can't be serious," Doug balked, ignoring Dani and keeping his eyes trained on Blade. "Please tell me you're not taking her with you."

Blade squared his jaw. "Yep, that's exactly what I'm doing."

Doug's face puckered like he'd sucked down the juice of a thousand lemons in one gulp. "She'll wreck everything!"

Dani chuckled as she jutted a thumb at Blade. "Somebody's gotta keep this guy in line. We don't want him freaking the big one and up-chucking all over Christian Ross, now do we?"

Blade shot her an annoyed look. "It was one incident! Are you really gonna hold that over me for the rest of my life?"

She pursed her lips. "I haven't decided yet."

"What's she talking about?" Doug muttered. "This woman climbed up the crazy tree and hit every branch on the way down. Are you really gonna listen to her drivel?"

The comment stung, but Dani shrugged it off with a nonchalant flick of her wrist. "What we're talking about, Dougie, is that one-shot deal you mentioned earlier. You know the chance of a lifetime, yada, yada, yada, all that crap." She winked at Doug who gave her a withering look. She'd certainly not made a friend out of him, but she didn't care. At this point, she was hamming it up to relax Blade. Heck, she'd even break into a song and dance if she had to. Even though Doug was a class A jerk, Dani could tell he'd spoken the truth. Blade was getting his shot, and she wasn't going to let him blow it on her watch. Maybe she was a good distraction. "Let's go throw-up boy."

"Quit calling me that," Blade growled, but he was smiling.

Dani rolled her eyes. "Chop, chop. Time's a wasting."

8

It was amazing how much it helped to have Dani at his side. When Blade was with her, he didn't focus as much on the myriad ways he could mess things up. The truth was that Doug was toxic. He tied Blade in knots. After the filming for this movie was over and they got back to LA, he'd have to find another manager and body double. Hopefully, whatever studio he worked with could handle the latter part. They'd put Doug in that position because it was an easy fix. Blade dreaded letting Doug go, knew his brother wouldn't step down easily. Still, it had to be done. But he wouldn't worry about that right now. He had bigger fish to fry. He offered up a silent prayer for help.

He and Dani paused outside the closed door of the large banquet hall where the film crew was set up. The plan was for Blade and Christian to film the next few days at the hotel and then at various locations around the island after the Christmas break. Blade's heart was pounding so hard he thought it might bust out of his chest. He took in a ragged breath.

Dani put a hand on his arm. "Hey."

He turned to face her.

"You've got this. One look at those baby blues and you'll have 'em eating out of your hand."

He grinned. "You like my eyes?" He stepped in closer as a rush of desire swirled through him. This girl was doing strange things to him. She was intoxicatingly beautiful and so alive.

She winked. "Don't let it go to your head."

Dani reminded him a little of his mom. Not in looks. His mom was petite and blonde with his same piercing blue eyes. She was a fighter, always choosing to view the glass as half full. She was determined to live her life on her own terms, regardless of what people thought of her. Blade hadn't realized until she was gone how much he'd loved her free spirit. It was a shock going to live with his dad and Doug, who were chronic worriers and complainers, always expecting the sky to fall. And they were so dang judgmental, ready to turn on people at the slightest provocation. He'd felt stifled, afraid to move for fear of messing up. It was miraculous that Blade had advanced as far as he had in his career with Doug constantly barking on his heels like a yappy dog.

Dani waved a hand in front of his eyes. "Earth to Blade. Don't zone out on me, throw-up boy. You've gotta focus."

He couldn't help but laugh. "Would you stop calling me that? It's disgusting."

"Well, what would you like to be called? Pretty boy? Hot-shot movie star?"

"How about Blade?"

She cocked her head, sizing him up. "Hmm ... Blade, who's got it made in the shade."

He wrinkled his nose. "That's even worse."

"Yeah, it kind of is," she chuckled. "I'll have to think about it— find something more appropriate for you." She held up a finger. "I know! Blue eyes."

"Do you always come up with your own nickname for people?"

"Pretty much." She grinned. "It makes life much more interesting, don't you think?"

"I suppose it does. I guess that means I'll have to come up with a name for you too." He held up a finger. "Oh, I've got it." He smiled. "Dani, who fell on her fanny."

Her jaw dropped. "What?"

"It fits because you fell in the pool."

"I knew what you meant," she pouted. "I just don't like it."

"Ah, you can dish it out, but you can't take it." He opened the door and let her go in first before following.

She glanced back at him over her shoulder. "Excuse me. I can take anything you can dish out, wise guy."

Her curls bounced happily on her slender shoulders. His eyes traced over her tapered waist, slim hips, and long legs. She walked with a bounce in her step, yet she still managed to look graceful. Dani was a ball of fire, and he loved it.

The assistant director approached with her entourage. "Hello, Mr. Sloan, we've got everything ready for you. Mr. Ross is already here. We'll have you both run through your lines, and possibly do a few takes today."

Blade motioned. "Andrea, this is Dani. Please give her anything she needs and make her feel at home."

Andrea nodded. "You bet." She extended a hand, flashing a brief smile. "Nice to meet you, Dani."

"You too," Dani said.

"This way," Andrea said briskly.

As they neared the area that had been sectioned off for the main actors, he spotted Christian right away.

At the same time, Dani nudged him. "Over there, talking to Trevor and Kat Spencer."

He caught the trace of awe in her voice, feeling a little awestruck himself. Sometimes it still felt surreal that he was an actor, rubbing shoulders with some of the biggest names in Hollywood. Blade's heart jumped in his throat, sending a jolt of adrenaline through his veins as he strode over with Dani beside him. When they reached the three, Christian smiled in recognition as he extended his hand.

"Blade, it's nice to finally meet you."

"Nice to meet you, too." Blade clasped Christian's hand, making sure to give it a firm shake; but not too hard, like he was volleying for power. Christian called all the shots and Blade was lucky to be along for the ride. It was a great honor to work with Christian, to be able to learn from him.

"This is my sister Kat and her husband Trevor."

"Howdy," Trevor boomed in his trademark drawl that had catapulted his show to stardom.

"We've met several times at the hotel," Kat said, offering a warm smile. "It's nice to see you again, Blade."

"Good to see you too, Kat." Blade wondered if she might mention something about the stalking incident and was relieved when she didn't. He didn't want that to tarnish his first meeting with Christian.

"Oh, yeah, that's right. Blade's staying here at the hotel," Christian said.

"It's a very nice place," Blade added, hoping he didn't sound like he was trying to kiss up. He was speaking the truth. The Windsurf was one of the nicest hotels he'd ever stayed in.

The conversation lagged as Blade sought for something halfway intelligent to say. But his mind was blank. Where in the heck was the blasted scriptwriter?

"Toasted marshmallows," Dani piped in.

Blade jerked. "What?" he said, turning to Dani.

"Toasted marshmallows," she repeated, an impish smile curving her lips.

He didn't have a clue where Dani was going with this, but it certainly wasn't helping the situation. Maybe he shouldn't have been so hasty in bringing Dani with him. He'd gotten a hoot out of her outlandish comments in the hotel room earlier when she'd put Doug in his place. But this was a very different situation. He hoped she realized that.

Kat and Trevor both started laughing. "You watch our show," Kat said, admiration sounding in her voice.

Dani's smile grew. "Yes, I really enjoy it."

"Would someone please explain to me what the heck just happened?" Christian said.

Kat rolled her eyes. "You obviously don't watch our show."

Christian looked at Blade. "Did you understand what they were talking about?"

Blade held up his hands. "I plead the fifth." Then he looked at Christian and lowered his voice, pretending everyone couldn't hear him. "I was as lost as you were." This earned him a smile from Christian.

"Movie stars." Kat clucked her tongue. "Have to be fed every line."

Dani put a hand on Blade's arm. "'Toasted marshmallows' is a nonsensical phrase Kat and Trevor came up with for whenever there's an awkward silence in the conversation."

"We have a lot of 'toasted marshmallows' on set," Trevor added.

Kat wrinkled her forehead. "Speak for yourself."

This brought laughs all around, completely erasing any remaining tension.

"And who might this lovely young lady be?" Trevor asked.

"This is Dani Fairchild. I hope you don't mind that I brought her on set today. She's my ..." Heat crawled up Blade's neck as he tried to figure out how to introduce Dani.

"I'm his good luck charm," Dani said smoothly.

Kat raised an eyebrow as she turned to Christian, laughter in her eyes. "Maybe you should've bought along your good luck charm."

Christian frowned. "I tried, but she was too busy helping out at the school today. My wife Everly," he explained.

"Speaking of your show, I'm always amazed at your transformations," Dani said.

"Thank you. We love it, don't we, hon?" Kat linked her arm through Trevor's.

He flashed a teasing grin. "You bet. The show gives her full license to boss me around."

She laughed. "And you don't listen to me any more on the air than you do at home."

"Ouch. That's hitting a little below the belt, darling."

"You can handle it, cowboy," she purred.

He draped an arm around her shoulder, pulling her close. "See why I love this woman? She keeps in me line."

"Somebody has to," Kat countered.

Blade tried to observe Christian without being obvious about it. He was about a half-inch taller than he with golden skin. His chiseled features gave him a warrior-like appearance, his eyes were a piercing turquoise. It was strange to see someone, other than his own mother, with eyes nearly identical to his own. Blade wondered if that's why he was chosen to co-star with Christian. Hopefully, his acting skills also had something to do with the screening process. Doug had made Christian out to be a hard-nosed veteran actor who had no patience with rookies, but Christian didn't strike him that way at all. It was probably too soon to say for sure, but from what Blade could tell, Christian was even-tempered and pleasant.

The director approached them. In his mid-thirties, Matt was on the heavy side with long hair that he kept wound in a man bun. He was a brilliant director and known for keeping on schedule. "Are we ready to get started?" he asked briskly.

"Let's do it," Christian said.

Kat sighed. "All right, I guess that's our cue to leave."

Christian shrugged. "You can hang around if you want." He wiggled his eyebrows. "Maybe we can teach you reality TV stars how the big league does it. Right, Blade?"

Not sure how to answer, Blade just laughed. He appreciated Christian including him in the banter like they were old friends.

Kat leaned over and gave Christian a playful shove. "Enough already."

"Sounds like somebody's gettin' too big for his britches," Trevor added, with a Texas-size grin.

"Seriously, bro. We would hang out and watch you in action," Kat continued, "but we've got lots do before we fly out on Friday."

"That's code for she wants to buy out the stores and haul all the gifts to Ft. Worth instead of just buying them when we get there," Trevor added.

Kat shook her head. "Men, they just don't understand."

"No, they don't," Dani agreed. "Are you headed to Ft. Worth for Christmas?"

"Yes, to visit Trevor's parents." Kat looked from Dani to Blade. "How about the two of you? Where are you headed?"

The inference was that they were a couple, which didn't hurt Blade's feelings. In fact, he rather liked the idea. He saw Dani's eyes widen, but she recovered quickly.

"I'm staying here for Christmas," Dani said. "I'm not sure what Blade's doing."

All eyes turned to him. He rubbed an eyebrow. "I'm still finalizing my plans," he said vaguely. Dani was going to be here for Christmas. Maybe he should stay here too. It would be wonderful to have her all to himself for a few days, if she would agree to it, that is. Was Dani single? He'd assumed she was. Hot prickles covered him. He didn't even want to think of her with anyone else.

"Are you guys coming over tonight?" Christian asked. "Everly's making chicken fingers."

For a split second, Blade thought Christian was talking to him, but then realized the question was directed to Kat and Trevor.

"You bet 'ya," Trevor replied. "Nobody in their right mind would pass up Everly's chicken fingers. You're a lucky man to get fed like that every night."

"Hey." Kat thrust out her lower lip in a pout.

Trevor caught her around the waist and planted a kiss on her cheek. "But not as lucky as I am to have this wonderful woman."

"Yeah, you just keep trying," she said, but her eyes sparkled. "What he's really saying is that he's tired of eating takeout."

"Honey, I'll eat takeout every night of my life, if it means I get to be with you," Trevor said.

"My silver-tongued rebel," Kat murmured, rewarding him with a brilliant smile as a tender look passed between them.

Blade was unprepared for the longing that hit him. He missed being part of a family—wanted to find someone he could build a life with. He wanted the type of relationship Trevor and Kat had. He looked at Dani and realized she was studying him, an enigmatic expression in her dark eyes. Suddenly, he wished it was just the two of them so he could ask her what she was thinking. He wanted to find out what made her tick, find out how she maintained her incredible zest for life.

"You should eat dinner with us tonight," Christian said.

Blade's eyes widened when he realized the statement was addressed to him. He pointed to himself. "Me?"

Amusement lit Christian's eyes. "Yes, both of you."

He felt a little foolish for acting so surprised. He turned to Dani, who looked as shocked as he did. "Would you like that?"

"Sure." She looked at Christian. "If you don't think your wife would mind feeding two extra guests."

Christian waved a hand. "Everly will be thrilled. She cooks enough for an army."

"I hate to be the bad guy here," Matt said, tapping his clipboard, "but we've got a schedule to keep."

Christian put a hand on Blade's shoulder. "I guess we'd better get to it." He grinned. "Let's see what you've got under the hood, wonder boy."

"I'm ready." Even as Blade spoke the words, he realized he meant it. He was completely relaxed. No inhibitions. Dani gave him a look that said, *You've got this.* "See ya in a bit."

She gave him a nod of encouragement. "I'll be close by."

Blade had been on set less than fifteen minutes and he'd already started to build rapport with Christian, and got a dinner invitation to his home, which was almost unheard of. Christian had a reputation for being reclusive, only allowing a few people into his circle of trust. Maybe Dani really was his good luck charm.

9

The wind felt good rushing in through the windows and whipping through Dani's hair. She kept one hand on the steering wheel, the other resting in her lap, as she followed the road that snaked along the coast. This was one of her favorite drives, with the waves rolling into the shore in a flurry of white. She glanced over at Blade to make sure he wasn't getting carsick. The last thing she wanted was him throwing up in her car. She'd just picked it up from the mechanic on her way to the hotel this morning. It was finally running well. She didn't want any more problems with it— certainly didn't want to have to have it shampooed. "You doing okay?"

"Fantastic," he breathed, giving her a lopsided grin that sent her stomach into flips. It wasn't fair for a man to be this good looking. As if his drop-dead gorgeous face weren't enough, the dude had perfect hair—messy in a stylish, sexy way. "This is much better than the bus," Blade added. He reached for her hand and gave it a squeeze, sending a jolt through her. She thought he might let her hand go, but he pulled it over into his lap. "Thanks for being my chauffeur."

Her heart began a wild dance against her ribcage. "Your chauffeur, massage therapist, muse, lucky charm. Whatever you need, I'm happy to oblige," she chirped, her voice sounding shrill in her ears.

She had the feeling she'd been dropped in the middle of a fairytale, except instead of the prince rescuing her, it was reversed. All she could think about was his hand over hers, and how he hadn't let go. She wondered if he could feel her pulse through her hand. *So much for trying to remain unaffected by him.*

"I hope you know how grateful I am for you, Dani. I mean it."

She caught the gravity of his words as she glanced his direction and saw appreciation in his striking eyes that looked so blue today, she swore she could dive into his soul.

The air between them crackled with electricity. "Thanks," she croaked. A few minutes later on a sharp turn that required her to place both hands on the wheel, she broke the connection. She needed to keep a little distance between them. Otherwise, she couldn't think clearly. *Oh, man,* at this rate, she'd be falling into his arms by the end of the night, begging him to kiss her. Heat burned her cheeks, and she was glad Blade couldn't read her thoughts. She couldn't think about that—how it would feel to become acquainted with those delectable lips.

"How much farther is it to your house?"

She chuckled. "You sound like Jaxson and Mason."

"Who?"

"My nephews."

"Your sister's boys?"

She cast a sidelong glance at him before turning her eyes back to the road. "I'm surprised you remembered that."

He tapped his temple. "A steel trap."

"And, oh so humble." She rolled her eyes.

"Hey!" He thrust out his lower lip in a mock pout, looking irresitible.

She pulled her eyes away from him and back to the road. She had to remain focused on driving.

"Let's see ... what was your sister's name? I know it started with a S. Sally ... no, Sandy."

"Bamp!" she blurted like he was on a talk show and had just gotten the wrong answer.

"Stephanie ... Sophia?"

"Samantha."

"Oh, that's right ... Samantha. Will she be at your house?"

"No, Samantha and her family are spending Christmas in Sacramento."

"I'm surprised you didn't go with them."

She shrugged. "I thought I'd be working my receptionist job at the time. But I guess things turned out okay, since I'm working for you now." It still hadn't completely sunk in that she was actually working for Blade, especially when he was holding her hand and confusing things.

"About that ... we stop filming the day before Christmas Eve and don't start back until the first of January. So, you would have time to go to Sacramento."

She pressed her lips together. "Thanks, but I'm good staying here."

He picked up on her hesitation. "You don't wanna go home for Christmas?"

She sighed. "I have mixed feelings about it. It's just my mom, now that my dad has passed away. I just saw her last month when she came for Thanksgiving, and I see Samantha and her family all the time. Plus, my mom will be too caught up in spending time with my nephews to notice anyone else. I've never stayed on the island for Christmas, so I thought I'd give it a shot ... see what it's like."

"Makes sense."

"How about you?" She glanced at him, then back to the road. "Are you going home for Christmas?" It hit her that she didn't even know where *home* was for him. "Where do you even live, anyway, Dr. Sloan?" Her voice rang with a heavy accusation.

He let out a nervous laugh. "LA."

"Not Denver?"

"I'm from Denver, but I live in LA now."

"My friend Rena Stanley's from Denver." She was getting off track. "So, are you going to Denver for Christmas?"

"I was thinking about going to LA." He paused. "But now I'm thinking I'd like to spend Christmas here."

Her eyes widened as she caught the meaning of his words. "Oh," she said casually. "That sounds good." She could feel his eyes, studying her. As she cast him a glance, she could tell that he'd read her like an open book. Knew the thought of him being here for Christmas was thrilling. Her cheeks went rosy. "What?"

He smiled. "Nothing." Blade's phone buzzed. He retrieved it from his pocket. "Doug, again."

"Maybe you should answer it. He's probably wondering where you are."

"Yeah, I guess." He clicked off the ringer and shoved the phone back into his pocket. "I'll call him at your house."

"You sure? That's the third time he's called. He's probably realized we gave Tal the slip."

"Yep, probably."

The edge in his voice told her she needed to drop it. "Okay," she said casually, her thoughts going back through all that had happened the past few hours. At the hotel, Blade and Christian spent a good two hours running through their lines. Then as the director was prepping the crew to do a few takes, Christian announced that he needed to call it a day. They decided to reconvene the following morning at ten a.m. to start filming.

When Dani told Blade she had to run to the Apple Store to get her phone repaired or get a new one, she was surprised when he offered to go with her. "I'm afraid if I let you out of my sight, you might disappear," he teased.

No, she wouldn't disappear. For better or worse, she'd made a commitment to stand by Blade until the filming was over. They'd still not discussed her pay, but Blade assured her they'd get everything worked out with his assistant, Natalie, tomorrow morning. Dani wasn't sure how that was going to work, seeing as how Natalie and Doug thought she was Blade's massage therapist. Dani wasn't going to exhaust her effort worrying about it though. Blade would have to sort things out.

Tal, Blade's bodyguard, tailed them to the Apple Store where Dani was forced to get a new phone because hers was beyond repair. Luckily, her data from her old phone could be transferred to the new one. As they were getting in Dani's car to head to the North Shore, Blade took Tal aside and pulled out a hundred-dollar bill. "This is yours if you'll let us 'lose' you until tomorrow morning."

Tal had been reluctant at first, fearing Doug's wrath. But then Blade reminded him that he was the boss, not Doug. Blade's relationship with Doug was turbulent, making Dani wonder why they chose to work together. From what she'd seen so far, all they did was fight 24/7. Then again, when it came to family, things often made no sense.

"We're here," she announced as she pulled into the driveway.

"Nice place," Blade said.

"Thanks," she said offhandedly, even though it wasn't her home. Still, she felt the need to acknowledge his compliment. She motioned with her head. "Come on in. I'll give you the grand tour, and then I'll get ready, quick like a flash, so we can head to Christian's place."

Walking around Samantha and Finn's empty house with Blade by her side felt intimate. She hadn't had a chance to call and tell Samantha everything that happened. Well, she wasn't planning on telling her everything. She'd leave out the part about approaching Chef Ray and falling into the pool. Samantha would be excited that she'd found another job so quickly, but wouldn't like hearing that Blade was spending the night in their home, while they were away. Yeah, she probably shouldn't mention that. Dani had debated about whether to invite Blade to stay over, but it was the only solution that made sense. It was a little over an hour's drive from Waikiki to Christian's estate in Pupukea with good traffic. Since Blade didn't have a car, he'd either have to take an Uber or get Dani to take him back; meaning she'd have another hour of driving to get home to the North Shore, only to turn around and go back to Waikiki the following morning. It was just easier to have him spend the night at Samantha and Finn's place and save a few hours driving.

She opened the door to the guest room and motioned. "This is where you'll be staying."

A teasing glimmer lit Blade's eyes. "I don't know how I feel about spending the night by myself in this big house. You sure you don't wanna sleep in the room next door? In case I get scared in the middle of the night?"

A smile tugged at her lips as she shoved him. "You're such a baby, Blade Sloan. I think you'll be okay. I'll be right next door in the guesthouse."

His lips pulled down in a frown. "Too bad," he murmured, stepping up to her.

Her breath hitched when he trailed a finger along the curve of her jaw.

"You are so beautiful," he said softly, his compelling eyes roving over her like he was absorbing every detail.

Delicious tingles rippled down Dani's spine. She wanted to fling her arms around Blade and kiss him until she couldn't see straight. His lips moved dangerously close to hers. Blood rushed like a waterfall through her veins as she swallowed. She had to be responsible. Had to—

He encircled her waist and pulled her to him. As his mouth came down on hers, she grunted in surprise. His lips were coaxing and smooth, like a dozen truffles rolled into one. She knew she should fight this, but it felt so good. When he deepened the kiss, a groan escaped her throat, as a river of fire rushed through her bringing with it a burst of glorious color. She slid her arms around his neck, threading her fingers through his thick, unruly hair. Kissing Blade was everything she'd hoped it would be and oh, so much more. He met her, fire for fire, their lips moving in a perfect dance. She had the fleeting impression of two souls connecting in a heady rush. *Two souls connecting.* Wait a minute, this was different from her past relationships—*lasting.* Except, it wasn't lasting. Blade would go back to LA after filming was done, and she'd be left here … alone, with a giant hole in her heart. A pang shot through her as she pulled back.

"I can't do this, not with you."

He frowned, searching her face. "Why not? That was fantastic. Admit it. You felt it too … this incredible energy between us."

She'd felt it all right, like a freight train hauling through her, pushing out all reason. She noticed he still had his arm around her waist. She tried to extricate herself, but he held her tight.

"Dani, what is it?"

The tenderness in his voice brought tears to her eyes. "I can't fall in love with you, not when you're leaving."

A stupid grin flitted over his lips. "You love me? *Wow.* I didn't know I had such a strong effect on you. We only met a couple of days ago."

Her eyes narrowed, heat crawling up her neck. "I don't mean I'm in love with you now, moron. I can't start a relationship with you and allow myself to fall in love with you ... eventually. Not when you're leaving."

He shook his head in confusion. "I'm not leaving, I'm right here."

She chuckled through her emotion. "I don't mean now. I mean at the end of January when filming is over. You'll go back to LA, and that'll be that." She gave him a sad smile. "Trust me, I know the drill. I've been through it enough times. And I don't want to go there with you."

His brows furrowed as he released her.

There. She'd said it, got it out in the open. As hard as it was to face, it was a relief. Now he'd understand and leave her be. A wave of remorse washed over her, even though she knew it was for the best. That kiss was spectacular, probably the best she'd ever had. Her lips still burned from the feel of him, and she wanted to kiss him again, not worrying about what would happen in the future.

He eyed her. "Exactly how many other guys have there been?"

"W-what?" She burst out laughing. "I tell you why we can't be together and you're worried about past boyfriends?" She threw her hands in the air. "Unbelievable."

He caught her arm. "I'm serious, Dani."

She could tell from his expression that he was. She didn't know whether to be flattered or ticked. "This is absurd," she muttered. "My past relationships are none of your dang business." She leaned forward into his personal space, her face nearly touching his. "What about you, blue eyes? How many girlfriends have you had?"

"A handful."

She barked out a laugh. "Exactly how many is a handful?"

"I dunno, four or five."

Her first thought was that she could double his number and it still wouldn't come close to the number of boyfriends she'd had. But when you counted serious relationships, they were about even.

"How about you?" he pressed, still up in her face. Her pulse drummed in her ears. Would he try to kiss her again? "About the same," she said casually, tracing the outline of his lips. He had just the right amount of scruff on his jaw line, and she liked the rough feel against her skin.

He cocked an eyebrow, amusement dancing in his eyes. "I assume that includes the surfer and artist?"

"Yep." A tight smile stretched over her lips.

A fierce look came into his eyes as he caught hold of her arm. "I don't give up easily. When I see something I want, I go after it."

She swallowed, her heart beating out a frenzied pace. "Is that right?" She laughed to ease the attraction as she tried to ignore the feel of his warm breath on her face. He smelled like cinnamon from the mint he'd eaten earlier in the car. Mixed with that was his clean, masculine scent that permeated her senses, tingling down through her toes. "Just because you have a good track record with all those other gullible girls you've met in the past, doesn't mean you stand a chance with me." His eyes shot open, and he was about to respond when she winked and patted his cheek. She had to put space between them ... fast! "Make yourself at home while I get changed. There's a TV in the living room, the remote is on the coffee table."

"I meant what I said," she heard him say as she hurried out of the room.

DANI WAS PUTTING the final touches on her makeup when her phone rang. It was Rena. *Shoot*, she'd forgotten to call her earlier when she got her new phone. Rena was probably beside herself, wondering why Dani had up and disappeared from the hotel.

"Hello."

"Dani," Rena breathed in relief. "I've been trying to reach you all afternoon. Is everything okay?"

Dani put down her blush brush, turning away from the mirror. "I'm fine."

"What happened? I searched all over for you."

"You won't believe it when I tell you. I was trying to talk to Chef Ray, who by the way is a conceited jerk, he treated me like dirt. I got all flustered because he was trying to turn me in to security."

"Are you serious?"

She grinned, hearing the angst in Rena's voice. She sounded as put-out as Dani had been. "Yes, but it gets worse. I was trying to get away without causing a scene, and I fell into the pool."

"What?" Rena exploded. "No!"

When she told Rena the rest, she let out a loud whoop. "Are you kidding me? You're working for an actor? And you're going to Christian Ross's house for dinner?" She clucked her tongue. "You're the only person I know who falls in a pool and then turns the catastrophe into the opportunity of a lifetime. Maybe you could get Blade or Christian to put a plug in for your blog."

"Yeah, maybe," she mumbled, but Dani had no intention of doing any such thing. Her relationship with Blade was stressful enough without adding an extra layer. And she didn't want to make things uncomfortable with Christian. She could joke about it with Rena, but still cringed remembering the disdainful way Chef Ray looked at her when she asked him for an endorsement. Dani's dad used to say that in business, you have to earn the right to ask certain questions. She should've remembered that little gem of advice before she went tromping up to Chef Ray before the competition started. Oh, well. Nothing she could do about it now.

"So, you're going to Christian's house for dinner and then Blade's spending the night with you?" A devilish laugh rumbled in Rena's throat. "That should be interesting."

Her stomach tightened. "It's not like that. Blade's staying in Samantha's guest room, and I'm sleeping in my own bed in the guest-house. It just didn't make sense to do all that extra driving back and forth between the North Shore and Waikiki."

"Don't get your panties in a wad. I'm just giving you a hard time."

She relaxed her shoulders. "Sorry, it's been a crazy day."

"It sounds like it."

"Were you able to get an autograph for your niece?"

"I was."

"Good." Dani glanced at the clock on the wall. They were supposed to be at Christian's estate in thirty minutes. "Rena, I'd better let you go. I'll catch up with you tomorrow."

Rena let out a long, drawn-out sigh. "All right. Have fun. Don't worry about me. I'll just be here in my apartment, eating a Lean Cuisine and watching hours of mind-numbing TV and living vicari-ously through my exciting friend, who's having dinner with movie stars."

"Yeah, yeah. It's not nearly as exciting as it sounds," Dani quipped, as flutters rippled through her. "Bye," she said, ending the call. *This was really happening!* She was having dinner with *the* Chris-tian Ross. Not just him, but Kat and Trevor Spencer too. And Blade! She kept replaying his words about how he went after the things he wanted. How could any girl resist him? That kiss! Her cheeks went hot just thinking about it. She drew in a breath, straightening her shoulders. "Hold it together, Dani," she muttered under her breath. "Remember, you're supposed to be responsible not some love-starved schoolgirl." She reached for her purse and shoved her phone in it. She slung the strap over her shoulder, checking her reflection in the mirror. She'd be strong and resist temptation. That was her only option. Otherwise, she'd be headed for a major heartbreak. And she couldn't handle that.

10

"That was delicious, but if I eat one more bite, I'm afraid I'll pop." Blade leaned back in his seat and touched his stomach as he looked at the remaining chicken finger on his plate. He'd lost count of the number of chicken fingers he'd already eaten. The minute he cleared his plate, Everly offered him more. When they first sat down at the table, Christian remarked that Everly was determined to feed the world. Blade, along with everyone else, laughed thinking it was a joke, but now he was starting to believe it.

"Well, I've got a little more room. I'll finish it off," Dani said as she lifted the chicken finger off his plate and took a bite. To be so thin, Dani could sure put away the food. He loved how free and open she was, even here in an environment most people would find intimidating.

"Now there's a girl after my own heart," Everly said, admiringly.

"Your food really is outstanding," Dani said. "Although if I ate like this every day, I wouldn't be able to fit in my clothes."

"Try living with her. She cooks like this every night," Christian said, draping an arm around Everly's chair. "I have to pace myself, especially when I'm making a movie and have to maintain my girlish figure."

Everyone laughed.

"I gave up worrying about my girlish figure long ago," Trevor interjected. He winked at Kat. "Must be a movie star thing."

"Must be," Kat laughed.

"Hey now," Everly warned, "don't be ganging up on my man."

"Yeah." Christian leaned over and planted a kiss on Everly's cheek. "Thanks for sticking up for me, babe."

She winked. "I've got your back."

"How do you cook like this every night and look so fabulous?" Dani asked.

"Thank you," Everly said, smiling at Dani.

Dani shrugged. "It's true."

Blade could've kissed Dani for that. She had them all eating out of the palm of her hand, and she wasn't even trying to impress them. He would've kissed her if he weren't afraid she'd slap him. Their kiss had been amazing, but then she suddenly withdrew. He was dead serious about what he told her. When he saw something he wanted, he went after it. And he wanted Dani. He'd been enamored with her the day they met, but after spending time with her today, he was smitten. Not that he wanted to rush things. He did want to continue their relationship—see where things led. He could tell Dani wanted the same thing, even though she was too stubborn to admit it.

"I hope everyone saved room for dessert. I made peach cobbler," Everly announced.

Blade's stomach was stretched to the point of pain. He couldn't stop a mortified expression from coming over his face. He tried to mask it, but too late. It was on display for the entire table as they broke into peals of laughter.

Dani put a hand on his arm. "You really should learn to mask your emotions. You're an actor, after all."

"Ouch!" Trevor hooted.

"Way to throw me under the bus," he growled at Dani, but didn't try to stop a grin from spilling over his lips. She shoved him, laughing.

Christian held up his fingers. "Blade ... Dani, there are two things you have to know about Southerners."

"Now this I've gotta hear," Trevor said.

"Every Southerner knows how to do at least one of two things," Christian continued.

Everly raised an eyebrow as she turned to him. "Really? I've gotta hear this too."

"It's true," Christian said straight-faced. "They either know how to fish or cook."

Trevor cocked his head, looking thoughtful. "Hmm ... he makes a good point."

"I don't know the first thing about fishing," Everly countered, wrinkling her nose. "Nor do I want to learn."

"But I know how to fish." Trevor motioned at Everly. "And you know how to cook. So between the two of us, we've got it covered."

Everly chuckled as she looked at Christian, shaking her head. "The things you come up with."

"Mom, can Sadie and I be excused?"

Blade looked down to the end of the table at the young boy who'd spoken. He was sitting across from a Polynesian girl about his same age. Christian had introduced them earlier. Jordan was Everly's son from a previous marriage, and Sadie was Kat's daughter from a previous marriage.

Everly nodded. "Yes, you may. But you need to make sure you get your homework done before you and Sadie play video games."

"But m-om," he countered.

"That goes for you too, Sadie," Kat added.

Sadie looked at Trevor. "Do I have to?"

"Yes, do as your mom tells you," Trevor said.

Sadie sighed dramatically. "O-kay."

They darted off.

Everly shook her head. "Kids."

Kat eyed Blade and Dani with interest. "So, how did you two meet?"

Blade nearly choked on his saliva as he turned to Dani.

"Do you wanna tell them, or should I," she chirped, a devilish glint in her dark eyes. A large smile broke over her lips. "Okay, I'll tell them. We met on the bus."

Blade thought for a millisecond she might leave it at that, but *no*, she had to tell the rest.

"I was sitting in a seat, minding my own business, when this guy stepped up beside me. There weren't any seats left on the bus. Blade, being a gentleman, let a woman and her child take his seat."

Dani made him sound so noble. He didn't dare tell them that part of the reason he gave up his seat was because he thought it might help to stand. He braced himself for the rest.

"Anyway, I looked up at him and realized something was wrong. So, I touched his arm and asked if he was feeling okay. To which he responded, *yes*." She paused. "And then he threw up all over me."

This brought bursts of hearty laughter from around the table. Kat was laughing so hard tears streamed down her face. "Are you serious?"

"Absolutely," Dani said.

Trevor winced. "That's disgusting."

"It was disgusting," Dani agreed. "For me, and for poor Blade." She touched his arm as she spoke, the warmth of her touch seeping into his skin. "We got off the bus as quickly as we could and showered off at Mokoli'i Park."

Christian shook his head. "A screenwriter couldn't have written that any better. That's awesome."

Blade sat back in his seat. "Dani didn't tell you the best part."

Her eyes widened as she turned to him. "I didn't?"

He slid an arm around her shoulders and pulled her close, thinking he could get away with it because she wouldn't want to cause a scene. "People on the bus were understandably upset. One guy was ready to punch me, but Dani came to my rescue. She told him off and led me off the bus. I tell you, she's my *hero*."

Blade loved the color that crept into Dani's cheeks as she looked down at her plate and said casually. "You're making more of it than it was. Anyone would've done the same."

"Not necessarily," Everly said. "What you did was pretty awesome."

"Yep, it was," Blade agreed.

They chatted for another fifteen minutes or so until Trevor pushed back his chair. "Well, Kat and I need to get home. Thanks for dinner, Everly. It was outstanding."

"But you haven't eaten dessert yet," Everly protested.

Trevor touched his stomach. "I'm afraid I'm too full."

Kat stood. "Me, too."

"Okay, I'll wrap some up for you to take home," Everly said.

Trevor smiled. "We'd love that."

Blade took this as a cue that it was time to leave. He scooted back his chair and stood as Dani did the same. "Thank you," he said. "Dinner was excellent."

"It was so nice meeting all of you," Dani added.

"We enjoyed meeting you too," Kat said, stepping around the table to give Dani a hug.

Trevor looked around. "I guess I'd better round up Sadie."

Kat offered a parting wave as they left.

"Thanks again," Blade said, placing an arm around Dani. "We'd better get going too." She tensed, but didn't pull away.

Christian frowned. "It's too bad you have to leave so soon." He looked at Blade. "I was hoping maybe the two of us could go out by the pool and talk shop."

"We've got plenty of time," Blade said quickly, looking at Dani who nodded in the affirmative. "We just didn't want to overstay our welcome."

Everly chuckled. "That's not possible with a Southerner and a Polynesian."

"That's right," Christian agreed, "if the Southern hospitality doesn't get you, the Aloha Spirit will."

"What he means is that we never meet a stranger," Everly added.

Christian stepped behind Everly and slid his arms around her waist, then kissed her cheek. "You outdid yourself, babe. Dinner was fabulous. Thank you."

Everly seemed to melt in his arms. "You're welcome."

Blade couldn't get over how warm and open Christian was at home as opposed to how aloof and reserved he was in the public eye. The exchange between Christian and Everly felt intimate, personal. He glanced at Dani who seemed to be reading his thoughts. Her dark eyes radiated warmth as she smiled, causing Blade to lose his train of thought for a second. He shook off the sensation with an inward laugh. It was insane how mesmerized he was by Dani Fairchild.

"Blade and I'll be out by the pool," Christian said to Everly.

"I see how it is. Running out before the cleanup," she teased.

Christian gave her a sheepish grin. "I wouldn't dream of it. I meant we'd go out after I help you clean up."

"Yes," Blade piped in. "How can I help?"

Everly waved a hand. "No worries. Go on out."

"I'll help clean up," Dani offered.

Everly rewarded her with an appreciative smile. "Thank you that would be nice."

Dani began stacking plates and carrying them to the sink.

"Dani, what do you do for a living?" Everly asked.

Blade caught Dani's slight hesitation, knew she was trying to figure out how to answer. He, too, wanted to hear what she would say. "I have a healthy cooking blog."

Everly's eyes lit up. "Wow, that's awesome."

Christian groaned. "Oh, no, don't get her talking about cooking, or you'll be here all night."

Everly shooed at Blade and Christian. "Go on now. Dani and I have lots to discuss."

EVEN IN THE DARK, Blade was awestruck by the splendor of Christian's estate. The pool was nice enough to be at a five-star resort with the picturesque waterfall framing the back section. Blade was doing well financially and would be doing even better when the new Jase Scott movie hit the box office. Still, Blade couldn't imagine amassing the kind of wealth Christian had. Then again, from what he'd read about Christian, it had been Kat's investments in her hotel chains that took Christian from millionaire to billionaire status. "This is incredible. I can see why you love it here."

"Yes, it's home." Christian motioned toward the patio table and chairs. "Have a seat."

They sat down. For the first time since he'd arrived at Christian's house, tension crept over Blade. He could tell this wasn't just a light-hearted chat. Christian had something important he wanted to say.

Christian crossed his legs and sat back in his seat. Blade then realized he was sitting ramrod straight, clutching the arms of the chair. He willed himself to relax. Maybe he was overthinking this—being too much like his dad and Doug who were always waiting for something bad to happen.

"You're probably wondering why I wanted to talk to you alone."

Blade attempted a smile. "The thought did cross my mind."

Christian stroked his chin. "You did well today."

"Really?" *Geez.* Could that have sounded any more juvenile? A rookie wet behind the ears? "Thanks," he added.

"I could tell you were a little nervous."

Sweat beaded across Blade's forehead as he swallowed. "Yeah, I'm working on that. Trying to stay loose, ya know?"

Christian waved a hand. "No worries. That'll come with time." A slight smile crept over his lips. "I've seen enough of your work to know you're the real deal. You've got the talent to make it in the business."

For a second, Blade was stunned by the compliment. "T-thanks." He gulped. He'd not been expecting that at all. Just as he was doing a victory dance in his head, he realized Christian was studying him. He rubbed his eyebrow. "What?"

"When *Hostile Territory* becomes a blockbuster hit, there are a few things you need to know."

Blade's veins thrummed like an electric current was running through them. Oh, how he hoped Christian was correct. He'd be a megastar, at the top of the food chain.

A slight smile crept over Christian's lips. "I remember being right where you are, on the cusp of attaining it all."

He leaned forward. "Thanks to you and the producers for giving me a shot. I want you to know how much I appreciate this. I won't let you down. I'll do what it takes to measure up."

Christian nodded. "I have no doubt," he said, but Blade could tell his mind was elsewhere. Christian was a hard man to figure out. "Are you familiar with the Solomon Islands in the South Pacific?"

"No, I'm not." Okay, he had no idea where this was going.

"The islands are breathtaking, a remote paradise. But one of the islands has a unique resource—timber. For the past sixty years, loggers have been extracting timber from the land in a massive deforestation with no regard for how it's affecting the ecosystem or the people. All the loggers are interested in is making a profit, exploiting the resources to fit their needs." He locked eyes with Blade. "Do you understand where I'm going with this?"

"Kind of, I guess. I'm the forest?" He felt like he was in school again.

"Exactly. You have a gift, which the Hollywood bigwigs will want. But if you're not careful, they'll use you up and then go on to the next person. All you'll be left with is ruin."

"But you're not ruined." Blade motioned, encompassing their surroundings. "On the contrary, you seem to have built a great life for yourself. And I'm not just talking about your estate. You and Everly are obviously close."

"Yes, I'm so grateful to have Everly. She grounds me, reminds me of what's truly important." Christian's eyes took on a faraway look. "It took me years, and a lifetime of hurt, to reach the point where I am now. I was taken in by the Hollywood glitz, thought my self-esteem hinged on my next role or the amount of money I was making. But then I had an accident, and everything changed."

Blade had done his homework, knew about the car accident that had left Christian's actor girlfriend paralyzed. The girl eventually took her own life. Blade couldn't imagine the turmoil that must've put Christian through, but he seemed to have made peace with it.

"You know all about my past." It was a statement rather than a question.

"Yes." Blade hoped it was okay to admit that.

Christian nodded. "I know about you too."

Blade jerked, eyes widening. "You do?"

"I make a point of getting to know my co-stars. And more importantly, to get to know the man to whom I'm handing over the keys to the Jase Scott series." He gave Blade a speculative look. "I know about your mom's skiing accident."

Blade clutched the arms of the chair.

"I know your mom was trying to get away from a stalker, which is why she was going so fast down the slope and crashed into a tree."

Blade's face burned as he gulped. He should've been used to having his private life on display, but hearing Christian detail it in cold, black and white facts was a kick in the gut.

"I also know about your stalker."

Blade's brows shot down in a V as he clenched his jaw. Had Doug been shooting off his mouth? He'd promised to keep that on the down low. "H-how?"

"Kat told me."

Blade nodded. Of course she would've told him. When she didn't bring it up at the shoot earlier today, he hoped it would just go away.

"Do the police have any leads?"

"Unfortunately, no."

Compassion touched Christian's features. "I hope they find and arrest the stalker soon. That's got to be unnerving."

A shiver went down Blade's spine. "You have no idea," he said quietly. The dark landscape around them seemed to close in as Blade hugged his arms. For all he knew the stalker was out there in the shadows, watching his every move. The conversation lagged as Blade rushed to fill the silence. "I can assure you, I won't let this interfere with my performance."

Christian waved away the comment, a trace of amusement in his eyes. "I told you, I know you've got what it takes. Or you wouldn't be here. That's not why I'm bringing it up."

"Why are you bringing it up?" Blade shot back, unable to hide the bite in his voice. He didn't like the idea of Christian toying with him.

Christian sat up straight in his seat, his voice taking on the weary tone of one who'd been there. "Because once you reach stardom, every media outlet from here to New York will work tirelessly to drag up every speck of dirt on you they can find. They'll dissect you, put you under a microscope, then shout your shortcomings from the rooftops. You have to be prepared to handle that."

He clutched his hands. How in the heck was a person supposed to get prepared for that? His mother's death. The stalker who contributed to it, a man who was never brought to justice. And then Blade's own stalker—a cruel coincidence considering his family history.

"It's not easy. Trust me, I know. But it's better to hear it from a friend, so you can get ready." He paused, his perceptive eyes scoping Blade. "You've got to learn to live life on your own terms. Realize that with or without the accolades you're okay with the person you are ... right here, right now. And when you become a star, protect yourself, set boundaries—make sure they don't drain you dry. You get what I'm saying?"

"Yeah, I have to hold to my principles. Get myself straight in here." Blade pointed to his head.

"No, you have to get yourself straight in here," Christian said, pointing to his chest. "Something that's hard to do in Hollywood, but it is possible." A smile played on his lips. "It helps to have a good woman by your side, which you obviously do. Dani seems like she's good at keeping you on your toes."

Blade chuckled. "Yes, she is. She's stubborn."

Christian laughed. "I know a thing or two about stubborn

women. Just ask Everly or my sister. You and Dani seem like a good fit. And she seems crazy about you."

A burst of warmth went through Blade. "Really? What makes you say that?"

He shrugged. "It's written all over her face when she looks at you."

He scowled. "She's determined to keep me at arm's length. Says she's afraid of falling for me because she thinks I'll leave her high and dry once the filming is done."

Christian lifted an eyebrow. "Would you?"

He squared his jaw, not appreciating the inference. "No way. I'd fight tooth and nail to hold onto Dani. She's the real deal. Any guy would be lucky to have her." He stopped when he saw the grin on Christian's face. "You're baiting me, aren't you?"

He spread his hands. "You're easy to get a rise out of, but no, I'm not baiting you. Only trying to help you keep your eye and heart trained on what really matters."

Blade cocked his head. "If you don't mind me asking, why are you helping me?"

A smile slid over Christian's lips. "Because you remind me of myself. I'm only telling you what I wish someone would've told me."

"Thank you."

"You're welcome. But the true thanks will come through your actions, after you get everything you think you've always wanted."

"Fair enough."

A comfortable silence settled between them as Blade let his thoughts get lost in the sound of rushing water and the gentle ripples of the dark, fathomless water as it lapped against the sides of the pool. Christian had given him a lot to think about. He didn't want his private life on display for the world—didn't want to rehash the pain of losing his mother in such a senseless accident. And he didn't want to get used up and thrown by the wayside, or lose himself in the Hollywood hoopla. He'd give his all on set, but his private life was his business. When the time came, maybe he needed to purchase a quiet estate like Christian's. Someplace he could go to recharge his battery. But he didn't want to go it alone. He needed Dani. He jerked slightly, laughing at himself. He'd only known Dani for a couple of days. It was too soon to start planning their future, but he couldn't stop thinking about her. Was Dani into him? Christian seemed to think so. The prospect was interesting ... thrilling. He could only hope Christian was right.

11

D ani scooted the chair around so she could prop her feet on the seat, then leaned back, enjoying the cool of the evening. The roar of the ocean was as soothing as a mother's lullaby. Blade had gone to the guest room to change into shorts and call Doug. He'd been in the bedroom a while, so Dani assumed the conversation wasn't going well.

The evening had gone well ... much better than Dani had hoped. Dinner was excellent, and she enjoyed the witty conversation between Christian and his family. It was fun getting to know Everly, and she'd shown genuine interest in Dani's blog. They could've talked all night about different recipes and cooking techniques. It was unreal to think of all the crazy turns Dani's life had taken in a matter of two days. Samantha wouldn't believe it if she told her.

Her phone vibrated against the table. *Speak of the devil.* "Hey, Sam."

"Hey, how are things going? What've you been up to?"

"Oh, you know ... the usual." She glanced at the sky, hoping lightning wouldn't strike. "Let's see ... what's new? I got a job."

"So soon? That's fantastic! Where are you working?"

Here's where it got tricky. She shifted in her seat, trying to figure out the best way to navigate this. "You remember the guy I told you about? Blake Stevens?"

"The doctor who vomited on you on the bus?"

"Yep, he's the one. Well, as it turns out, he's not really a doctor."

"O-kay. Then why did he tell you he was?"

Dani cringed at the wariness in Samantha's voice. She couldn't blame Samantha for being paranoid, especially considering how many times Dani had gotten herself in a jam.

"He's an actor ... here filming a movie."

Silence.

She tightened her hold on the phone. "Sam? Are you there?"

"I'm here." She let out a long breath. "Why did he lie to you?"

Dani's throat went dry as she swallowed. "He didn't want anyone to know who he really was because he was embarrassed about the situation—throwing up on the bus."

"What does this have to do with a job?"

"Blade hired me as his ... sort of, as his personal assistant."

"Who in the heck is Blade? And what do you mean by *sort of*?"

"His real name is Blake Stevens, like he told me. But his acting name is Blade Sloan. I act as a personal coach, help him loosen up so he can perform." She heard Samantha's sudden intake of breath, realized she was digging herself deeper and deeper, but she couldn't seem to stop her mouth from rambling. "He gets stressed due to the acting. I give him positive reinforcement. It really helped him today as he ran through his lines."

"Is this a legitimate job?"

She pictured how Samantha would look, a deep crease between her brows as she frowned. "Absolutely. He's paying me more than I was making as a receptionist." The excitement was too much to contain as her voice bubbled. "You won't believe who Blade and I had dinner with tonight."

"The Pope?"

Her brows bunched together. "Quit being a smart alec."

"Sorry." Long pause. "Okay, who'd you have dinner with?"

Samantha's voice was flat like she was bracing herself for bad news. "Never mind," Dani huffed. Samantha could be such a downer.

"Come on," Samantha growled. "Don't be a baby."

"I'm not." She thrust out her lower lip, knowing she was.

"Tell me," she pleaded, her tone starting to thaw.

Dani couldn't hold it in any longer. "Christian Ross and his wife. And Trevor and Kat Spencer."

"What?" Samantha boomed. "Are you serious? The Christian Ross, from the Jase Scott series?"

"Yep, the very one."

"And Kat and Trevor Spencer from *Fix it Up Hawaii*? Oh my gosh! That's crazy." Samantha giggled. "How in the heck did you manage that? I've only been gone for a couple of days and now you're dining with movie stars?"

The awe in Samantha's voice was gratifying. Dani leaned back, trailing a hand through her hair as she let out a throaty laugh. "That's how I roll."

"So, is Blake, um Blade?" She paused. "What did you say his last name was?"

"Sloan."

"Oh yeah. That's right. Blade Stone. Is he a big-time actor too? I've never heard of him."

"He's starring in the new Jase Scott movie with Christian. This is Blade's shot at making it to the big league. That's why he's been so stressed."

"I guess that makes sense." A beat of silence stretched between them. "Just be careful. Don't go gaga over Blade. Take things slow, okay?"

"I will."

"Promise?"

She rolled her eyes. "Yes." She jumped as Blade slid his arms around her.

"Take what slow?" he murmured in her ear. His voice had a husky edge that sent a quiver of awareness through her.

Her first thought was that he felt strong and warm, and she liked how the muscles in his arms moved against her. She stiffened. No, no, no! She had to fight this!

"Is someone there with you?" Samantha asked.

"Nope. Just me." Her voice had an unnatural edge that screamed suspicious. Delicious tingles circled down her spine as Blade trailed light kisses down her neck. She tried to wiggle away from him, but he held her tight. The nerve! He knew exactly what he was doing— getting all lovey-dovey when she couldn't get away from him, not without Samantha knowing something was up. "Samantha. I've gotta let you go."

"Why? Are you sure you're okay?"

"I'm fine." Dani's head swam with desire when Blade nipped the tender spot behind her earlobe.

"Mom wants to say hello."

"Tell her I'll call her tomorrow. I'm getting another call. It's probably Rena."

"Oh, okay, I love you."

"Love you too. Bye." Quickly, she ended the call, then spun around. "What do you think you're doing?" she spat indignantly. "You can't just kiss me like that! Get me all confused."

"You're confused," he drawled with a chuckle. "That's a good thing, right?" He sat down in the chair where her feet had been and pulled it so close he was a breath away.

Her heart started hammering so fast she could hardly breathe. "No, it's not a good thing," she fired back.

He cocked a confident smile. "Why not?"

"Because, we're not a couple!" she blustered. "And if you think I'm just gonna melt at your feet because you're flashing those baby blues at me, you've got another thing coming, mister."

He trailed a finger along the naked flesh of her arm, sending her cells swirling. "We could be a couple," he said softly, searching her face. "Would it be so bad if we gave *us* a chance?" A hopeful smile tipped up the corners of his lips. "See where things lead? I like you, Dani. A lot."

"I like you too." *Crap!* Had she just said that out loud? Well, it was true. She did like him. In fact, she was crazy about him.

A quirky grin flitted over his lips. "I like you. You like me. What's the problem?"

"Geography."

He sputtered out a laugh. "What?"

"Geography. You live in LA. I live here." She squared her jaw. "I've been through this too many times to count. I'm tired of getting my heart stomped on." She gave him a remorseful smile. "Sorry, but that's just the way it is." She could tell from his wounded look that her comments cut. But she owed it to Blade to tell him the truth.

His jaw tightened. "I'm not buying it."

She had a flashback to earlier in the day when Doug said he wasn't buying the idea of her being Blade's massage therapist. She lifted her chin. "Well, that's too bad, because it's the truth."

"It's not fair," he muttered.

"No, it's not, but life rarely is," she snipped.

He continued as if she hadn't spoken, "... Making me pay for the sins of past guys who've hurt you."

She rocked back, not expecting that. "Huh?"

He cupped her jaw. Even in the semi-darkness with only the deck light, his intense gaze pierced her to the core. "I know you've been hurt before, but eventually you're gonna find the right guy." His eyes held hers, and when he spoke his voice was tender, almost a whisper. "And who's to say that guy isn't me?"

Any response she could've given died in her throat as he leaned in and gave her a long, drugging kiss that sent all rebuttals flying to the wind. All she could think about was the insistent feel of his lips against hers as he deepened the kiss, sending shock waves rippling through her.

He pulled back, searching her face. "Can I take that as a yes?"

She couldn't help but laugh. "*Geez.* You're like a dog who won't let go of a bone."

He fingered one of her curls. "Please."

A sense of reckless abandon surged over her, and she felt a sliver of the old Dani return, as she lowered her voice to a throaty whisper. "Kiss me again, and I'll think about it."

———

THIS IS A DREAM, Blade kept repeating, but it felt so real. They were on a boat with the sun sparkling on the water like an endless sea of glass. Dani's laughter floated like delicate chimes in the salty breeze, her nut-brown eyes shining with adventure. Her impish smile held just enough mystery to keep him guessing, but she was also warm and open. He loved the freedom of being with her—like he could conquer the world. She tilted her head to the sun, her glorious mane of curls cascading down her slender back. He stepped up behind her and wrapped his arms around her. She leaned back, resting her head on his chest. He'd never felt this content, yet so alive.

Dani reached back and caressed his face, but her fingers were ice. Blade was cold, so cold he feared he'd never be warm again. Dani's expression changed to terror as water engulfed them. He dove into the black ocean to find her, but there was only emptiness where she should've been. A suffocating panic cloaked Blade, shutting out all the light until the darkness was complete and terrible.

The scene changed, Blade was on a ski slope, the glittering snow so white it hurt his eyes. He saw her from a distance at first. Then he was right upon her. He could feel his mother's fear as if it were his own, oozing out and bleeding into the snow, blotting out all reason. She had to get away. She glanced over her shoulder and saw the stalker closing in. She dug her poles deep into the snow as she pushed off, whizzing down the double black diamond slope like a jailbird out of his cell. Suddenly Blade was falling. He felt the brute impact when she hit the tree, pain splintering through him, eclipsing all else.

Blade shot up in bed, his heart pounding as his hands wrung the covers. It took a second for him to get oriented. *It was a stupid dream*, he muttered, rubbing his hands through his hair. He was about to rest back against the pillow when he saw the door. It was partially open.

He distinctly remembered closing it. Hot prickles pelted over him like needles, then, he went cold. He heard a noise. He jerked, his body tensing as he craned his ears. There it was again—a slight muffled sound. Footsteps? He got out of bed and made his way to the door. He looked around wildly, searching for something that could be used as a weapon. But he came up empty handed. His heart in his throat, he peered into the hall. Nothing.

He stepped out and made his way to the living room, half-expecting someone to jump out and attack him any second. When he got to the front door, he heard another sound. Frantic footsteps—someone running. He flung open the door and nearly choked when he saw Dani standing there. Her face was chalky, her eyes large, brown coins.

She let out a cry and rushed into his arms. "Someone was in the guesthouse."

He looked around at the black night, the darkness shrouding them like a curtain. The person could be anywhere, watching. A sense of foreboding trickled over him. "Someone was in here too," he said quietly. "Let's go in." He didn't want to be out here like sitting ducks.

When they stepped inside, he closed the door and locked it. Then something occurred to him. What if the person was in here, with them? Instead of outside? What would he do? How could he protect Dani? He took a breath, willing himself to calm down. Panicking wouldn't solve anything. Then he realized Dani was trembling. He put his arms around her, drawing her close.

"Oh my gosh! I can't believe this is happening."

"Me neither." The words seemed to fall out between them like meaningless drivel as he rubbed her back.

She pulled back, her face tight with fear. "What should we do? Call the police?"

His first instinct was to not call the cops, because he was so used to trying to keep things on the down low—fight this battle privately away from the public eye. But now Dani was involved. And they didn't even know for sure if this was related to the stalker. Maybe someone had just broken into Dani's house. He looked around. "Did you notice if anything was taken?" From what he could tell, everything looked untouched. Chances were, it was the stalker.

"No, I just got up and ran here."

They jumped when they heard a loud whack.

"They're still out there." Tears filled Dani's eyes.

Something in Blade shifted. It was one thing for this blasted stalker to hound him, but terrorizing Dani was another thing altogether. His eyes narrowed as adrenaline coursed through his veins. "Where do you keep your knives?"

Dani's jaw dropped. "What?"

He rushed to the kitchen. "I'm going out there to put a stop to this once and for all."

She followed on his heels. "You can't. What if something happens to you?"

"This has gone on long enough," he muttered, pulling open drawers until he found the knives. He grabbed a butcher knife and clutched it like a dagger.

"Maybe we should call the police," Dani said, wringing her hands.

He squared his jaw. "Good idea. Call them now. In the meantime, I'll see if I catch the person. I'll be back," he growled. "Lock the door behind me. Don't open the door unless it's me."

"How will I know it's you?" A crazed look came into her eyes as she clutched the back of the chair.

"I'll knock three times."

She nodded. "Be careful."

A look passed between them. "I will."

Blade tightened his grip on the knife as he stepped outside. He heard the click of the lock behind him. *Good.* At least Dani would be safe. He stole down the wooden staircase as quietly as possible. But in his ears, his every step sounded like a firecracker going off. He scoped the empty space around him, anticipating an attack. The air had turned cool, raising goose bumps over his arms, reminding him that he only had on shorts and a flimsy t-shirt. There wasn't another soul in sight. He got to the bottom of the stairs and planted his feet in a battle stance, ready to pounce, glaring into the darkness. If the intruder was watching, he'd know Blade meant business. He scoured the empty yard and driveway. Nothing.

"Who are you?" he said, the sound of his words lifting into the salty air. The only response was the steady pounding of the waves on the beach behind him. "What do you want?"

Silence.

He walked around the entire house, even doing a sweep of the beach. No one was there. Finally, there was nothing else he could do except return to the house. Dani was probably beside herself with worry. When he reached the staircase, he saw it on the bottom step. A single white rose, tipped in blood. His breath froze. Someone had placed it there when he was checking the beach. He whirled around, trying to catch a glimpse of the stalker. His skin crawled like it was trying to leave his body. The person had to be close by, watching. He glared out across the driveway, then at the yard, and to the dark houses on either side. "If you want me. I'm right here," he taunted.

A burst of anger seared through him as he picked up the rose by the stem and flung it across the yard. He swore loud enough for the person to hear. "You're a coward, lurking around in the dark. A pathetic coward with no life of your own. Otherwise you wouldn't be trying to leech onto me."

He stood, waiting for the stalker to retaliate. He didn't know what he would do, exactly, if the person did attack. But he was tired of doing nothing. He was tired of being afraid. He stood there a full five minutes or more, but nothing happened.

Finally, he turned around and walked back up the stairs.

12

Dani paced back and forth—three steps forward, three steps back—clenching and unclenching her hands. Blade had been gone a long time. She was going to do as she'd said and call the police. Then she realized that she'd run out of the guest-house without her phone. Had Blade taken his phone with him, or was it still in his room? She went into the guest room. His phone was on the dresser. She picked it up to call and realized she didn't know his pass code. *Crap!* Then she spotted the word "emergency" on the bottom left side of the screen. She pressed it and called 911.

"911, what is the address of your emergency?"

Dani rattled off the address, practically screaming into the phone. She also gave her name when the dispatcher asked for it.

"What is your emergency?"

"Someone broke into my house."

"Is the intruder there now?"

"No, but my friend went out to look and hasn't come back. I'm afraid something happened." Her voice quivered, dread knotting her stomach. *Please let Blade be okay*, she silently prayed. Dani nearly jumped out of her skin when she heard the knock at the door, letting out a startled gasp.

"Ms. Fairchild, are you okay?" she heard the dispatcher say, but she was listening for the knocks. She'd heard the first. She tensed ... waiting ... two ...three. A giddy relief pulsed through her making her dizzy.

"Are you okay? Is someone there with you?" the dispatcher asked.

"My friend's coming back in. Hold on."

"Ms. Fairchild, I need you to stay on the phone with me until the police arrive."

"I'm here." She moved the phone away from her ear.

"Blade? Is that you?" The door didn't have a peephole. Generally, people felt safe on the North Shore. In fact, most of the neighbors didn't even lock their doors.

"It's me."

She let out a sigh of relief as she opened the door. "Oh my gosh! I'm glad you're okay!" Tears rushed to her eyes. She'd not realized how much she was starting to care about him until this moment. She heard someone talking and realized the dispatcher was still on the phone.

"Ms. Fairchild. Are you okay?"

"I'm fine," she barked, then saw blood on Blade's hands. She let out a cry, her knees going weak. "Oh, no!"

"What?" he asked, then looked down at his hands.

The phone fell to the floor as she put her hands to her mouth. "W-what happened? Did you hurt someone?" This was like something out of a horror movie.

"No, I didn't see anyone."

"But the blood."

"A white rose was left on the bottom step. The petals were tipped in blood. There must've been some on the stem as well. I threw it across the yard, ranting at the stalker, hoping to draw her out. But it didn't work." The corners of his jaws twitched, a haunted expression in his eyes. "I'm sure she was out there though, watching the whole thing."

Dani's stomach lurched. The sight of the knife and the blood on

Blade's hands was too much. The floor seemed to give way beneath her as she stumbled, then caught herself before she fell.

"Are you okay?"

She nodded numbly, looking at the knife in his hand. "Maybe you should put that away and clean your hands before the cops arrive." If the cops rushed in and saw him, they'd arrest him on the spot, thinking he was the intruder.

He nodded and went to the sink.

Oh, crap. The 911 dispatcher. She'd forgotten all about her. She bent down and picked up the phone. "Hello?"

No one was on the line. Either the woman had hung up or the call had gotten disconnected when she dropped the phone. It buzzed. She was going to answer it, but then realized it was a text.

Blade wiped his hands on a dishtowel and went to her side. "You're getting a text," she announced unnecessarily, handing him the phone.

She saw the stricken look on his face, heard him moan. Her temples pounded more furiously than the surf outside. "What?"

He held the phone out to her. At first, it didn't register what she was seeing. Then she realized it was images. The first was of her sleeping in her bedroom and the second was of Blade. This was followed by a text that said, "Next time, I won't just take your picture." Dani's hands began to shake as tremors racked her body. Her knees turned to jelly as she clutched the back of the couch for support. "Those are of us."

"Yes," he croaked, his face paler than sand.

Dani's mind whirled, trying to put everything together. "Someone broke in and took pictures of us sleeping." Alarm spiked through her, nearly leaving her breathless. The pictures were taken at close range. "Whoever took these was right next to us." The room started to spin.

"Are you okay?" Blade reached for her arm and led her to the sofa, where they both sat down.

Tears sprang to her eyes as she turned to him. "What have I done? The stalker knows where I live ... where my family lives." She clutched her hands.

Blade put an arm around her. "I'm so sorry."

The remorse on his face cut her to the quick. "I won't let anyone hurt you," he said vehemently, fire flashing in his eyes.

"You can't promise that," she said dully. "If the person had wanted to harm us, he or she could have."

He put his free hand over hers to stay the trembling. His lips thinned, eyes narrowing. "This is all my fault. I shouldn't have given Tal the evening off. If he'd been here, this wouldn't have happened."

Dani only shook her head.

He tightened his hold on her, putting his lips to her hair. "It'll be all right."

She leaned into him, hoping he was right.

A succession of loud knocks caused Dani to jump.

"This is the police."

"About time," she muttered dryly. It was a dang good thing the intruder was gone and not an immediate threat or they would've been dead by the time the police arrived. Everything operated at a slower pace in Hawaii, but this was ridiculous. She went to the door and answered it. Two officers stood outside.

"Are you Dani Fairchild, the one who called 911?"

"Yes, I am." She motioned. "Come in."

THE OFFICERS WEREN'T happy when they learned Blade had thrown the rose across the yard, tampering with the evidence. But Blade had been through this enough to know that the stalker hadn't left any prints or other incriminating evidence. He showed them the texts, which he figured were sent from a burner phone. Blade explained that these were the first texts he'd received, but he'd been harassed for months. He gave them Doug's number so they could follow up with him. Further, he explained that Doug was working with detectives from the Honolulu Police Department. They assured Blade they'd follow up with Honolulu district the following day. The officers did a thorough search of the house, guesthouse interiors, and outside premises before leaving.

It was now three a.m. While Blade was exhausted, he wasn't the least bit sleepy. He wondered if he should call Doug and let him know what was happening. He'd called him earlier when he and Dani returned from Christian's place. Doug was livid that he'd ditched Tal, but was rendered speechless when Blade told him about having dinner at Christian's place. "Well, it's good that you're getting to know Christian. Maybe that'll help you loosen up," he finally said.

Blade knew that Doug had a hard time with his success, and if the situation had been reversed—if he'd wanted to be an actor ever since he was a kid and his brother ended up being the one discovered— Blade might've had a hard time with it too. So he really couldn't fault Doug. But still, it got old. He needed someone in his corner, now more than ever. And Doug didn't seem capable of anything except tearing him down. He'd asked the police officers to keep this incident under wraps, and they assured him they would. But there were no guarantees. For all he knew, news of the stalker could be broadcast everywhere by morning. Christian was right. He had to look this in the eye and face it, come what may.

He watched as Dani poured two cups of hot water and placed tea bags in them. He felt terrible for involving her in this. "I called Tal. He's coming over."

She nodded, drawing her lips into a tight line.

He stepped up to her and placed his arms around her. "I'm so sorry," he said again, pressing his lips into her hair. He was relieved when she didn't pull away. Her warmth radiated over him, helping to ease some of the tension. A part of him wanted to scoop Dani up in his arms and run away with her. Forget he was an actor. Forget there was a stalker out there waiting to do him harm. He wanted it to just be him and Dani, away from all the problems.

"It all seems surreal."

"Yeah, for me too."

She turned to face him, her dark eyes filling with some indefinable emotion. "When you were outside, I was afraid." Her voice caught as she took in a breath and began again. "I was afraid you weren't coming back." A long, brittle silence stretched between them. "And then when I saw you holding the knife with blood on your hands ..." She shuddered, her voice trailing off. She studied his face with such intensity he had the impression she was staring into his soul. "I can't imagine what you've been through."

The tenderness in her voice caused his throat to thicken. "It's been hard."

"No wonder you were sick that day on the bus. I would've been too." She swallowed. "Do I need to be worried?" Her voice faltered as her lower lip trembled. "I just keep thinking about that person being in my room." A crazed look came into her eyes.

He rubbed her arms. "The stalker's after me, not you."

She let out a humorless laugh. "Yeah, I know. I'm just collateral damage, right?"

He cringed at the bite in her voice. He didn't blame her for being upset. "I promise, I won't let anything happen to you. I'll hire ten bodyguards if necessary and make sure they never leave your side." He realized that was the wrong thing to say when he saw the mortified look on her face.

"So, I'll never have any more privacy, is that what you're saying?"

He wanted to punch something—to scream at the top of his lungs for the insanity to stop. Whoever this person was, he or she was stripping everything from him bit by bit. Now that he'd found Dani, he didn't want to lose her. But he didn't want her to get hurt because of him either. "No, that's not what I'm saying. It would just be temporary ... until we can find out who's doing this."

"Didn't you say the stalker has been doing things in LA, months before you came?"

He clenched his teeth. "Yes." His gut churned like it was full of rocks. Even though it would kill him to let her go, he couldn't let Dani become a victim because of him. His voice sounded dead and flat in his ears. "If you don't feel comfortable being with me, I'll understand. You're under no obligation to keep working for me. And as much as I like you, if you don't want a relationship ... well, I can't blame you."

He let go of her arms, his hands dropping to his sides. This is where it would end. She'd take the *out*, and that would be that. The knowledge settled over him like a concrete block around his neck, dragging him deeper and deeper into despair.

She cocked an eyebrow. "Really?"

He was taken aback by the defiance in her voice. "That's what you want, isn't it?"

Her brows slanted down as she lifted her chin, giving him a blistering look. "If you think I'm the kind of person who tucks her tail and runs at the first sign of trouble, then you don't know me very well, Blade Sloan."

An incredulous laugh bubbled in his throat, and he felt a rush of admiration for this feisty woman filling his grayscale world with brilliant hues. "So, you're okay with continuing our relationship?"

The beginnings of a smile tipped the corners of her lips as she patted his cheek. Her eyes seemed to grow brighter with an inner fire that kindled hope within him. For one tiny moment, he felt invincible like there was nothing he couldn't accomplish with Dani by his side. "Yes, blue eyes, I think we should keep moving forward." She turned to move away, but he caught hold of her wrist and moved her back around.

"You're incredible," he murmured, taking in her delicately sculpted features and luscious lips. Her hair was a tangled mass of happy corkscrews that flowed over her shoulders. Without her makeup, she looked younger, but still stunningly beautiful. "How did I ever get lucky enough to find you?"

She chuckled, her thick, black lashes brushing against her cheekbones. "As long as you always remember that, we'll be just fine."

Her silky voice resonated deep inside him. "Every minute of every day," he said before pulling her to him. He threaded his hands through her glorious hair and pressed his lips to hers in a long, ardent kiss that left them both breathless.

13

Dani squirmed in her seat as Detective Kalia Kalama studied her with black, hawk eyes that missed nothing. This woman was no-nonsense, smart. When Dani and Blade arrived at the hotel, Kalia and her partner Luke Ripley were there waiting to question them about the night before. The officers who'd responded to the call had updated them on all that had occurred. Unfortunately, before they could delve into the nitty gritty of the stalker issue, Detective Kalama became preoccupied with Dani.

"Dani Fairchild," Kalia mused. "Where have I heard that name before?"

"I'm not sure." If Kalia had heard her name, it could only mean one thing—she was familiar with the Jett Barnes debacle. Blade was sitting beside Dani on the sofa in his suite, the detectives sitting in chairs across from them. Blade turned, giving Dani a questioning look, to which she shrugged.

Kalia bunched her brows. "Do you know Maurie Barclay?"

Heat crawled up Dani's neck. Maurie was Liam's business partner, whom he eventually married. Liam was the artist and billionaire heir that Dani jilted at the altar. When Dani took off to the club in Waikiki to meet Jett Barnes, Liam grew worried and asked Maurie's friend on the police force to check Jett out. Dani could only assume Kalia had been that friend. She owed Kalia a great debt. Through her they realized Jett had a criminal record, and then Liam and Samantha came rushing to her aid, saving her in the nick of time. Still, Dani didn't want her foible to be broadcast to Blade. She wanted to forget the dreadful event ever occurred and didn't want to be reminded of how naïve and stupid she'd been to fall for Jett Barnes. "Yes, she admitted. I know Liam."

Kalia pointed, a broad smile parting her lips. "Of course, you were the one who almost got kidnapped by Jett Barnes."

Blade's head whipped around. "What?"

Dani waved a hand. "That was another life. I'll tell you about it later," she added with a wan smile when he kept probing her with penetrating eyes.

"It's good to put a face behind the name," Kalia said. "You're lucky to be sitting here, alive and unscathed. Do you keep in touch with Maurie and Liam?"

Dani could tell Blade was about to burst with questions. "No, not really." *Please don't mention my engagement to Liam*, Dani prayed, balling her fist, her fingernails digging into her palm.

"Weren't you engaged to Liam?" Kalia asked.

Crap! "Yes," she muttered through tight lips as she looked at Blade, who was frowning.

"You were engaged?" he asked, his voice accusing.

Kalia laughed. "Yeah, she left the poor guy at the altar."

Blade shook his head. "Why didn't you tell me?"

Dani straightened in her seat. "I didn't feel the need to dredge up the past. Liam was the artist I told you about."

"Oh, yeah." He rubbed his eyebrow. "But I only thought he was your boyfriend."

This was ridiculous. Blast Kalia for opening her big mouth. "Boyfriend, fiancé ... what does it matter? I didn't marry him," she snapped. She turned to Detective Kalia, her eyes burning. "Did you come here to get the rundown on my past love life, or do you want to know what happened last night?"

Kalia chuckled. "Tell us everything. And I want every detail."

Blade began with Dani helping to fill the gaps. When they finished, they waited for the detectives to respond.

Luke Ripley leaned forward. "May I see your phone? I'd like to take a look at those texts."

Blade handed it over.

"We'll need to get access to your cell phone records," Detective Ripley said after he scrolled through them, "see if we can track the texts."

"Sure, talk to Doug. He can give you access." He spread his hands. "But I don't know if it'll lead to anything. The stalker's too smart to leave obvious bread crumbs."

Luke nodded. "That may be true. But we have to check all the angles."

Dani could hear the tension in Blade's voice, knew this was eating him up inside. She'd never tell Blade this, but right after everything happened, it had rattled her to the point where she'd considered walking away from him. But then she saw the pain in his eyes when he told her she didn't have to stick by him. Something had shifted inside her, and she knew she couldn't leave him. She had to see this through.

Kalia looked around. "Where is Doug, by the way? I wanted to tell him, and you," she said to Blade, "about the information we found when we looked at the security camera footage."

"What did you find?" Blade said. Dani heard the hope in his voice. Had they found something that would help put an end to this ordeal?

A looked passed between the two detectives before Kalia spoke. "Nothing."

Dani's heart dropped as she looked at Blade who shook his head. "That's not possible." His jaw tightened, his voice rising. "Someone came into my room and put the rose on the bed. The cameras had to pick that up."

Kalia spread her hands. "Yes, unless someone got access to the security feed and tampered with it."

Dani made a face. "Is that even possible? I would think a nice hotel like this would have top-notch security." Kat Spencer seemed like a thorough person who would make sure correct protocols were in place. Dani wished they'd known about the cameras last night so they could ask Kat about it.

"I suppose it's possible," Luke said. "Even the best systems aren't fool proof. We've called in a specialist to examine the footage to see if it was tampered with."

Kalia crossed her legs and adjusted her pants so the crease was straight. "There's also another possibility." She paused, like she was hesitant to speak.

"What?" Blade asked.

"It could be an inside job."

Dani heard Blade's breath catch. She reached for his hand and gave him a reassuring squeeze.

"That's why I need to speak to Doug," Kalia continued. "I need a list of everyone who has access to your suite—maids, security detail, everyone. In the meantime, I suggest you keep your bodyguards close. We don't want a repeat of what happened last night ..." her face clouded "... or worse."

Blade let out a long breath. "I just can't believe someone close to me would do this."

Kalia looked at Dani. "We're in the process of interviewing all of your neighbors to see if anyone saw anything out of the ordinary during the time of the break-in."

Crap! If the neighbors got questioned, one of them was sure to call Samantha and ask her about it. Oh, well. It had to be done. If Samantha found out, Dani would have to find a way to put her at ease. Otherwise, she'd be on the next plane back here. Dani didn't want that. Samantha deserved to have a worry-free Christmas.

The detectives stood, signaling the conversation had come to an end. Dani and Blade also rose to their feet. Kalia handed Blade her card. "We're not sure what the situation is, but we're covering all the bases in the hope we can bring an end to this quickly. Have Doug call me."

"Will do."

"We'll be in touch," Kalia said with a brisk nod as they left the room.

When it was just the two of them, Blade turned to Dani. "This whole thing makes me sick." He barked out a laugh. "I wish I could get my hands on the person behind this."

She put a hand on his arm. "Kalia and her partner seem sharp. Hopefully, they'll be able to find out who's responsible."

He nodded, but she could tell from the doubtful look on his face that he didn't believe her.

She touched his cheek. "Hey, it'll be okay."

He sighed. "Yeah." Then he tipped his head, giving her a speculative look. "So, tell me about Liam Barclay." He frowned. "And Jett Barnes. What's this about you almost getting kidnapped?"

She laughed lightly. "I'll tell you all about it when we have more time."

He encircled her waist. "Oh, no. You're not getting away that easily."

His biceps rippled against her as he held her in an iron grip. Desire sizzled through her when she saw his smoldering look that turned his eyes a deep blue. She drank in his rugged features, loving how he had that rough and tumble look she found so appealing.

He leaned forward and feather-kissed her nose, then his lips moved to her neck, brushing against her skin and evoking a tender ache that melted through her. She could get lost in his arms and stay this way forever. "Maybe you just need some persuading," he uttered in a low, husky tone. She parted her lips, expecting a kiss. "Or maybe I should just do this instead." She let out a squeal when he tickled her.

"Stop," she pled, laughing so hard she was crying as she broke away from him and tried to dart out of his reach, but he was faster. He grabbed her waist, tickling her mercilessly.

"Well, well. What do we have here?"

Dani and Blade froze as they looked at the blonde standing in the doorway.

"I did knock," she sniffed, glowering at Blade, "but you were preoccupied."

The blonde, from the pool. Dani didn't like how possessive she acted towards Blade then or now.

Blade cleared his throat, still holding onto Dani's arm. "Um, Dani, this is Eden Howard my co-star. Eden, Dani Fairchild, my massage therapist ..." He turned to Dani, amusement dancing in his eyes as he cocked a smile "... and my girlfriend. Right, Dani?"

She flashed a large smile as she put her arm around Blade. "Right." If Eden held any romantic delusions about Blade, Dani was determined to squelch them here and now.

Eden smiled, her eyes remaining cold. "This is new." She zeroed in on Blade, like Dani didn't exist. "You were single the other night when we went to dinner. We had so much fun together," she hummed.

Eden reminded Dani of a Malibu Barbie with her surfer blonde hair and perfect figure. She was the pampered type, expecting every guy to fall at her feet because she was beautiful. Dani straightened to her full height. "Things have changed."

"Evidently." Eden fluffed her hair. "Anyway, Doug sent me up here to collect you."

Dani arched an eyebrow. *Collect.* Really?

Blade frowned. "Where has he been all morning?"

"Meeting with Matt to go over director's notes for the scenes."

Blade jerked, his jaw tightening. "What? And he didn't think to include me? As the actor, I should be involved in anything the director has to say."

Eden shrugged. "Don't blame me. I'm just the messenger," she said flippantly, like it was no big deal. She made a flourish with her hand. "Ta ta" She turned on her heel and strutted away. "See ya on set, Blade," she slung over her shoulder.

Dani didn't appreciate the innuendo in Eden's voice or the brazen way she'd looked at Blade like he was a hunk of meat to be served up however she pleased. She'd have to keep an eye on Eden Howard.

"I can't believe Doug met with the director without telling me," Blade fumed.

Dani shook her head, not sure how to respond. From what she'd seen of Doug, she wasn't impressed. But she'd only met him once, and he'd been under a lot of stress. "Maybe there was some sort of misunderstanding."

"Or maybe my brother's a jerk, determined to undermine me."

"If you feel that way, then why did you hire him as your manager?"

"That's a dang good question," he grumbled, taking her hand. "Come on. I don't wanna be late for filming and give Doug another thing to hold over my head."

14

D ani just kept nodding like she knew what was going on as Natalie pointed out the paraphernalia she'd gathered for the hot stone massage treatment.

Natalie touched the black slow cooker. "I put the stones in water and turned them on high. They should be warm enough. Also, the bottle of coconut oil is on top. You can use these tongs for the larger stones and the slotted spoon for the smaller. I also got lots of extra towels." She motioned to the portable massage table. "I wasn't sure what type you use, but Doug told me to get what I thought. I hope this is okay."

Dani looked at the table in question with the rolled white towel at the head, acting as a pillow. "That looks great," she said nonchalantly, even though she was trying not to panic. The thoughts of rubbing oil over Blade's back and shoulders sent a heat wave simmering through her. The only consolation in the whole situation was that Blade was just as uncomfortable as she. After the film crew wrapped up for the day, Doug announced that he had a surprise for Blade. Then he motioned at Natalie. In a breath of excitement, Natalie told how she'd gone and purchased all the supplies so Dani could give Blade a massage. An exuberant smile stretched over Natalie's lips. "I figured since you're an expert, this would be a real treat for Blade."

Dani turned to Blade whose eyes turned to saucers. "Huh? You bought what?" he asked Natalie.

Natalie patted Dani's arm. "Dani knows all about it. She'll explain how everything works."

Doug was watching the scene with an amused expression. Dani figured Doug knew she wasn't a real massage therapist and was trying to put them on the spot.

Blade turned to her. "It's been a long day. Maybe you could give me a massage another day."

Natalie's face registered disappointment and Doug looked smug.

"No, I'm fine." Dani looked Doug in the eye. Two could play this game. "I'll be happy to give you a massage. That is what you hired me for, after all."

Blade raised an eyebrow. "Are you sure?"

A plastic smile formed over her face. "Absolutely." She looked at Natalie and Doug. "But I'm going to have to ask the two of you to step out of the room and give us some privacy. Otherwise, Blade won't be able to relax."

"That's convenient," Doug chuckled.

Dani shot him a blistering look. "On second thought, I guess you could stay, if that's how you get your jollies—watching your brother get a massage."

Blade laughed as Doug's face turned scarlet. He looked like he wanted to strangle Dani. "No thanks," he grunted. "I've got plenty of other things to keep me busy." He skulked out of the main room and down the hall. A second later, they heard a bedroom door slam.

"If you need anything else, let me know," Natalie said. "I've got some paperwork to catch up on."

After Natalie left, Blade stepped up to Dani, a devilish glint in his eyes. "So, you're really gonna give me a massage?"

She sighed in resolve. "Looks that way."

He grinned. "I guess I'll need to get ready. Should I take my shirt and jeans off?"

"I think you're enjoying this a little too much," Dani quipped. She hoped Blade wouldn't notice that her face was flaming.

He jutted his thumb toward the thermostat, a deadpan expression on his handsome face. "Should I turn up the air? You look a little warm."

She shoved his chest, noticing how muscular he was. "Go on and change." She pulled a frown. "And for goodness' sake, if you're gonna take off your jeans, make sure you put some shorts on."

He let out a low chuckle as he leaned in and whispered. "I can hardly wait."

"How did a nice little girl like me get mixed up in all this crap?" she muttered to herself as she watched Blade saunter down the hall. It was hard enough to keep from gawking at him when he was fully dressed. She'd seen him without a shirt before, so she knew how great he looked. But now she had to rub oil all over him in the pretense of a massage. She fanned her face. *Hold it together, Dani.* People gave massages all the time, and it was just that—a massage. She could do this! She'd just have to picture herself somewhere else, like walking on the beach. Yes, that's how she'd get through it.

Dani wiped her sweaty hands on her shorts as she walked over to the makeshift massage station. The slower cooker containing the stones was set up on the coffee table. She lifted the lid and jumped backed as steam rose. Quickly she put it back down. Too bad she didn't have time to watch a Youtube video about hot stone massage therapy. She'd have to make it up as she went. Good thing she was used to improvising.

Her breath hitched when Blade came striding back in like he was king of the world. She couldn't help but take in his sculpted pecs and abs. He was lean and sinewy, his body perfectly proportioned. His movements were lithe and graceful, his muscles rolling under his skin like a sleek race car. How was it possible for a man to look that good? A quirky grin flitted over his lips when he saw her checking him out, causing her face to blaze like a neon sign.

"Where would you like me?"

Her pulse hammered in her chest as she motioned. "On the table, of course."

He lay face down, which was good, because that meant he couldn't see Dani's cheeks burning hotter than the summer sun at Waikiki. Natalie said she'd put the oil in the slow cooker to warm it up. She lifted the lid and grabbed it, then squirted a quarter-sized amount into her hands. She drew in a deep breath. *Just put the oil on him already*, her mind screamed. Tingles bust through her fingertips when she touched his skin. She drew in a sharp breath, and then flinched when he laughed.

"Is it that bad?"

Or at least that's what she thought he said, but the words were muffled due to the towel. She leaned forward. "I beg your pardon."

He turned his head sideways. "I can't even see you, but I can feel your anxiety. I don't bite," he said dryly.

"I am not anxious," she shot back, lightly slapping his shoulder blade with the palm of her hand.

"Oh, yeah? Prove it."

That's all it took for her to dive in full force as she began massaging his shoulders with a vengeance.

"Not so hard. That hurts."

"Ultra-sensitive, huh, blue eyes?"

"It's a massage, not a clay-molding session."

She smiled, her nervousness vanishing. Then she eased up, her hands gliding over his shoulders and underneath his shoulder blades. She tried not to think about his muscles and how his broad shoulders tapered into a perfect V. *Just rub*, she commanded herself. Despite her determination to remain unaffected by Blade, the heat of his body seeped into her fingers, and she felt an intimate connection. A slow-burning desire churned in her stomach as she swallowed and tried to squelch the attraction. It was crazy how quickly she was falling for Blade. All the talks she'd been having with herself about responsibility weren't helping one iota. In the past, the guys she'd dated had been more enamored with her than she with them. That wasn't a bad thing, because it gave Dani the upper hand. But this thing with Blade was different. She didn't even want to contemplate how lonely it would be to not have him in her life. And that was dangerous territory, seeing as how he'd leave in a month. She wondered again what the relationship was between Blade and Eden Howard. Had they dated? Eden must've had some hope of them being a couple for her to act so possessive of him.

Her hands moved to Blade's neck. *Geez.* Even his nape reeked of masculinity. His hair curled slightly against his skin, as if begging her to run her fingers through it. Kissing Blade had been like getting a taste of heaven, and she wanted more.

Blade's neck and shoulders were tense. For a moment, she forgot about her discomfort in giving him the massage and focused on loosening up his muscles. She used her thumb to press deeper into his muscle tissue, making circular motions.

"Yeah, right there," he slurred like he was half asleep. "That's where it hurts."

"No wonder. You're tied in knots." She put more oil on her hands and massaged deeper, trying to loosen the muscles. Then she went down his back, massaging out from his spine. In a real massage, the therapist would have worked on Blade's legs. But there was no way Dani was going there. She had to draw the line somewhere. When she got to his waist, she went up his back, repeating the same process.

"Are you going to use the stones?" Blade asked.

"Oh, yeah." She'd forgotten about those. She lifted the lid of the slow cooker and used metal tongs to lift out a medium-sized stone. She had no idea where she was supposed to put it—maybe on his spine? It seemed logical. She placed the stone on his lower back. The instant it touched his skin, he yelped and jumped at the same time. The stone fell to the floor with a loud thud as Blade turned to face her.

"Ouch! That hurt."

She held up her hands in surrender. "Sorry, I didn't realize it was that hot."

"You're supposed to take the stones out of the cooker and let them cool a minute on a towel before placing them on my back."

She rolled her eyes, her free hand going to her hip. "Well, excuse me. It's not like I've ever given a massage before," she hissed.

"Yeah, but you've gotten a massage before, right?"

She gave him a steely look. "No, I haven't."

He frowned. "Really?"

"Really," she retorted. "I don't want some strange person touching me."

He laughed, shaking his head. "You really are something."

She wasn't sure if that was an insult or compliment so she just looked at him. "Do you want to continue with the massage, or not?" she snapped.

He lay back down. "Yeah, the first part was great ... until you scalded me."

Guilt pummeled over her when she saw the red mark on his back. "Maybe we'll skip the stone part and just let me finish the massage. How's that?"

"Sounds good."

She did another round on his back, going through the same process as she had before. His shoulders and neck felt looser. She massaged him until her hands got tired. Finally, she sighed, patting his shoulder. "Okay, you're done."

He sat up on the bench and turned to face her. "You're not doing the front side?"

Her horror must've been written all over her face because he chuckled. "I'm just kidding. You're good." He winked. "You might just make a good massage therapist, after all, Dani Fairchild."

She furrowed her brows. "Don't hold your breath."

His eyes held hers, and all she could think about was how blue they were. "Thank you." He reached for her hands. "It really did help."

"You're welcome." Suddenly, she felt shy, standing here facing him ... when he was shirtless. She was so glad he couldn't read her thoughts, wouldn't know how sexy she thought he looked with his six-pack and ripped biceps. He stood and reached for the towel. She was surprised when he lifted it over her head and brought it behind her waist like a belt, using it to pull her to him.

Mischief danced in his eyes as he pumped his eyebrows. "Now what?"

She arched an eyebrow. "Do you always capture your massage therapists?"

His laughter held a playful edge. "Just the beautiful ones with thick curls and a tongue sharp enough to cut metal."

She rested her hands against his chest, resisting the temptation to rub her hands over his pec muscles. She felt the pounding of his heart, or was that her own heart, beating so furiously?

"I don't know whether to tickle you or kiss you."

The husky tone in his voice sent tingles circling down her spine.

She wanted him to kiss her. She let herself melt into him as she lifted her face to his. Then she remembered where they were. A flutter of panic went through her. "We can't. Not here."

He frowned in confusion. "Why not?"

"What if Doug or Natalie sees us?"

"I don't care what they see." He let the towel fall to the floor and gathered her in his arms as he searched her face. "I don't care if the whole world knows we're together."

"But I'm your employee, remember?"

"Yeah, but that's a technicality." A lopsided grin tugged at the corner of his lip. "I was just trying to figure out a way to keep you in my life. And it seemed like a good solution at the time."

"I can't take your money, if I'm not doing something useful."

"You are. You help me loosen up on set. Even if we weren't in a relationship, I'd fight tooth and nail to keep you around." The fierce look in his eyes left no room for argument. He leaned in to kiss her, but she pulled back.

"I still don't want them to catch us kissing," she whispered. "They think I'm your massage therapist. And despite what you're saying, you must care what they think or you wouldn't have gone along with the charade of me massaging you."

His smile grew larger, a wicked glint lighting his eyes. "Wouldn't I?"

She was getting the feeling she'd been had. "What do you mean?"

He pursed his lips. "Hmm ... let's see, I just got a massage from this amazing woman I happen to be crazy about. And you did a pretty good job," He winced, "except for when you burned me."

"W-what?" she sputtered. She should've been angry, but a laugh bubbled in her throat as she slapped his chest. "You're such a dork. I can't believe I fell for that." She ran the phrase through her head again, the part where he said he was crazy about her.

"You stepped up to the plate, determined to prove yourself. I didn't have the heart to stop you."

"Uh, huh." She clucked her tongue. "Payback is rough. You know that, don't ya?"

"That's what I hear."

"Your time's coming." And to think, she'd been a nervous wreck about the whole massage thing.

He moved in closer. "So, do I get that kiss now?"

She parted her lips in response. But right before his lips touched hers, she drew back. "Psyche!" She patted his cheek. "Go get a shower. I'm ready to get out of here." They'd decided the night before that Blade was going to stay at Dani's until the stalker was apprehended. Dani was grateful Blade and Tal would both be there. Hopefully knowing a bodyguard was on the premises would curtail the stalker from trying anything else. Then again, it didn't stop the stalker from breaking into Blade's suite. Still, if anything were to happen, Dani wanted to have other people around. And it was a good excuse to spend every minute with Blade.

"Okay, but we've got a stop to make before we head to your place."

She cocked her head. "Where?"

He flashed a mischievous grin. "You'll see." He picked up the towel and strode down the hall to his bedroom and closed the door. Dani couldn't stop the large smile from spreading over her lips. She couldn't believe Blade had tricked her into giving him a massage. He was such a dork! A handsome, thrilling, lovable dork. But still a dork.

She went over to the slower cooker and unplugged it. Then she closed the cap on the oil. Other than that, there wasn't much else she could do to tidy up. She wasn't sure where Natalie wanted to store these items. The massage table looked like it could be collapsed, but she wasn't sure how. She was squatted down, looking underneath it when Doug came into the room.

"I can't figure out how to collapse the table," she explained, standing up.

Doug scowled. "You don't know the first thing about giving massages, do you?"

The hair on her neck bristled. "I beg your pardon."

"I checked you out. You're not a massage therapist." He ground out the words like he was a judge delivering a prison sentence to a convicted felon. "You're a wannabe food blogger."

The words were an invisible fist that left Dani breathless for a second as her heart pounded like the wings of a caged bird against her ribcage.

A self-satisfied smile curled Doug's lips. "That's right. I did my homework. I talked to Chef Ray. I know you came to the hotel to beg an endorsement off him. Pathetic," he muttered.

Dani's eyes misted, but she blinked the moisture away as she straightened her shoulders. It was hard to believe this jerk was Blade's brother. No wonder the two of them had problems. She balled her fists. "Who or what I am is none of your concern."

"Anything that concerns my brother concerns me. And I make a point of weeding out the gold diggers."

Dani's blood started to boil. "You don't know the first thing about me. And from where I'm standing, the only gold digger here is you."

He rocked back, jaw going slack. Then his eyes narrowed to hard slits. "How dare you accuse me of that."

She lifted her chin. "How dare you accuse me. Maybe it's time you found your own life, instead of riding on the coattails of your younger brother's success."

"I'm his manager," he thundered.

He was dang intimidating, towering over her, the veins in his neck protruding like roots from a tree trunk. If she hadn't been so furious, she might've been a little scared. "Is that why you went behind his back to go over the director's notes this morning?" Blade had confronted Doug about that the moment he got on set. The two of them stood in a corner and argued for a good fifteen minutes until Christian arrived. Doug's face turned a blistering red, and he looked like he might rush at her any minute. It went through Dani's mind that she was saying too much; but once she got fired up, there was no stopping her. The rest seemed to slip out of its own accord. "You're not helping Blade. You're tying him in knots, undermining him at every turn. Blade loves you because you're his brother. But if you don't change your ways, he'll eventually see you for what you are." She squared her jaw. "Furthermore, in case you're wondering, Blade is perfectly aware of my background and intentions."

Doug pointed at her. "I've got your number. You'd better watch yourself," he growled, storming out of the suite and slamming the door behind him.

It wasn't until Doug had left the room that Dani realized her knees were shaking. She went to the couch and fell back into the seat cushion. She'd let her tongue get the best of her again, but Doug had attacked her first. Her impulse was to tell Blade everything the minute he came out of the shower, but then he'd have war with Doug. Dani didn't want to be the cause of adding any more stress to Blade's life. The best thing to do was to keep her mouth shut and let things with Doug play out. She could only hope his true nature would be revealed sooner rather than later.

15

"How does it look?"

The hopeful expression on Blade's face had a childlike quality which tugged at Dani's heartstrings. He was probably just as adorable when he was a kid, as now, leaving a long trail of broken hearts in his wake. Her lips tipped in a broad smile. "Perfect." She glanced at Tal who was sitting on the couch watching a football game. "Tal, what do you think?"

"Looks good to me." A teasing grin touched his lips. "For a Haole tree."

She put her hands on her hips. "Just because we didn't get colored, blinking lights doesn't mean it's a Haole tree."

Blade cocked his head. "What does Haole mean?"

"A Hawaiian term for white people," Dani explained.

Tal waved a hand. "Da white lights are boring. You could've at least made them blink already."

Dani shook her head. "Then I'd feel like we were in a disco." She did a little dance as she spoke.

"Do that again," Blade said, open admiration shining in his eyes.

She held up a finger. "You know what we need? Some music to liven things up." Even though they were having a wonderful evening, the events from the night before permeated everything around them. Dani hated how the stalker made her feel uneasy in her own home, or Samantha's home, rather. If the stalker wasn't found by the time Samantha and Finn returned, she'd have to come clean about everything, so they could take precautions to protect themselves and the boys. The irony of the whole thing was that Finn installed a topnotch security system a couple of years ago, when a slew of bikes were getting stolen on the North Shore. They were diligent about keeping it armed for several months, but then drifted back into old habits. Dani had no clue how to work the system. She didn't want to ask Samantha, because she'd know something was wrong. Thankfully, Tal knew a little about security systems and got it semi-working.

"Just let me know before you open any doors," he warned. "I couldn't figure out how to set it the regular way, but it's on silent mode. You won't hear a thing, but it'll trigger the police."

It was a pain to have to think before opening the door, but comforting that if anyone came in, the police would be notified. For the next few days, Dani planned to sleep in the main house with Blade and Tal. She was glad she wasn't here alone. A shiver ran down her spine as she glanced at the large window and menacing black from the evening, peeking through the edges of the curtains. Was someone out there, waiting for them to go to sleep before wreaking more havoc? She pushed aside the negative thoughts. No need to let her imagination run wild. She went to her phone and turned on her music app. She started dancing, swaying her hips as she stepped up to Blade. "Let's dance," she said, reaching for his hands. He twirled her around and did a few token moves. She pressed her lips together. "Not bad."

Blade wrinkled his forehead. "Not bad? I thought that was pretty good."

"What do you think, Tal?" Dani asked. She glanced over her shoulder and realized he'd turned his attention back to the game. She laughed. "See, even Tal lost interest."

"Hey," Blade growled reaching to tickle her. "That was uncalled for."

She jumped back, evading him. When they settled down, she turned her attention to the tree, a wave of tenderness gushing over her. "It looks fantastic. Thank you."

Blade wrinkled his nose. "You're a terrible liar. It looks pathetic."

She laughed. "It's the thought that counts. I love it." Blade insisted that they had to put up a Christmas tree, so they left the hotel and went straight to Lowe's to purchase one. Pickings were slim, however, and all they could find was a tiny tree that reminded Dani of a Charlie Brown Christmas Tree. They'd gotten a few decorations, but the tree was so ugly it was cute.

Tal had dutifully tagged along. At first, it had been annoying to have someone hovering over them, watching their every move. After the trip to Lowe's, they'd gone to the grocery store where Dani picked up items for dinner. Finally, when they returned to the house, Dani couldn't handle the awkwardness any longer, so she started including Tal in the conversation and got him to help Blade bring in the tree. Tal was on the quiet side, but he seemed like a nice guy. He grew up on the North Shore and graduated from Kahuku High before venturing into the security field.

Blade stepped up behind Dani, wrapping his arms around her, swaying to the beat of the music. "Thanks for dinner. It was amazing." He leaned in, his mouth grazing her ear. "I could get used to this … the two of us coming home after a long day of work, eating dinner together."

She placed her hands over his, loving the protective feel of his strong arms around her. "Tal watching the game."

Blade grunted. "Maybe not that."

She wriggled around to face him. "I like being here with you too." She didn't want to ruin the moment by opening up a conversation about the future, but that's where her thoughts were going. What would happen after filming ended? She was falling hard for Blade. In fact, if she were truly honest with herself, she'd never been this head over heels for anyone before. She thought feelings like this came on slowly after spending a lot of time with a person. But this thing with Blade was happening so fast she could hardly process it.

Blade looked toward the sliding glass doors leading out to the back deck. "It's a beautiful evening. Would you like to take a walk on the beach?"

She tensed, eyes widening. "After what happened last night?" She arched an eyebrow. "You want to go outside, in the dark? Do you really think that's wise?"

He let out a heavy sigh. "What happened last night was rough."

"Yes, it was," she answered quickly.

"But for you, it's new and fresh. For me, it's been going on for months."

The pain in his eyes shot a dart through her. She couldn't imagine living like this for months, fearing every minute something terrible would happen. "I haven't thought about it that way. I'm so sorry."

He nodded, offering a tight smile. "I guess a walk on the beach is off the table, huh?" He brightened. "But we have the weekend stretching before us. What's on the agenda for tomorrow?"

The thrill of adventure tingled over her. Blade was going to be excited about what she had planned. "How would you like to go kayaking? To Chinaman's Hat?"

His smile grew. "Are you serious?"

"Yep." She eyed him with mock concern. "You don't get seasick, do you?"

He leaned closer, amusement shimmering like sunlight in his light eyes. "Afraid I'll puke on you again?"

She made a face. "Ugh! I hope not. Once is enough to last me a lifetime."

"Yeah, me too," he chuckled wryly.

"After we explore Chinaman's Hat, I thought we'd grab lunch at the shrimp truck in Kahuku."

"A shrimp truck?"

"It's legendary. You'll love it."

He caressed her hair, his hands cupping her cheeks. "I know I will, as long as I'm with you."

Desire simmered over her as she raised her face to his.

His lips brushed against hers with the softness of silk that sang through to her toes. Lightly, he kissed one side of her mouth and then the other. Tantalizing shivers circled down her spine as she put her arms around his neck and pressed her lips to his. He slid his arms around her waist and up her back, pulling her closer. She let out a tiny moan as the kiss became more demanding, sending her pulse soaring and knees trembling. When the kiss ended, Blade rested his forehead against hers as Dani threaded her fingers through his.

"I hope you know how incredible you are."

His words flowed over her like warm honey as she smiled. "Thanks. You're not so bad yourself."

He pulled back, his eyes roving over her face like a gentle caress. "I'm so grateful you came into my life."

"I feel the same way about you." A burst of sheer exhilaration raced through her. These feelings were different from anything she'd felt before. Was it possible that she'd finally met her match? Emotion lodged in her throat as the answer came shining through. Yes, it was very possible. She straightened her shoulders, a sense of recklessness coming over her. "You know what? I think we should go for a walk on the beach?"

Blade tipped his head in surprise. "Really?"

"Really. We can't stop living our lives because of some stalker. If we do that, then the stalker has won."

He rewarded her with an appreciative smile. "That's exactly how I feel." He looked toward the couch. "Tal, we're going for a walk on the beach."

Tal instantly jumped up. "Okay, let's do it. I'll only be a few steps behind you."

A FEELING of contentment settled over Blade as he put his arm around Dani, drawing her closer to him. For a moment, he let his mind get lost in the fluidity of the flames as they licked at the wood. The cozy fire felt good against the moist night air, the surf pounding against the shore. Dani had invited Tal to join them around the fire, but he told them he'd rather stay back to have a full view of the situation. Blade was glad Tal was keeping his distance, because that meant more alone time with Dani. The past two days had been glorious, and Blade wasn't ready to go back to work tomorrow. On Saturday, they'd done just as Dani suggested and took a sea kayak over to Chinaman's Hat and explored the island. The shrimp truck was just as good as Dani had said. Afterwards, they lounged on the beach behind Dani's house, soaking up the sun and being lazy. Dani cooked a fabulous dinner of salmon, mango salsa, brown rice, and green beans. Then they spent a quiet evening watching a movie. Today, they'd gotten up early and gone to a sunrise service at Turtle Bay Resort. Blade enjoyed hearing the sermon taught by Pastor Steve, who looked like a throwback surfer from the 1970s. Something Pastor Steve said had stuck with him. He spoke of faith and how we're often required to walk those few steps into the dark before coming into the light. Then he spoke of how God is in the details of our lives. "There are no coincidences," he said. "Everything that happens is known to God, and it happens for a reason."

Thinking back, it wasn't that Pastor Steve said anything monumental, but rather, it was the quiet peace that came over Blade when he spoke. For so many years, Blade had been carrying the pain and guilt of what had happened to his mom. Oh, how he wished he could live the day of her death over again. Had he been there, he could've protected her. She wouldn't have been alone on that mountain, trying to escape. It seemed a cruel coincidence that Blade would also be hounded by a stalker. For months, he'd prayed to be delivered from this, and the answer kept coming to him in the form of the scripture from Proverbs. "Trust in the Lord with all thine heart, and lean not unto thine own understanding." He'd been trying to trust, but the uncertainty stretched before him like a long, black road with no end in sight. Today, however, was different. He'd offered up the same prayer, but the feeling he received was that all would be revealed soon. He hoped with all his heart that was the case. He wanted to be free of this—free to live his life. Free to love Dani. Since meeting

Dani, he felt a renewed sense of strength, like he could accomplish anything he put his mind to.

"What're you thinking about?"

He removed his arm from her shoulders and angled to face her. "I really enjoyed the service at Turtle Bay."

"Pastor Steve's great. His wife Madelyn is wonderful too. I wish you could've met her, but she's expecting her fourth child and is at home on bed rest."

He was surprised Dani knew Pastor Steve and his family so well. "Do you attend the sunrise service every week?"

"I try to. I go with Samantha, Finn, and their boys. It recharges my battery for the upcoming week. And I love Turtle Bay. It's the first place I stayed when I came to Hawaii."

"You never did tell me about your engagement or how you almost got kidnapped." When her jaw tightened, he placed a hand over hers. "There's no judgment. I just want to know more about you." A smile tugged at his lips. "I want to know everything about you."

She took in a breath as she nodded. "Okay, I'll give you the Cliffs-Notes version. My father died suddenly of a heart attack when I was in my early twenties. He left my mom, Samantha, and me with a lot of debts." A sad smile touched her lips. "My dad was a great man. He never intended to hurt us. He was a real estate investor and took a lot of risks. He'd always come out on top before, so he thought he always would. Anyway, we were in dire straits, faced with losing our house, and my mom has a heart condition. I know, ironic, right? Mom has a heart condition, and she's been fine; whereas my dad was healthy as a horse, then fell over dead." She stopped. "Am I boring you to tears?"

He squeezed her hand. "No, not at all."

"Samantha got engaged to a rich guy, thinking it would solve all of our problems. As the oldest, she felt like it was her duty to fix everything. Anyway, Anthony was working a deal in Hawaii, so he brought Samantha along. I signed Samantha up for surf lessons at Turtle Bay and Finn was her instructor."

Blade spurted out a laugh. "Really? She fell in love with her surf instructor? This sounds like a book or movie."

She suppressed a giggle. "Yeah, it kind of does. Anthony, Saman-tha's then-fiancé, had a next-door neighbor named Liam." She wrin-kled her nose. "He was the artist."

"Oh." A dart of jealousy went through Blade. He didn't like picturing Dani with anyone else, past or present.

"We were just friends, at first." She hesitated. "I was a bit of a wild child back then, I'm afraid."

His eyes rounded in mock astonishment. "You? No!" He could totally see that, Dani was so free-spirited.

Her cheeks colored. "I didn't do anything bad. I just thought everything was fun and games. I met this guy on the beach, Jett Barnes. He invited me to a club in Waikiki. Deep down, I knew it wasn't a good idea, but I went anyway." Her features hardened. "Jett put a date-rape drug in my drink and was leading me out to his truck when Samantha and Liam showed up and saved me."

For an instant, Blade was at a loss for words. Then anger took hold. "Whatever happened to Jett?"

"I had to testify." She shuddered. "Which was a whole other ordeal I'd rather not go into, if you don't mind. Nothing happened to him, at that time. But eventually more charges were brought, more girls testified, and he was sent to prison."

A feeling of vindication settled over Blade. "Good, I'm glad he went to prison." He paused. "I'm so glad you were okay." He couldn't stand the thought of anything bad happening to Dani. "What happened between you and the artist?"

She sighed. "I broke up with him the day of our wedding."

A laugh gurgled in his throat. "Ouch."

"Yeah, it wasn't one of my finest moments. I just couldn't go through with it. I cared about Liam, but I didn't love him."

He began tracing circles over the top of her hand, his pulse esca-lating. "What about now? With us?"

A hint of a smile ruffled her lips. "Blade Sloan, are you asking if I love you?" She'd asked the question lightly enough, but her eyes were serious, questioning. Time seemed to stand still as he locked gazes with her.

"Yes," he uttered.

"I think I might," she admitted, coughing slightly to clear her throat.

He couldn't stop the monster-sized grin from spilling over his lips as a shot of adrenaline raced through him. Up 'til now, the greatest thing that had ever happened to Blade was getting the starring role in the Jase Scott film. But this was so much better! "That's good."

She let out a shaky laugh. "It is?"

"Yes, because I love you too." Now that he'd said it out loud, he could breathe easier.

"But we haven't known each other for very long."

"I know. It's crazy. But I have to be honest about how I feel."

She nodded. "Me too." She touched his face. "Tell me about you."

"What do you want to know?"

A grin radiated over her. "Everything."

"Hmm ... let's see ... where to start. I was born a middle-class white boy." He cleared his throat. "Or Haole boy." He laughed inwardly when he heard Tal grunt.

Dani shoved him, her lower lip jutting out in a pout. "Hey, now. I was forthcoming with you. What's the story between you and Doug? You obviously don't get along." She wrinkled her nose. "Why in the heck did you hire him as your manager?"

He frowned. "You go right for the jugular vein."

"It saves time," she shrugged.

"Yeah, I suppose it does." He rubbed his eyebrow, trying to collect his thoughts. "Doug and I didn't grow up together. Our parents got divorced when I was three. Doug went to live with our dad, and our mom kept me. The divorce was nasty. I only saw my dad and Doug a couple of times a year, on holidays. I wish you could've met my mom." He smiled, remembering. "She was this little, petite thing, always dressed to the nines. But she was feisty, like you."

Dani's mouth rounded to an O as her face fell. "You think I'm feisty?"

For a blip of a second, he thought he might've said something wrong and was trying to figure out how to respond when she laughed.

"Just teasing. I know I'm a handful. Anyway, didn't mean to interrupt."

"My mom was a real estate agent."

"Oh, wow. I guess our parents had something in common. Sort of. My dad was more a real estate investor in large-scale ventures like malls and shopping plazas."

"My mom sold houses." He hesitated. He wanted Dani to hear it all, but it was still so hard to talk about.

She touched his arm. "Are you okay?"

"Yeah. She sold a house to this investment banker who became fixated on her."

Dani's mouth dropped. "Was it a stalker situation?"

He nodded, his jaw tightening. "Yes, I didn't realize it was going on. The banker came to her work, left her notes, kept showing up where she was, even followed her home a couple of times. My mom went to the police, hoping they'd take care of it, but didn't say a word about it to me. She went to Aspen to go skiing. And, I'm sure, to get away from the situation. She tried to get me to go with her." His voice caught. He swallowed, trying to get out the rest. "I wanted to stay home and hang out with friends. I liked the idea of having the house to myself. My mom was on a slope, about to go down, when she realized the stalker had followed her to the resort. She was trying to get away, lost control, and crashed into a tree." He couldn't stop tears from pooling in his eyes.

Dani scooted next to him and gathered his hands in hers. "I'm so sorry."

He nodded, a tear dribbling down his cheek.

"What happened? To the banker?"

His eyes narrowed, the familiar anger burning through his veins like acid. "Nothing."

"What?" she blustered. "How could that be?"

"He claimed he was there, skiing."

"Did she not have a restraining order against him?"

"Yeah, but the guy had money and influence. The police told me after the fact all that had taken place. But they didn't have enough to make a case against the guy that would stick."

Dani shook her head. "That makes me sick," she muttered.

"Yeah, it was terrible. But I was a teenager. There was nothing I could do." The injustice of it all sliced through him like a knife, gutting his insides. Would the pain ever go away?

"What happened to the banker?"

"He died of cancer a few years later."

She nodded, biting her lower lip. Her eyes flashed. "This may sound terrible, but I'm glad he died."

"I was too," he admitted. Silence stretched between them. Blade stared into the fire, his thoughts a jumble.

"What happened after that?"

"I went to live with my dad and Doug." A dry laugh escaped his throat. "I was as much a stranger to them as they were to me. We kind of tiptoed around each other for a couple of years."

Dani touched his arm. "I'm sorry. That must've been hard."

The compassion in her eyes struck something deep inside him. "It was." He'd never told anyone all of this before, kept it hidden in some dark place where it couldn't hurt him. "Doug always wanted to become an actor. He went to LA and got cast in a handful of commercials. Finally, he landed a small part on a soap opera. After I graduated from high school, I didn't know what I wanted to do with my life. My dad suggested I go live with Doug. To make a long story short, Doug got me a job working on the set of the soap opera, and I got discovered instead of him."

"Ah," she drawled. "Makes sense."

"What?"

"Why he resents you so much and why you keep him around. You feel guilty because you became the star instead of him."

He let out a humorless laugh. "Is it that obvious?"

"Now, that I know the story. Yes, it is." She ran a hand through her hair. "That's tough. It makes me sad for both of you."

His lips formed a grim line as he stared into the flames. Too bad they couldn't burn away the hurt.

"It's not your fault."

He turned to her. "Isn't it?"

"No. You're a talented actor. You have an energy that draws people to you. It's your gift."

The compliment meant more than he could express. "Thank you. I do love acting. And despite the fact that I didn't grow up dreaming of becoming an actor, I've worked hard to get where I am." Resentment sounded in his own ears. "I just wish Doug would recognize everything I'm putting into this." His voice trembled. "That day my mom died, I lost everything." He coughed to choke back the emotion. "All I've ever wanted was for Doug and me to truly be brothers." He wiped at his tears using his palms. "I don't think that's too much to ask, you know?"

Dani put an arm around him. "Look at me."

He turned to her.

"I don't know what will happen between you and Doug, but I can promise you this." Her eyes misted. "You've got me now. You never have to be alone again. You got that?"

Looking at her with the light from the fire reflecting off her profile, he had the feeling she was an angel sent straight from heaven. "Yes. I love you, Dani Fairchild. And I'm saying it out loud with no reservations."

She laughed through her tears. "I love you too."

"You hear that, Tal?" Blade said loudly.

"I hear ya," Tal answered dryly. "I'm sure the whole beach heard it."

"Well, you'd better avert your eyes or you might see more than you bargained for," Blade said as his lips captured Dani's.

16

When Dani's phone vibrated, she stepped away from the set so she wouldn't interrupt the filming, which involved a chase scene through the lobby, halls, and a hotel room on the second floor where Blade and Christian, along with the villain, would crash through a window and land in the pool. Tomorrow would be the last day of filming with Christian until after the Christmas break. Wednesday and Thursday, the shoot included segments with Blade, Eden Howard, and a few of the other actors, wrapping up all remaining scenes at the hotel. After the Christmas break, filming would commence at other locations around the island.

"Hello. Rena, how are you doing?"

"Running like crazy. How are you?"

"Good. Things have been hectic here too."

"How's the new job?"

"Great."

Rena's voice went juicy. "And Blade? How are things with him?"

A smile filled her face. "Really well."

"You'll have to give me all the details."

She heard shuffling in the background, could tell Rena was in a hurry. "Is everything okay?"

"Yeah, sorry to ask you this, but would you mind helping me out tonight?"

"What's going on?" Dani hated to break the routine of spending her evening with Blade. But Rena had never asked for help before, and she didn't want to be a lousy friend.

"It's Mr. Hadler."

Dani cocked an eyebrow. "What's the tyrant up to this time?"

"Tyrant's right," Rena muttered. "I made the mistake of telling Mr. Hadler that I make homemade chocolates for friends and neighbors."

"You do?" This was the first Dani had heard about it.

"Yeah, I thought I told you that. Of course, this is my first time making them in Hawaii. We'll see how my recipe turns out at sea level."

"That's right. This is your first Christmas here." Rena moved to Hawaii only a month before Dani met her.

"Mr. Hadler wants me to make candy for all the tenants and deliver them tomorrow."

"Really? Why can't he just buy a few boxes of macadamia nuts like everyone else does?"

Rena blew out a frustrated breath. "I know. That would be the sensible thing to do, right?"

"Yeah, but remember who we're talking about. Sense doesn't factor into the equation."

Rena chuckled dryly. "I hear ya." She paused. "Would you mind helping me? If you can't, it's okay, I just thought I'd ask."

"I can probably do that." Dani mulled it over. "Let me talk to Blade and see what we have going tonight."

"Ooh, that sounds so official." She trilled her tongue. "If you have other plans, then no big deal."

"I'll check with him and get back to you."

"Okay, sounds good."

A few hours later, Dani called Rena back. "I can come."

"That's fantastic."

"Yeah, it works out well, actually. Christian's been wanting to take Blade out on his boat. Blade's going to do that while I come to your house." She didn't mention that she'd have a bodyguard in tow. Unfortunately, Tal had a much-needed day off since he'd been working around the clock, so Blade had someone else to fill in. "Should I stop by and grab us some takeout on the way to your house?"

"That would be great. I really appreciate you helping me. Otherwise, I'd be up all night making chocolates."

"No worries. It'll be good to catch up." Just as she ended the call, her phone vibrated again. It was her mom. "Hey there."

"Hi, honey. How are you doing?"

"Really well."

"We miss you. It's not too late to hop a plane, so you can be here for Christmas. Jaxson and Mason have been asking for you every day."

Dani's heart softened at the mention of her nephews. "Tell them I miss them."

"I can't believe how much they've grown." She told Dani all about their cute antics. It was good to hear her mom so bubbly and happy, but Dani didn't need the detailed run-through of everything going on. Still, she listened politely until the conversation lagged.

"I guess I should let you go, Mom. I need to get back to work."

"Hold on. Don't hang up yet. I'll get you a ticket."

Dani scraped a hand through her hair, the words gushing out. "That's so nice of you, but I think I'm gonna stay around here."

"By yourself? That's no way to spend Christmas."

Dani heard talking in the background.

"What was that?" Katia said, speaking to someone else, her voice was muffled like she'd put a hand over the mic. "Oh, I'd forgotten about that. Well, that should be fun for Dani."

What should be fun for me? Dani rolled her eyes. "Mom, are you still there?"

"Oh, yes. Sorry. Samantha was just telling me that you have to stay there so you can pick up Finn's friend Gibson at the airport on Thursday."

Crapola! Dani had forgotten all about that. Hot needles pelted over her as she clutched her throat. When she'd committed to that, she and Blade weren't together. But she couldn't tell Samantha they were together now, not without telling her everything else. On the other hand, Blade wouldn't like her picking up some guy at the airport and showing him around the island. She realized her mother was waiting for her to answer. "Oh, yeah, I forgot about that."

"Samantha was afraid you might forget, so she emailed you Gibson's itinerary." Innuendo coated Katia's voice. "Who knows, this might be the one. According to Samantha, Gibson's a great catch."

"I can hardly wait," she grumbled.

Katia made kissing sounds into the phone. "I love you."

"Love you too, Mom. Bye."

Dani blew out a long breath. *Great.* Another problem to deal with. Well, if worse came to worse, she'd simply explain the situation to Blade and bring him, and Tal, along. She chuckled, picturing Gibson's reaction when she showed up with another guy and a Polynesian bodyguard. *Welcome to Hawaii, where everything operates by its own set of rules. Allow me to give you a lift to your hotel, and hopefully we'll never cross paths again.* Dani sighed. "Samantha ... Samantha, what have you gotten me into?" she said under her breath.

DANI JUGGLED the Chinese takeout with one hand and knocked on Rena's door with the other.

"Come in," Rena called.

Not wanting to freak Rena out, Dani instructed the bodyguard to stay in his car. "I promise you, I'll be perfectly fine," she assured him.

Reluctantly, he agreed.

"Hey." Rena was standing at the kitchen countertop, stirring a glass bowl of melted chocolate. Beside her was a tall stack of gold boxes. She wiped her forehead. "I'd forgotten how much work this is."

Dani held up the bag of Chinese food. "Would you like to take a break and eat something? Then I'll help you."

"That sounds great. I'm starved. Let me just dump this batch of nuts in the chocolate and dip them onto wax paper to dry while we eat."

"Sounds good, I'll just put this on the table."

Dani was setting down the food when she heard the crash, then Rena swore. Gold boxes were scattered across the floor.

"This is turning out to be a disaster," Rena moaned.

"Here, I'll pick them up while you finish the chocolate."

She flashed a grateful smile. "Thank you."

Rena pointed. "Maybe stack them over there, out of the way."

"Sure." A few minutes later, Dani noticed Rena was wearing rubber gloves. "I'm afraid I didn't bring any gloves."

"Oh, no worries. The only reason I'm wearing them is because I have on compression gloves underneath and don't want to get them wet. It's a pain wearing gloves when you're trying to cook."

"Why're you wearing compression gloves?"

"My wrists have been bothering me, probably from typing all the time."

"Ew, I hope you don't have carpal tunnel."

Rena winced. "Me too. My fingers on my right hand were giving me fits last night. I couldn't even sleep."

"I'm sorry. It probably doesn't help that you're making all of this."

"I know, which is why I really appreciate your help." She shook her head. "Enough about me. I wanna hear about you and Blade."

Dani watched as Rena scooped the chocolate-coated nuts onto the paper. She told Rena the whole story, starting from the beginning. It felt good to rehash everything, making her realize how much she missed her evening talks with Samantha. When Dani got to the part about the stalker and intruder that broke into her house, Rena looked shocked, reminding Dani how terrifying the ordeal was.

"That's terrible. Did you call the police?"

"Yes, we did."

"Have they turned up anything?"

"Not yet, unfortunately."

"I hope they catch the person soon."

"You and me both."

Rena put the empty bowl in the sink and ran water over it. Then she wiped her hands on a nearby towel and removed the plastic gloves. Dani smiled inwardly at the bright pink compression gloves. Rena was only a few years older than Dani, but she was an old soul, which made her seem much older and wiser. Rena was an attractive woman with her stylish blonde bob and lively eyes. She'd never mentioned having anyone in her life, but there must've been someone. Dani hated to think of her being all alone. Rena retrieved a couple of glasses from the cabinet. "Would you like some juice or tea?"

"Water sounds great."

"Would you like ice with that?"

"Yes, please."

They sat down at the table. Dani removed the containers of orange chicken and broccoli beef from the bag, along with the fried rice. As they ate, Dani rambled on about how wonderful Blade was. They giggled like teenagers when Dani talked about the massage. Then she told Rena about her conversation with Doug and how horrible he was. "Blade feels obligated to Doug because he's his brother, but I wouldn't put up with Doug's crap for two minutes, if it were me."

Rena smiled, shaking her head. "You're a pistol. I admire your frankness and how you look the world in the eye and tell everyone to go to the devil."

Dani nearly choked on a piece of broccoli as she hiccuped a laugh. "You make me sound so terrible and fierce." She reached for her napkin, wiping her mouth. "Unfortunately, I'm just a hothead."

"I wish I could've been a fly on the wall when you told Mr. Hadler to stick it."

She grimaced. "Yeah, not one of my finest moments."

Rena grew thoughtful. "I dunno. If it hadn't happened, you wouldn't have met Blade."

"True." She took a long drink of water. "You also played a part in my getting together with Blade."

"Really? How?"

"If you hadn't talked me into going to the hotel to talk to Chef Ray, I never would've fallen into the pool. And I never would've connected with Blade again. That's the day everything came together."

"I guess we owe it to my niece, for wanting Aiden Anderson's autograph."

"Yes, we do."

They had just put the food away, and Rena was slipping on her rubber gloves to get back to work, when a knock sounded at the door.

Dani's heart lurched. Was that the bodyguard, coming to check on her? Then again, she didn't know why she was worried. At this point, it hardly mattered. She'd told Rena the whole story, so she'd understand.

Rena went to open it.

A delivery man handed Rena a bundle of flowers in pink wrapping. She laughed in surprise. "These are for me? Are you sure you have the right address?"

"Are you Rena Stanley?"

"Yes, I am."

"Then I have the right address. Have a good evening."

"Thanks." Rena closed the door.

Dani rushed to her side. "They're beautiful. Who are they from?"

Rena pulled out the card and read it, her face going flush. "It says it's from a secret admirer."

"That's awesome. Any guesses as to who it might be? I always thought Henley from accounting had a thing for you."

Rena blinked rapidly. "I don't know about that." She brought them to her nose. "Umm, they smell good." She held them out for Dani to smell.

"Yes, they do."

"Would you mind arranging them for me in a vase?"

"Me?" Dani touched her chest.

"Yeah, you're good at that."

"I am?"

"I remember when you arranged the flowers we gave to Kim Ashby from all of us at the office."

"Oh, yeah, I'd forgotten about that. Sure, do you have a vase?"

"Somewhere." Rena placed the flowers on the counter, her hand going to her mouth. "Where did I put that thing? Oh, yeah. It's in the cabinet." She stood on her tiptoes and reached for it. Dani stepped up beside her, "Here allow me." She reached on the top shelf and grabbed the vase.

"It must be nice to be that tall," Rena said.

"Yeah, sometimes."

Rena pointed to the nearby drawer. "The scissors are in there."

"You with a secret admirer, me with a boyfriend. Our mundane lives have certainly stepped up a notch," Dani mused.

"Yours is a little more exciting than mine." A smile played on Rena's lips. "But a secret admirer is kind of nice, especially at my age."

"Whatever. You're beautiful and young."

Rena touched her hair, batting her eyelashes. "Thank you. You need to come over more often."

"Yes, I do." She motioned, scrunching her nose. "Just not when you have all this chocolate to make. How many boxes are you doing anyway?"

"Twenty-two."

Dani blew out a breath. "Wowser, I guess we'd better get busy."

"If you can help me make it, I can pack it in the morning."

"Are you sure?"

"Absolutely, that way, you won't be here all night." She gave Dani a coy look. "I'm sure a certain movie star wants to get you home."

"Yeah, right," she said, but couldn't stop the goofy grin from stretching over her face.

17

Blade could feel Dani's animosity radiating from across the room. He glanced over and made eye contact. Bad idea. She shot him a death glare, and then looked away. The whole thing was ridiculous. Yes, he'd kissed Eden a dozen times or more today, but it was only acting. He'd tried to explain that to Dani, but it fell on deaf ears. He understood how Dani felt. It would be torture to sit back and watch her make out with another guy, even if it was acting. But he didn't know any other way around this. When he realized which scenes were on the docket today, he suggested that Dani hang out in the hotel suite and relax. Big mistake! That only made things worse. If they could just get through the next few hours, he had a surprise for Dani, which would fix everything.

Dani really should've been more understanding about the situation, considering he'd reacted okay when she told him she had to pick up some guy from the airport and take him to his hotel. Granted, it had taken every bit of self-control he could muster to control his temper, but he had. If Dani knew how many kissing scenes Blade had done in the past, she'd blow her cork. Heaven forbid if she ever watched any episodes of the soap opera *Hope for Tomorrow*. Writers sprinkled in kisses like commas when they couldn't come up with anything witty for the characters to say. Yeah, at first, it had been uncomfortable, but like anything, Blade got used to it. Kissing those actresses was nothing like kissing Dani. No other woman was like Dani. Even though she was fighting mad at him, he couldn't help but think how beautiful she looked with fire raging in her liquid brown eyes.

"Trouble in paradise," Eden draped an arm around Blade's neck as she cast a surly look in Dani's direction.

He removed Eden's hand. "Mind your own business," he growled.

She laughed, trailing a fingernail down his jaw line. "Touché."

The director stepped up to them, focusing on Blade. "This time, I want you to really get into the kiss. Dip Eden back and lay it on her. Take control. Make me believe you love her."

With Dani here, Blade was tied up in knots. But he knew that Matt was right. He had to make this look real. Otherwise, they'd be here all day. And he couldn't let that happen, not with what he had planned for later. "Okay, I'll get it right this time."

"This is gonna be fun," Eden purred.

REVULSION CHURNED DANI'S GUT. After today she'd have images of Blade kissing Eden seared into her mind. And to make matters worse, Eden had cornered her earlier in the restroom. "I'm looking forward to my scene with Blade," she'd said.

"You really need to learn the difference between acting and real life," Dani snipped.

A taunting smile spread like a virus over Eden's Botoxed lips. "In case you haven't read the script, let me tell you how this ends. I get the guy." Her cool eyes appraised Dani as she smirked. "One thing you'll learn about me, darling, is that I always win." She flipped her hair and sauntered out.

Eden's promise kept running through Dani's head as she watched Blade kiss her over and over. An inferno raged in her gut, to the point where Dani feared she'd combust. No girl should have to witness her boyfriend kissing another girl. She probably should've stayed in the suite, but that wouldn't change what was happening. No wonder the divorce rate was so freaking high in Hollywood. How did Christian and Everly navigate this? They'd already left for the mainland the day before, or she would've paid Everly a visit. Earlier, Blade accused her of being unreasonable. Maybe she was, but she'd had about as much of this as she could stomach.

She looked at Blade who had Eden in a lip lock, their bodies wrapped together.

"Cut," the director announced. "Perfect. That looked believable to me."

Dani couldn't have said it better herself. It looked totally believable, and heart-wrenching. Tears burned her eyes. It was too much. She wasn't cut out for this kind of life. In the next second, she was on her feet, bolting out of the hotel lobby. She made it to the front steps when Blade came running after her.

"Dani, where're you going?"

She whirled around to face him. "I'm sorry, but I can't take any more of that," she spat.

"It's just acting. It doesn't mean anything."

She gritted her teeth. "It means something to me," she yelled, pointing to her chest.

He rocked back, his face draining. "I don't know what to say. You knew I was an actor. You've seen Jase Scott movies. You know how it goes."

The condescension in his voice sent her over the edge as her head burned like it was on fire. She let out a harsh laugh. "I know Eden Howard is dying to get her claws into you. She's been throwing the kissing scene in my face with her taunts and pompous looks."

He caught hold of her arms. "I don't give a crap about Eden. I love you."

The fierce look in his eyes was almost enough to persuade her, but then she looked at his lips. Those same lips that had touched hers had been touching Eden, and scores of other girls. He'd evoked a passion in her she didn't know was possible, and she loved him to the point of hurting; but it wasn't in her to share him with anyone else—whether it was acting or not.

"I'm sorry," she squeaked, breaking out of his grasp and hurrying away.

"What should I do?"

Blade turned. "What?"

"Should I go after her?" Tal asked, concern etching his features.

"Yes, please." Blade ran a hand over his jaw.

"But if I'm with her, I can't protect you."

"Go. She's more important."

A SPLITTING HEADACHE pounded across the bridge of Blade's nose. He rested his head against the back of the couch, eyes closed. How in the heck had things gone so wrong? He was glad Tal had gone after Dani. He couldn't live with himself if anything bad happened to her. The whole thing was absurd. Maybe after Dani cooled down, she'd realize that she'd overreacted. Panic raced through him. What if she didn't come around? He didn't want to lose her. He'd give up acting all together if that's what it required. Or maybe he could refuse to do any kissing scenes. He noticed that in the last few movies Christian had done, the relationship scenes were limited to longing gazes or hugs. Who was he kidding? Christian had reached the point where he could do whatever the heck he wanted. But Blade was nowhere near that point. And like he told Dani, he might not have always wanted to be an actor, but he wanted it now. He wanted his career and Dani. Was that too much to ask? A harsh laugh rippled in his throat. Yeah, probably, no one was lucky enough to have it all. That's just the way it worked.

"Rough day?"

He opened his eyes as Doug sat down in a chair across from him. "I'm not in the mood to fight with you, Doug."

"Is this about Dani?"

He sat up, a sour grin twisting his lips. "You know it is, brother.

Don't pretend that the entire film crew didn't watch the whole thing through the glass doors."

"The two of you did cause quite a stir. She couldn't handle the kissing, huh?"

"Did you come in here to rub it in? Tell me how foolish I was for believing I could find someone?" His voice rose. "Is that what this is about?"

"I suppose I could tell you all those things. And I'd be right."

He scratched out a scornful laugh. "You never stop, do you?"

Doug brought his hands together. "Actually, I came in here to tell you that if you don't go after Dani, you're making the biggest mistake of your life." He shrugged. "But if you're determined to make me out to be the villain, then so be it." He moved to stand.

Blade held out his hand. "Wait a minute. What?"

Doug sat back down. "I know we don't always see eye-to-eye. And I didn't care much for Dani, initially. But these last few days you've been with her, you seem happy."

"Since when have you cared about my happiness?"

"Yep, you're right. All I care about is the bottom line." Doug used the arms of the chair to propel himself to his feet. "Anyway, I've said my peace. I just wanted you to know that I booked the boat like you asked. Everything is ready to go for 4:30. Go ... don't go. Take Dani with you ... or don't. I don't really care. But if you do decide to take Dani, Natalie bought her a suit from the boutique downstairs, and packed your basket dinner." He was almost out of the room when Blade spoke.

"Doug?"

He turned. "Yeah."

"Thanks."

He brought his lips together in a firm line. "You're welcome."

Blade's phone vibrated in his pocket. He fished it out, hoping it was Dani. Disappointment swallowed him. Not her. "Hello."

"Blade Sloan?" a female voice said in a brisk tone.

"Yes."

"This is Detective Kalama from the Honolulu Police Department."

"Oh, hey."

"I've got some additional information on your case that I know you'll want to hear."

IT WASN'T until Dani got to baggage claim that she realized her predicament. She had no idea what Gibson looked like. She should've thought to bring a poster with his name on it. She was sure she looked like crap with swollen eyes and a red nose. She'd cried all the way to the airport. All she wanted to do was pick up Gibson Hobbs, take him to his hotel, and go home and sleep. Heck, she might even call her mom and ask her to buy that ticket to Sacramento, after all.

She could tell from Blade's stunned reaction that he thought she was being stupid, which made the situation worse. Blade was like one of those Nazi concentration camp guards who'd become so desensitized by his profession that he didn't think anything was wrong with it. But she doubted Blade would be as blasé about the whole thing if the situation were reversed.

A large group of passengers made their way to baggage claim number five, designated for Gibson's flight. She reached in her purse for her phone and called Samantha. "Hey, it's me. I'm at the airport," she said dully.

"Are you okay?"

"Peachy," she chirped, the word burning her throat like poison.

"You don't sound peachy."

She sidestepped the comment. "I don't know what Gibson looks like."

"Dani, what's wrong?"

Tears sprang to her eyes, her throat going thick. "I'm okay." Hurriedly, she brushed away the tears. She was determined not to fall apart at the airport.

"What happened?"

"Blade and I had a fight. I'll tell you about it later," she barked. "What does Gibson look like?"

"He's tall, on the thin side, with brown hair."

"Okay." She glanced around. That description fit at least three guys in her view.

"Anything else?"

"He wears glasses. Oh, and he looks a little like Clark Kent from *Superman*."

She let out a heavy sigh. "Really? Superman? I doubt that." She glanced over and saw him. He did look sort of like Clark Kent. "I think I see him. But if you ask me, he looks more like a grown-up Alfalfa from *The Little Rascals*."

Samantha balked. "He does not. He's really cute."

"For a geek." In reality, he was a cross between Clark Kent and Alfalfa. Not that Dani cared what the guy looked like. She had eyes for only one man. Too bad his profession mandated that he kiss nearly every actress in the nation.

"Be nice, Dani," Samantha warned. "And remember, you're supposed to show him around the island."

"Yeah, yeah. Got it. Bye." She ended the call before Samantha could respond. She straightened her shoulders, plastering on a smile as she stepped up to him. "Gibson?"

He nodded and touched his glasses.

"I'm Dani. It's nice to meet you."

A pleased smile broke over his face as he pumped her hand. "Nice to meet you, Dani. Thanks for picking me up."

He was cute in a bookish way, but unfortunately, all she could think about was how his eyes looked normal when they should've been a piercing blue. His hair was tame when it should've been messy. And he could get lost in any crowd, rather than exuding the chemistry that drew people to him. *Blast you, Blade Sloan.* To have finally found love and have it ripped away so suddenly. A sharp pain shot through her heart, and for a second she felt like she couldn't breathe.

Gibson gave her a concerned look. "Are you okay."

She held up a hand, offering a weak smile. "I'm fine." She swallowed back the tears gathering like storm clouds on the horizon, threatening to spill. Her stomach churned, and she felt shaky. She sucked in a ragged breath, trying to get control of her emotions. This was pathetic. How could she have let herself fall so hard for Blade? She'd known it was a bad idea from the beginning and promised herself she'd be responsible. A buzzer sounded as the baggage carousel started turning. "How many suitcases did you bring?"

"Just one."

Good. Less to fool with. Normally, Dani would've tried to wade through polite conversation, but just getting here and not ripping the guy's head off was the best she could do right now.

Gibson leaned forward and grabbed the handle of his suitcase, lifting it off the carousel. Then he smiled at Dani. "Okay, all set."

She motioned. "This way." *Geez.* This was awkward. She had no idea what to say to Gibson, and he didn't seem to be one for conversation. With Blade the conversation simply flowed. An image of his teasing grin filled her mind, bringing a longing that physically hurt.

They were almost to the exit doors when she saw a familiar face. Her heart skipped a beat as she stopped dead in her tracks. Gibson got a couple of steps in front of her before realizing she wasn't there. He turned, giving her a questioning look, which she brushed off. "Tal, what're you doing here?" Her brows scrunched.

Tal chuckled out a nervous laugh. "Hey, Dani. How ya doin'?"

A spurt of anger went through her. "Have you been following me?" The guilty look on his face was his answer. She straightened to her full height, glowering at him. "Blade put you up to this, didn't he?"

"He just wanted to make sure you're okay," Tal said. "He worries about you, know what I mean?"

Gibson pushed his glasses back up on his nose. "Who's Blade?"

"You tell Blade that I don't need him or anyone else to protect me. The stalker was after him, not me," Dani spat. "Now that we're not together anymore, I won't be in any danger."

"Stalker?" Gibson said. "What stalker?"

Dani narrowed her eyes. "You tell Blade to stay out of my business."

Tal gave her a quirky smile. "Tell him yourself."

"Huh?" Her pulse started sprinting as she looked past Tal and saw Blade rushing through the doors.

"Dani," he said breathlessly, waving.

A feeling of exhilaration shot through her, and she had the impulse to rush into his arms. Then she remembered she was fighting mad at him. He'd hurt her, kissing another woman dozens of times in front of her face.

"Uh, what's going on here?" Gibson asked.

In that second, a wickedly brilliant plan took shape. Something that would let Blade know exactly how she felt. She turned to Gibson, grabbed his shirt, and pressed her lips to his. At first, he jerked in surprise, but she didn't let go. She kept forcing the kiss until he halfway responded. His lips were loose and moist like a wet sponge. She pulled back, flashing Blade a triumphant look.

Blade's face turned dark, his jaw dropping. "What're you doing?"

She lifted her chin. "How does it feel? Watching your girlfriend kiss another guy, right in front of your nose?"

"Girlfriend? I thought you were single." Gibson held up his hands, shaking his head. "I don't know what's going on here, but I don't want any part of it."

"I am single," Dani barked.

Fury crossed Blade's features as he leveled a menacing glare at Gibson. "She is not. She's with me."

Her hands flew to her hips. "I was with you, 'til you started sticking your tongue down Eden's throat."

"That was acting! I told you it meant nothing."

"Well, it meant something to me."

Blade shook his head. "You're the most stubborn, infuriating woman I've ever met."

"And you're a jerk!" Okay, not the wittiest comeback, but it was all she could think up at the moment. She looked at Gibson, her words grinding like metal. "Let's go. We've got a date."

She started marching forward as Blade ran after her. "You're being ridiculous, Dani. Stop being a baby."

She spun around. "I love you, Blade Sloan."

He grinned in surprise. "I love you too."

Anger boiled over her. "But I won't share you with the world. You got that? Let's go, Gibson," she ordered. She barreled forward, keeping her gaze fixed straight ahead. Wretched tears pressed against her eyes, but she'd be darned if she'd let one escape.

When they got to the car, she pushed the clicker to open the trunk. Gibson put his suitcase in. She got behind the wheel. Gibson also got in. She started the engine, then flinched when the back door opened. She turned, realizing Blade had gotten into the car. "What the heck!"

"If you're determined to go on a date with him," he gave Gibson a scornful look, "then I'm coming too."

"Hey, I don't want any trouble," Gibson said. "I can call a cab to take me to my hotel."

Dani cackled. "Oh, no. You're staying. I'm not spending one minute alone with him." She jutted her thumb back to Blade.

Blade laughed lightly. "Good, then it's all settled. But we need to hurry. We've got an appointment at 4:30 at the dock in Waikiki."

Dani made a face as she looked at him through the rearview mirror. "What're you talking about?"

She caught a smidgen of a sparkle in his eyes. "I rented us a boat for the afternoon."

Despite her best effort to squelch it, excitement thrummed in Dani's stomach. "You got us a boat?"

A boyish grin tugged at his lips. "Yep. Christian and I had such an amazing time that I wanted you ... us ... to experience it."

"I don't do boats," Gibson said. "All that open water makes me nauseated."

Blade patted his shoulder. "I've got news for ya. You're on an island, bud. Surrounded by open water. You'll be fine."

Dani's shell started to crack. No one had rented a boat for her before. That was really sweet. Then it hit her. Even though she was furious with Blade, she was glad he was here. She glanced back at him through the mirror, their eyes locking. The familiar desire swelled through her as he gave her a crooked smile.

"Go with me on the boat. Please?"

Those blue eyes had the power to melt through any defense she could put up. And she knew she'd never be able to resist him. He'd eventually wear her down. She sighed. "Fine. What's the address? Let me plug it into my phone."

He held up his phone. "No need. I've got it right here. I'll start the navigation."

18
_____

The boat was a good idea. Blade looked out at the open expanse of ocean, glittering in the afternoon sun. The salty breeze was just cool enough to be invigorating without being too cold. He tightened his hold on the wheel and looked back at Dani who was lounging on the deck, her face lifted to the sun, brown ringlets cascading over her shoulders. She was a vision in the red, two-piece Natalie purchased at the boutique, her toned, tan skin glistening in the sun. "Isn't this great?"

"It's okay," she said nonchalantly, but he could tell she loved it. He bit back a smile. She was certainly making him pay for kissing Eden, but he could tell she was softening. It would only be a matter of time before he wore her down, and he was determined to stay close by her side until that happened. He was dying to tell her what Detective Kalama had told him in hope Dani could help make sense of it, but that would have to wait until she wasn't still ticked at him. He looked at Gibson, who was clutching the rail, his face gray.

"How are you?"

"Okay," Gibson croaked through tight lips.

"I've got some Dramamine in my bag," Blade offered. He felt for the guy, especially considering he'd probably be feeling the same way if he'd not taken two pills before they pushed off.

Gibson grimaced. "No thanks. That stuff makes my heart race."

Lucky for Blade, the only side effect he had from the drug was a heightened sense of awareness, which only added to the splendor of the experience. He felt a little guilty for dragging Gibson into the middle of his and Dani's argument. But at least the guy was getting a chance to go out on a boat.

"How far out should we go?" Blade asked.

"To Fiji," Dani exclaimed, her musical laughter floating in the air.

A sense of adventure wicked through Blade as he fixed his sight straight ahead. "You got it," he said, upping the speed. He leaned forward, feeling like he was one with the ski boat as it skipped over the waves. It was nice to be out here without Tal looming over him, although he was kind of growing fond of the big guy. When they'd gotten on the boat, Tal planned to come along. But Blade assured him they'd be perfectly fine and that it was better for him to wait at the dock. When Tal protested, Blade laughed saying, "No one can get to Dani and me in the water, and I'm pretty sure Gibson's not a stalker." Tal had put up with a lot from Blade and never complained. Blade was going to give him a hefty Christmas bonus.

Twenty minutes later, Blade eased off the throttle, bringing the boat to a stop. There was nothing but ocean on all sides. The perfect spot to break out the dinner Natalie had packed. He got up from the driver's seat and went to grab the basket. "Anyone hungry?"

Gibson looked like he might puke any second. "No thanks."

Dani sat up, giving him the once-over, her eyes sparking in a challenge. "I'm surprised you don't have motion sickness too."

He sat down beside her. "I took Dramamine as soon as we got on the boat."

"Oh." She lifted her chin and looked away.

He leaned in and whispered in her ear. "You look fabulous, by the way."

"Thanks," she said frostily.

He opened the basket, not sure what to expect. "Let's see ... what do we have? A couple of deli sandwiches, chips, grapes, hard candy. It looks like Natalie packed us a bit of everything."

Interest lit Dani's eyes. "I'd like a sandwich."

"Have anything to drink?" Gibson asked.

Blade pointed. "Yep, in the Styrofoam cooler over there. Nice and cool."

Blade unwrapped his sandwich and took a large bite. Then he nudged Dani. "This is fun, isn't it?"

"Yeah, it's nice," she said mechanically.

He frowned, frustration mounting inside him. What was it gonna take to get her to warm up to him? He'd already apologized profusely. What else could he do? He looked at Gibson who was clutching a water bottle in one hand and holding onto the rail with the other. The boat was barely rocking, but he was holding on for dear life like he was getting thrashed in a storm. "What do you do for a living?"

"I'm a programmer."

"Did you come here for a vacation?"

"No, I work for Finn's company. I'm opening up a satellite office here."

Blade turned to Dani, his brows furrowing. "Is he talking about Finn, your brother-in-law? The surfer?"

Her face turned pink as she shifted in her seat. "Yeah."

Gibson chuckled. "Finn likes to surf, but he also owns one of the largest software companies on the West Coast."

"Is that right?" Blade eyed Dani, who gave him a sheepish grin. "I thought your house was awfully nice. Why didn't you tell me?" It hurt to think she was keeping things from him.

She picked at her sandwich, peeling off the wilted edge of the lettuce and dropping it over the side of the boat. "Samantha and Finn don't like having their wealth broadcasted. So I make a practice of keeping it on the down low." She wrinkled her nose. "Kind of like how you hid your identity from me."

"But I came clean right away." He searched her face, his voice taking on an accusing tone. "I told you personal things about me, things I've never told anyone else."

She sighed. "I would've told you, but with everything going on it slipped my mind. I wasn't trying to keep it from you, honest."

He could tell from the sincerity in her eyes that she was telling the truth. Dani had the most expressive eyes of anyone he'd ever met, and they really were windows to her soul. No longer hungry, he placed his sandwich down on the seat beside him and turned to her. "I want us to work ... whatever it takes." He stroked her hair, relieved when she didn't move away. "I don't have the answer to the kissing thing, but I'll give it all up—the acting, everything—if that's what it takes." The certainty of his words reverberated through him. As much as he loved acting, he loved Dani more. And he wasn't about to lose her. The only sound was her sudden intake of breath. Then tears pooled in her eyes.

Her features softened. "You'd do that ... for me?" she gulped.

"Absolutely, I don't want to lose you."

She rewarded him with a large smile that shot rays of sunshine through him. Then she threw down her sandwich and jumped in his lap, flinging her arms around him. She laughed through her tears. "I love you." She crushed her lips to his, kissing him with a fervent passion that sent him soaring to the clouds above.

"Um, the boat is sinking."

"What?" Blade pulled back in a daze, still feeling the burn from Dani's lips.

Gibson went bug-eyed like he was staring into the jaws of death. "The boat is sinking!"

Blade grunted. "That's absurd. We're not sinking."

Dani clutched his arm, her face tightening. "I believe Gibson's right."

"No, we're not sinking," Blade chuckled wrapping his arms tighter around Dani. Then his throat clutched as he looked around and realized they were!

Dani scuttled out of his lap as Blade sprang up. "What the heck?" he muttered. He peered over the edge scouring the boat for any signs of damage. "It looks fine over here."

Dani, realizing what he was doing, went to the other side. "Uh, oh, we've got a problem." Her lips thinned into a tight line. "Come and look at this."

Blade rushed to her side and looked over. His heart lurched when he saw a two-foot gash running horizontally along the back quarter of the boat, like someone had crashed into something. "The boat's taking on water because we're sitting still. Once we start moving, it'll be fine." He jumped in the driver's seat and started the engine. It sputtered a few times like it was trying to turn over, then died. A trickle of sweat ran between his shoulder blades as he pulled at his t-shirt and tried again. This time, he got nothing but the hollow click of the starter. He swore and pounded a hand on the boat. Dani put a hand on his shoulder.

"Try again," she encouraged.

He did. Nothing. They were dead in the water.

He reached for the hand-held transmitter attached to the VHF Boat Radio and turned on the knob. It was dead.

Dani's voice had a panicked edge to it. "How are we gonna tell them where we are when we don't even know the coordinates?"

"The radio's not working," Blade said, the full scope of their predicament washing over him.

Gibson sprang to his feet. "What? This can't be happening."

Blade ran the sequence of events through his mind. The gash in the boat, the engine stalling, the radio not working. Too many coincidences. Pastor Steve's sermon came rushing back. "This is not a coincidence," he said aloud. He caught hold of Dani's arm. "Someone tampered with the boat."

The stricken look on her face mirrored his own feelings. "That's what's happening here?" she asked hoarsely.

"I'm afraid so." He ran both hands through his hair. Now what?

"The cell phones," he and Dani said simultaneously.

They each went for their phones. Neither of them had a signal.

"Figures," Dani muttered. She turned to Gibson. "Do you have a signal?"

He shook his head slowly back and forth like he was in a daze.

Alarm trickled over Blade as he looked at the rising water.

Another foot and it would be coming into the boat. He tried to think. "Are there any life jackets on board?" He knew before he opened the storage bin what the answer would be, but they had to look anyway. "Nada."

Dani looked at him. "I'm scared."

"Me too," he admitted. The ocean on all sides felt menacing, whereas it was liberating earlier. It had been stupid to charge so far out without checking the radio first. Why hadn't he thought to do a sweep of the boat, make sure they at least had life preservers? The gash was on the side of the boat opposite from where they boarded. And it was low enough on the boat to go unnoticed. He balled his fists. Who was behind this?

He slumped down on the bench where he and Dani had been sitting earlier. Dani sat down beside him. He reached for her hand, which was trembling. "Everything will be okay," he said.

"You can't promise her that," Gibson yelled. "No one can." His face crumbled as his words poured out in a whimper. "We're gonna die out here." He started pacing in circles, a wild look in his eyes. Then he let out a high-pitched laugh. Rage twisted over his features as he pointed at Dani. "This is all your fault!"

Her jaw went slack. "What?"

"If you hadn't tricked me into coming out here with you to make Blade jealous, I'd be safe and sound in my hotel right now."

The hair on Blade's neck bristled, astonished at how quickly Gibson was turning on Dani. "That's enough," he warned. "You're a grown man. No one put a gun to your head and made you step on this boat. You were free to leave at any time."

Gibson belted out a derisive laugh. "Right. Dani was my ride, remember?" He waved a hand, shaking his head in disgust. "Whatever, dude. As bad as you have it for Dani, you'd defend her to your dying breath."

Blade certainly couldn't argue with that. Any other time, he would've jumped up and knocked Gibson into next week for badmouthing Dani, but he had bigger problems. The water was an inch from coming into the boat. A quiet desperation settled over him.

They were going into the water. No doubt about that. As far out as they were, they had little hope of anyone rescuing them. But they wouldn't go down without a fight. "There must be some sort of emergency kit on here, maybe a flare."

Her dark eyes radiated fear. "Yeah, if the stalker didn't take it."

He opened the bin. It was completely empty.

"What now?" Dani asked, a quiver in her voice.

The nightmare he'd had the night the intruder broke into Dani's house flashed through his mind. He and Dani had been on a boat, and then water closed in around them. He put an arm around her, trying to keep the shakes out of his own voice. "We pray."

THIS WAS something out of a nightmare. Was this how it was going to end? Tears burned Dani's eyes as she blinked them back. Crying wouldn't help, but what else could she do. Samantha didn't even know where she was and might never know what happened to her. Her heart broke into a million pieces as a scream shattered her mind, wracking her body. She didn't want to die. She looked at Blade, a rush of love coming over her. At least she was with him. He offered a reassuring smile. He was scared too, although he was trying hard to be brave. Gibson was trembling like a scared kitten. She felt bad that she'd dragged him along.

Dani felt like she was standing back, watching it all unfold from a distance as water poured over the sides of the boat, spilling onto the deck. Gibson let out a shriek and started weeping. Dani felt like weeping too, but she had to hold it together. Still, she couldn't stop tears from streaming down her face.

She'd offered a thousand prayers since they realized their predicament. Even so, she said another one in her mind and was surprised at the peace that came over her. Somehow, in a way that defied words, she knew it would be okay. Maybe that meant that they'd die. *Please don't let us die*, she prayed.

Water was up to their waists. "We have to find something to hold onto," Blade said. "Something that will float."

Dani looked around wildly, her eye stopping on the Styrofoam cooler bobbing in the water. She pointed. "That!"

Gibson raced for it, grabbing onto it. "It's mine," he pronounced savagely like he was a concentration camp prisoner, fighting for the last scrap of bread.

Blade pounced on him, dragging him away.

"What're you doing?" Gibson cried, his voice sounding like a wounded animal.

Dani had heard about people going berserk in the face of death, but she'd never witnessed it before.

"Stop it!" Blade yelled, holding Gibson's arms behind him. "Listen to me," he growled. "You need to pull yourself together. If we fight over the cooler, we'll rip it to shreds. We can all take turns holding onto it."

Gibson laughed maniacally, wrestling against Blade. Dani waded through the water and slapped Gibson hard across the jaw. "Enough!" This rendered Gibson silent. His glasses were hanging, about to fall into the water. Dani pushed them back onto his nose and got in his face. "What you said earlier was right. I shouldn't have gotten you in the middle of this. I'm terribly sorry about that. Truly, to the depth of my soul." She tightened her jaw. "But right now, you need to get a grip, man. Or we'll have no other option but to leave your butt here with the sinking boat."

He nodded, averting his eyes.

"Are we good here?" Blade asked.

Gibson nodded, so Blade released him.

Blade's voice grew practical. "Okay, here's what we need to do. Go into the water now, so we won't get sucked under when the boat sinks. One of us will hold onto the cooler while the other two tread water, then we'll switch. Got it?"

"Got it," Dani said, glad they had a plan to focus on, rather than the horror of going down in the ocean.

Blade turned to Gibson, the savage look in his eyes leaving no room for argument. "Agreed?"

"Agreed," Gibson mumbled.

There was something so magnificent and pure about the calm way Blade was taking charge. Whatever happened to them, Dani was so grateful she'd found him. And if they were fortunate enough to make it out of this alive, she'd never let him go.

Blade looked at her. "You okay?"

A smile touched her lips. "Yeah." Her heart was pounding so ferociously she could hardly breathe. The water rising around them was colder than she thought it'd be, but not frigid.

"Let's go. Dani, you hold onto the cooler first. Let's dump everything out."

"But what if we need the water?" Gibson argued.

"We need the cooler to float more than we need water right now," Blade said. He lifted it and dumped out the contents. Gibson scrambled for a water bottle and shoved it in his pocket.

Dani let out an involuntary cry as she clutched the cooler and leapt into the open water. The cooler escaped her grip when she hit the water, but she managed to grab hold of it. Blade and Gibson followed behind her, treading water. It took Gibson only a couple of minutes to realize the water bottle weighed him down, so he removed it from his pocket where it began bobbing on the water.

"Swim away from the boat," Blade urged.

The cooler was more buoyant than Dani thought it would be. She held onto it for dear life as she used her legs to push through the water. They watched in silence as the boat disappeared in a whoosh. There were a few bubbles and then nothing. A couple of minutes later, water bottles floated to the surface followed by their towels and extra clothes. The items floated out in a gigantic circle, moving away from them. Dani's eye caught on the colorful fabric of her floral shirt. It had been a gift from her mother, a special order from Katia's boutique. Dani really liked that shirt! Gloom cloaked over her as she rushed to think of the positives. She was grateful the water was calm and that it was still light outside. Even as the thoughts went through her mind, a shudder raced through her. They only had about an hour before sunset. They were completely vulnerable, tiny specks in an endless sea of water. Panic threatened to engulf her as she swallowed, offering another prayer. She couldn't lose it now.

Blade and Gibson were nearby, treading water. "How ya doing?" Blade asked.

"I'm good. Do you wanna trade?"

"Yes," Gibson said, reaching for the cooler. The irrational part of her didn't want to let it go, but she knew she had to. They'd take turns, just as Blade said. The minute she let go, Gibson grabbed it. They treaded water for what felt like a good ten minutes or so before Blade said he needed a turn. He held onto it for what seemed like a very short time before offering it to Dani.

"I'm okay for a few more minutes. You need to rest," she said.

"Let's do five minute intervals," Blade suggested.

"But we don't have a watch," Gibson said.

"He means, let's estimate five-minute intervals," Dani said. It was a tense situation for all of them, but Gibson was really getting on her nerves. *Gibson, the Geek.* That's what she'd dubbed him initially, and she'd been correct. She laughed inwardly, dispelling some of the gloom. Then she instantly felt bad. If they died out here, Gibson's death would be on her head ... *sort of.* She had no way of knowing this would happen when they got on the boat.

The water rippled around them, their bodies rising and falling with the rhythm of the current. Dani tried not to focus on *what if*, but kept her thoughts focused on the rotation schedule. Her strength was waning, and she didn't know how much longer she could keep doing this. She looked at Blade, treading water beside her. "I want you to know how grateful I am to have met you." She touched her fingertips to his.

His eyes narrowed. "We're gonna get through this, Dani. I don't know how, but somehow, we will."

Hot tears pooled in her eyes. It was a nice notion, but she was starting to lose hope. The sky above them was ablaze with purple and orange streaks from the setting sun, ironically beautiful considering their current circumstance. The sunset meant dusk was setting in. She didn't even want to think about what was lurking beneath them in the dark water. Shivers pulsed through her, bringing a wave of nausea. Sharks fed at dusk. A bleak despair settled over her.

"I'll never forget that day on the bus," Blade said chuckling. "The way you faced down that muscle man wearing the wife-beater shirt."

She knew he was trying to take her mind off their desperate situation. She smiled. "I couldn't help but feel sorry for you, standing there, green around the gills." She paused. "I saw you earlier."

"You did?"

"Yeah, you command attention wherever you go."

"I don't know about that."

"It's true." She loved how unassuming Blade was. "I was arguing with myself. I wanted to get to know you, but I didn't want to fall in love with someone who would only be on the island temporarily." The irony of what she was saying hit her full force as she laughed. "Of course, none of that matters now." It was her turn to hold the cooler. She reached for it, grateful for a reprieve. "I wouldn't have made you give up acting for me."

He looked surprised. "But the kissing?"

She smiled. "I know. It's torture for me to see you kissing someone else, even in the name of acting. But it's also torture not being with you. The fact that you were willing to give it up means everything."

"I would've given it up in a heartbeat to keep you."

"The only thing worse than being out here in the wretched ocean is hearing you too go back and forth with all your gooey nonsense," Gibson said. "Blah, blah, blah, blah," he droned.

Dani and Blade looked at each other wide-eyed, and then burst out laughing.

Gibson scowled. "What's so funny?"

Blade looked at him. "You really are a piece of work, man. It's remarkable that you've been able to keep your glasses on."

"How were you able to do that?" Dani asked. It felt good to focus on something other than their impending demise.

"I put on my strap, just before I went in the water."

"Oh, wow. I didn't even realize that." She looked at Blade. "Did you see that?"

"Nope, it must've escaped my attention when I was trying to pry the cooler out of his hands," he said dryly.

Dani hooted. "For sure. Gibson, it seems like you have more ingenuity than we gave you credit for."

"Thanks." A sarcastic smile stretched like a rubber band over his lips. "If I never see the two of you again, that's perfectly fine with me."

"Suits us too, buddy," Blade said. He touched Dani's arm. "Hey, there's something I need to tell you. In case ..."

Her breath caught. This was the first time Blade had intimated they might not make it. "Yeah."

"Detective Kalama called after we had our fight." He paused, gulping a breath. "The analysis came back on the video footage from the suite."

"And?"

"It wasn't tampered with, meaning it was for sure an inside job."

Blade's voice was breathy, like he was running a race ... or treading water. She chuckled inwardly at the metaphor. "Here," Dani offered. "It's your turn to take the cooler." They switched places. Now that she was the one treading water, she should probably stop talking and save her breath. But if they didn't make it back alive, she wanted to at least know the person who'd been the cause of it all. Dani forced her brain to focus on what Blade said, trying to gauge what it meant.

"They interviewed your neighbors."

"Most were asleep that time of the night."

"Yep, all except for the elderly man across the street. He has a hard time sleeping and was out walking his dog."

"Mr. Finch."

"Yeah, that was the name. Mr. Finch said he saw a man and woman, dressed in black, roaming around your house around the time of the break-in."

She jerked, sucking in a labored breath, her sentences coming out in short bursts. "Is he sure? It was two people? Why would two people be stalking you?"

"That's what the detectives are asking. They're wondering if maybe someone's pretending to stalk me."

"Why?"

"To do me in ... and pin it on a stalker."

The horror of it rolled over her. "Who?" she squeaked.

"Mr. Finch told Detective Kalama that earlier that day, he'd seen the man—the intruder—getting out of the car with you and going into the house."

Chills ran through her. "Is Mr. Finch saying that I know the stalker?" Anger surged through her, giving her a burst of renewed strength. "That's absurd."

"Yeah, that's what I thought, too, when she first told me. Even when we went on the boat, I didn't put any stock in what Detective Kalama said. I thought she was barking up the wrong tree. I mean, I went outside and looked around. At first, I wondered if Mr. Finch might've seen me." His voice trailed off.

"And then everything happened with the boat," she finished for him.

He nodded. "Out here, with nothing but time on our hands, I got to thinking. Mr. Finch said the guy was dressed in all black. I was wearing shorts and a t-shirt, so it wasn't me he saw. There's one other person who looks enough like me from a distance to be my double."

"Doug," she exploded. Her mind began to spin. "Do you really think he'd try to kill you?" Sure he was a jerk and super resentful of Blade, but murder?

"He talked me into coming on the boat with you."

"Why would he do that?" She barked out a laugh. "Doug hates my guts."

"Exactly."

"And, Doug's the one who arranged everything for the boat."

"I hope you're wrong. I hope Doug wasn't behind this." It carved out her heart to think Blade's own brother would try to kill him. The idea seemed preposterous. And yet, someone was trying to kill him. "Do you really think Doug's capable of murder?"

"Well, someone obviously is," Gibson piped in. "I mean, look where we are."

Dani's thoughts caught on something Blade had said. "Who's the woman that was with him ... assuming it's Doug. Please don't say Natalie." Natalie was one of the sweetest women she'd ever met.

"No, it couldn't be her. The woman had on a hoodie, but Mr. Finch saw blonde hair peeking out underneath."

"Does anyone who works for you have blonde hair?" Dani's chest was tight, constricting her breathing. She'd only be able to talk a few minutes longer and then had to conserve her energy. "Eden!" She looked at Blade and could tell he was thinking the same thing.

"It's possible," he admitted.

"What motive would Doug have for getting rid of you? If you're no longer around ..." she gulped in a gush of air "... then he's out of a job."

"Not if he takes my place as the star."

"Doug doesn't have a hundredth of the charisma that you do."

"He doesn't know that. And that's probably exactly what will happen if we don't make it. Doug will take my place to make things easier on the producers."

Dani was getting lightheaded. She'd talked all she could for a while. Her mind ran through everything Blade had said, going through it again and again. The more she thought about it, the more it made sense. Although she couldn't figure out what motive Eden would have for harming Blade. She was crazy about him. Then again, maybe it was a case of sour grapes because he'd chosen Dani. Still, it was a stretch to think Eden had jumped from scorned woman to murder accomplice in a few days.

Blade and Gibson changed places, letting Gibson have his turn resting on the cooler. Dani's mind began to wander. She thought about her dad and the pain she felt over losing him. Her mom had seemed so fragile then, so inept at facing the world on her own. But she'd survived ... thrived even. Her thoughts went to Samantha—her rock. Samantha would be devastated by Dani's death, would feel guilty that she'd gone to Sacramento for Christmas and left Dani home alone. Dani was glad Samantha had Finn and the boys. Hopefully that would help ease the sting of loss. Dani got the eerie feeling of being suspended in time. Had it been hours or days since they'd been out here? Now that she'd stopped talking, she found that she could float, using mostly her hands, keeping her nose and mouth just above the water. She exerted less effort that way. The cold was penetrating every cell of her body, her limbs getting heavy. Maybe she could last longer, if she could conserve her strength. She let out a scream when her calf muscle seized up.

Blade grabbed her arm, panic ripping through his voice. "What's wrong?"

"I've got a cramp."

Blade reached for the cooler, grabbing it from Gibson. "Let Dani rest."

"But it's not her turn," he argued.

Dani went under, salt water filling her throat as she sputtered, hands batting against the water to stay afloat.

"Here, hold on." Blade wrapped her arm around the cooler.

Agonizing pain stabbed Dani's leg, and her throat felt raw from the salt. She gagged trying to expel it. Blade reached for her calf and massaged it. She could no longer hold back the tears. Suddenly, it was too much. "I can't do it," she sputtered. "I'm too tired."

"Look at me," Blade ordered, determination radiating from his eyes. "You can. Don't give up on me, Dani. We're in this together. You got that?" he asked gruffly. "Me and you!"

"Yeah." She drew in a ragged breath. Blade's ferocity was comforting, helping her to settle down. "You're right." She offered a rubbery smile. "I'm okay." She decided then and there that so long as Blade was here by her side she'd keep fighting with every ounce of strength she had left. If they were going to go down, then by golly, they'd go down together.

"Hey!" Gibson screamed, waving his arms.

"What now?" Blade muttered. "I feel bad that he got dragged into this. But I swear, if we make it out of here alive, I'm gonna knock that guy into next week."

Dani gurgled out a laugh. "You'll have to get in line behind me. He's tromping on my last nerve." What in the heck had made Samantha believe she and Gibson would be a good match?

"Is your calf okay?"

"Yeah, it's better." It still hurt, but nothing like it had a moment ago. She felt her strength returning.

"Hey! Over here. Hey!"

Dani turned to see what Gibson was yelling at. Hope fluttered in her breast when she saw the dot in the distance. "It's a boat."

"Hey!" Blade yelled.

All three of them started yelling and waving.

"I'm going to swim closer to see if I can get their attention," Blade said.

Dani grabbed his shirt, a swift panic overtaking her. "No!" she blurted. If she let him swim away, she might never see him again.

He gave her a tender smile, placing a hand on her shoulder. "I'll be right back. I promise." A long beat stretched between them until she finally nodded, biting her lip. He took off with long, swift strokes. Dani marveled that he had enough energy to swim left, much less to swim so quickly. *Please come back to me*, she prayed.

Blade got about a football field's length away before he raised up and started waving his hands. "Hey! Over here."

"Hey," Dani and Gibson yelled, also waving their arms.

"The boat's coming toward us," Dani exclaimed, bursting into tears. She lifted her face to the darkening sky. "Thank you!" Her prayers had been answered. "We're gonna make it," she said, relief flooding her.

19

Exhaustion settled over Blade as he drew Dani closer. It was hard to concentrate on answering questions when all he wanted to do was snuggle next to Dani and rest. Detective Kalia Kalama and her partner Luke Ripley were kind enough to come to Dani's house to question them, rather than making them go to the police station.

Kalia leaned forward, her forehead wrinkling. "I still can't get over the Styrofoam cooler." She shook her head. "Or the fishing boat that found you. Do you know how lucky you are to be alive?" she mused.

"Yes, we do," Dani answered for them both. "Although, I don't think it had much to do with luck."

Kalia tilted her head. "What do you mean?"

Blade spoke first. "The father and son who were fishing rarely stayed out past sunset, but for some inexplicable reason they decided to stay out longer this time. The father felt impressed to go to a new area, which is where they found us."

Kalia smiled. "A happy coincidence, it seems fate is on your side."

"No, it wasn't coincidence or fate, but providence." A blanket of warmth rose in Blade's chest as he spoke, bringing home the truth of his words. "It's a miracle we were found." He looked at Dani who had tears in her eyes.

"Yes," she agreed, "our prayers were answered."

"So it would seem." Kalia cleared her throat like she was uncomfortable talking about deity. "Has Doug contacted you since you were rescued?"

A wry grin tipped Blade's lips. "No, that would be hard to do seeing as how my phone is at the bottom of the ocean."

Dani shook her head. "I just realized that's the second phone I've ruined in the past few days. My phone was lost too," she explained to the detectives.

Luke brought his hands together. "We stopped by the hotel to question Doug, but he wasn't there. We've left a message for him to contact us ASAP."

Blade was still having a hard time wrapping his mind around the fact that Doug might be behind all of this. "Do you really think Doug's involved?"

Kalia looked thoughtful. "It's one of two theories we're working on."

Blade's interest was piqued. "What do you mean?"

Luke slid a photo from his folder and handed it to Blade. "Do you recognize this woman?"

Blade's heart picked up a notch as he looked at the picture of the forty-something-year-old blonde woman with frizzy hair. Was she the stalker? "I don't recognize her." He didn't know if he should feel disappointed or relieved. He handed the photo back to Luke, waiting for the detectives to expound.

"Hotel security found this woman, Lindsey Williams, lurking around the hallway leading to your suite this afternoon. She claimed she's a fan of *Hope for Tomorrow* and was trying to get close enough to take a selfie with you. Supposedly, she's a school teacher from Wisconsin who's only been on the island for a couple of days. We're checking into her story."

"If the woman's story checks out, then it's likely she's not the stalker," Dani said.

Blade frowned. "And it seems strange that she would've been at the hotel, trying to get my autograph if she orchestrated the boat sinking."

Luke leaned forward. "Unless she was trying to set up an alibi by getting caught at the same time the boat was sinking."

They sat quietly, pondering the scenario until Kalia spoke. "Like I said, that's one theory." She paused. "But my gut tells me the stalker is not Lindsey Williams." She studied Blade. "Do you think your brother could be behind this?"

Blade mulled over the question. "If you'd asked me earlier, before the boat, I would've said *no way*. But now ... I'm not sure."

A look passed between the detectives. Luke drummed his fingers on the arms of his chair. "You said Doug was the one who rented the boat, is that correct?"

"Yes." They were certainly acting like they thought Doug was guilty.

"We spoke to the owner of the boat. He told us that when he rented the boat to Doug this morning, it was in good condition. The radio was working, and it was well-stocked with life jackets." Kalia glanced down at her notepad. "Six jackets, to be exact."

Blade frowned, his pulse increasing. "Did you say Doug rented the boat this morning?"

"Yes." She glanced down. "At 10:00 a.m. Doug met him at the dock."

"We didn't get on the boat until 4:30." Blade rubbed a hand across his forehead. All the evidence was pointing to Doug. He didn't want to believe it. It was insane to think his own brother tried to kill him. Blood rushed to his temples and he felt shaky. He hoped it was the frizzy-haired lady or another stranger with no connections to him.

Dani gave him a concerned look. "Are you okay?"

He forced a smile. "Just tired."

Kalia stood, as did Luke. "I'm sure you're both exhausted," Kalia said.

Blade and Dani rose to their feet. Every muscle in Blade's body ached and he was so weary he could barely move. He was sure Dani felt the same way. His nerves felt rattled and raw, like he was expecting something else bad to happen. He was sure it was post-traumatic stress. Feeling as he did now, it would be a long time, if ever, before he got on another boat. "Thank you for coming here to take our statement."

Kalia nodded. "Of course. You've been through a lot. It's the least we can do. Things will slow down the next couple of days, but after Christmas, we'll get back on this. In the meantime, if you need anything, give us a call." She caught herself. "Um, when you get a new phone, that is."

Blade thought of something. "Speaking of phones, did you find out who sent the texts?"

Kalia brought her lips together in a grim line. "No, our tech team wasn't able to trace the source."

He nodded in disappointment. No surprise there.

A brief smile touched Kalia's lips. "Have a good evening. And Merry Christmas. Mele Kalikimaka," she said to Tal, who responded with the same. The detectives gave a parting nod and then left.

Blade turned to Tal who was sitting at the kitchen table. "Are you okay staying here tonight? I feel like I've been working you like crazy." Tal was beside himself when he realized all that happened with the boat. He kept saying he knew he should've gone with them. Blade explained that it was better that he wasn't there. He wasn't sure the Styrofoam cooler would've been strong enough to keep Tal afloat. And there was nothing he could've done to fix the situation. Still, Tal felt responsible. Dani had such a wonderful way with people and brought Tal into their circle, transcending him from employee to friend. Blade was very grateful to have him.

Tal looked him in the eye, a quiet strength sounding in the timbre of his voice. "I'm good. I'll feel better knowing I'm here to make sure everything's okay."

"Well, I feel much better knowing you're here." Blade put an arm around Dani who yawned.

"Me too."

The doorbell rang. Blade frowned. "Maybe the detectives forgot something."

Dani held up a finger. "We were going to tell them to check out Eden."

"Oh, yeah. That's right. The blonde hair thing."

She shrugged. "It's probably a long shot, but they need to cover every angle."

Tal stood. "Let me get the door." The determined set of his jaw suggested he was ready to take down anyone who tried to harm them.

It was crazy how fast tension crackled through the room. It was doubtful the stalker would show up here, ringing the doorbell. Then again, maybe he or she would. Blade didn't know what to think anymore.

Tal opened the door. "May I help you?"

"Merry Christmas," a woman boomed. "You must be the bodyguard."

Tal glanced back for their approval. Blade was about to say he'd never seen this woman before, but Dani stepped forward. "This is my friend Rena." She hugged her. "Hey."

Rena held up a plate. "I brought you some chocolate. I figured it was the least I could do since you went to all the trouble of helping me make it."

Recognition dawned. "You're Dani's friend that she used to work with at the industrial park."

A bright smile tipped Rena's lips. "Yep, that's me." Her eyes sparkled. "And you must be the handsome movie star I keep hearing all about." She handed Dani the plate of chocolate and stepped up to Blade. He went to shake her hand, but she hugged him instead. "I've heard all about you," she drawled, giving Dani a coy smile.

It was cute how Dani's cheeks went rosy. Blade cocked his head. "You've been talking about me?"

Dani gave him a sheepish grin. "A little."

Rena waved a hand. "It was all good."

Dani placed the plate on the table.

Blade hoped the visit would be short. Not that he didn't want to get to know Dani's friend, but he was so flipping exhausted.

Dani stifled a yawn. "Excuse me."

Rena looked back and forth between Dani and Blade. "Is everything all right? You both look so worn out."

"It's been a rough day," Dani admitted.

Rena drew her brows together. "What happened?"

Blade was tempted to say they could talk about it another time, but Rena sat down in a chair. Dani sat down on the couch. Finally, Blade also sat down next to Dani. Tal took his seat back at the table.

Rena leaned forward slightly, waiting for Dani to speak.

"The boat we were on sank, and we nearly drowned," Dani began.

"What?" Rena's eyes bulged. She shook her head. "What happened?"

For the second time this evening, Dani and Blade told the story. When they were done, Rena just sat there, looking stunned. "I'm so glad you were okay. It's a miracle the fishing boat ran upon you."

"Yes."

"Do you care if I have one of these candies?" Tal asked.

Rena looked surprised, and a little put-out as she turned to Dani. "I brought those for you and Blade."

"It's okay," Dani said quickly. "We don't mind sharing. Tal's like family."

"Oh, okay," Rena said, but it was obvious she wasn't happy about it.

That was a strange reaction, and a little rude, Blade thought. Then again, maybe he was being overly sensitive since he was so tired. Rena and Dani chitchatted a few more minutes. Blade's eyelids were getting so heavy he could barely hold his eyes open. At this rate, he'd fall onto the floor. He must've nodded off because the next thing he knew, Dani was nudging him. "Hey, babe, you fell asleep." She turned to Rena. "I'm sorry, but we're both so exhausted."

Rena stood. "I guess so ... after everything that happened. Before I go, I'd really like for you both to try a piece of my chocolate."

Blade shook his head. "I would love some, but my stomach's still a little off. I'd better not."

Dani chuckled. "Yeah, you'd better not is right. I don't want a repeat of the bus fiasco."

"If I eat chocolate this late, that's probably what you'll get," Blade countered.

Dani flashed Rena an apologetic smile. "Unfortunately, I'm not feeling so great myself. We'll both eat some tomorrow. It'll be a nice treat for Christmas Eve."

Rena looked like she might argue, but smiled instead. "Sounds good. I'll let you two get some rest." She hugged Dani. "Merry Christmas, if I don't see you."

"Merry Christmas," Dani said.

"It was nice to meet you, Blade. I'm sure we'll meet again."

"For sure."

Blade let out a sigh of relief when Rena left. "I thought she'd never leave."

Dani made a face. "Be nice. She's my friend."

He put his arms around her. "I know. And she seems nice. But I'm exhausted."

"Me too. I was ready for her to go too," she admitted.

He cocked an eyebrow.

"So I could do this." She lifted her chin and planted a kiss on his lips.

He drew her close. "I love you so much."

"I love you too." She rested her head on his chest. "And I'm so tired," she groaned. "Let's watch a movie together and fall asleep on the couch. I don't want to be away from you for a minute."

"Good idea." Blade looked back over his shoulder. "Tal, you wanna watch a movie with us?"

"Sure. You care if I have one more of these chocolates? They're excellent."

"Help yourself," Dani laughed, shaking her head. "We'd better set our alarm. We've got to get new phones before the stores close tomorrow."

He groaned. "I forgot about that." Dani made Gibson promise not to breathe a word of the boat sinking to Finn until Dani had a chance to talk to Samantha. Blade was doubtful the weasel would keep his word. Dani was probably thinking the same thing, which is why she was so anxious to get to the store.

They sat down on the couch. Blade put his arm around Dani as she snuggled into the curve of his shoulder. They didn't make it past the first fifteen minutes of the movie before they were both sound asleep.

DANI JERKED when she heard the noise. She opened her eyes as she sat up and looked around, her heart pounding. She'd been having a nightmare where they were back in the water, a heavy weight pushing her deeper and deeper into the blackness of the ocean. She shivered, hugging her arms as she looked at Blade, sleeping beside her. Tal was in the overstuffed chair snoring loudly. Unease trickled over her. Had the sound been part of her dream? She flinched when she saw a shadow out of the corner of her eye. She let out a scream, grabbing Blade's arm.

Blade sat up in a daze. "What's wrong?"

Her voice was frozen as she pointed. The shadow stepped forward. Dani's stomach lurched when she saw the flash of metal and realized the person was holding a gun. Blade sprang to his feet.

"Hold it right there," a woman ordered.

Dani's mind reeled. She knew that voice. "Rena?"

Rena removed the hood from her head, her blonde hair catching the pale moonlight streaming in through the double-glass doors.

Dani stumbled to her feet, clutching Blade's arm. "W-what're you doing?" She felt like she'd left reality and entered some alien world where everything was turned upside down. A knot formed in the pit of Dani's stomach as she looked at the woman she'd thought was her friend. Hurt rankled her. "Why?"

Rena snorted. "This has nothing to do with you. You just happened to get in the way."

Dani looked at Tal, snoring loudly. Why was he still sleeping?

A snide laugh rumbled from Rena's lips as she followed Dani's trail of vision. "Lughead's down for the count. One too many chocolates." Her voice grew brittle. "If you had been a good little boy and girl and eaten your chocolates, you'd be sleeping peacefully right now and all of this would be so much easier."

"Meaning we'd be dead," Blade said, a hard edge to his voice. "Who are you? Is your name even Rena?"

She grunted. "Of course my name's Rena."

"Who are you working with?"

"With me." Doug stepped up beside Rena.

Dani heard Blade's sudden intake of breath. Realized the blow this must be to him. It was one thing to suspect your brother, but to watch it unfold before your very eyes was much, much worse. Panic raced over Dani, making her go weak in the knees as she used Blade to steady herself. They'd drugged Tal, so he was no use to them. Had he thought to arm the security system? She could only hope he had. The last time, it took the police forever to arrive. They'd be dead by the time they got here. After all she and Blade had been through, it seemed utterly unfair that they would die here in Samantha's living room.

"How could you do it?" Blade demanded, his voice shaking with fury. He balled his fists. "All these months, you pretended to be a stalker. Knowing how that would rattle me, considering how our mother died."

"Poetic justice, little brother." Doug's eyes narrowed to black slashes. "You took everything from me."

"What're you talking about? I took nothing from you."

"Our mother chose you instead of me." Doug's voice broke.

"That's a lie," Blade countered. "I was three years old when our parents divorced. The only reason Mom kept me was because Dad didn't know how to take care of a toddler."

Dani picked up on the note of disbelief in Blade's voice. A chill slithered down her spine. Doug was irrational. It would be impossible to reason with him.

Doug's voice escalated to a rant as he pointed to his chest. "It should've been me in the Jase Scott movie, instead of playing nursemaid to you." Rage contorted his features, making him look more monster than human. "Well, that's all about to change."

Blade swore under his breath and moved to pounce. He stopped cold when Rena's voice cracked like thunder through the room. "One more move, and you'll die this instant."

Doug laughed to himself. "I had you right where I wanted you, so tied up in knots you hardly knew your own name." He shot Dani an accusing look, hatred burning in his eyes. "Until she came along and ruined everything."

The room started to spin as Dani fought to steady herself.

"You leave Dani out of this," Blade roared.

"With your little cheerleader by your side, you could do no wrong," Doug continued as if Blade hadn't spoken. "You actually started acting, got chummy with Christian Ross. Dani transformed you into a new man," he sneered. A peculiar glint shone in his eyes as he smiled. "And sadly, she'll contribute to your death."

A sickening dread pulsed over Dani nearly closing off her throat. She swallowed, trying to get a good breath. Then her anger took hold when she realized Rena was studying her, a satisfied smirk on her face. Dani steeled herself up, meeting Rena's gaze. "What's your involvement in all this?"

Rena flashed a victorious smile. "You may be a spitfire, but you're not the sharpest tool in the shed, Dani. Doug and I are together in a relationship."

Rena had only been on the island a couple of months and was from Denver. Dani tried to make sense of it. "So you planned this whole thing from the beginning? Is that why you started working for Mr. Hadler, because I was there?"

"No, stupid," Rena snorted. "Our working together was just a coincidence. Believe it or not, I really was your friend." Her lips puckered. "Then in a crazy turn of events, you had to meet Blade and fall in love with him."

Dani's mind clicked through the events. "You didn't go to the hotel to get an autograph for your niece. You went to help Doug play stalker, didn't you? You're the one who left the roses and notes." She shook her head in disgust. "I can't believe I thought you were my friend." The betrayal hit her like a punch in the gut, making her sick.

"You won't get away with this," Blade said, keeping his eyes fixed on Doug. "The detectives were here earlier, they know it was an inside job, and that there was no stalker." His voice had the cutting edge of steel. "They know it was you, Doug."

For one blessed second, a sliver of uncertainty crept into Doug's eyes. Then he shook it off. "Like I said, you've gotten pretty good at acting." He barked out a laugh. "Too bad it happened too late to help you." He looked at Rena. "Let's get this over with."

The cold, dispassionate tone in Doug's voice was more terrifying to Dani than his rage. She scrambled for something to stall. "You're wrong about Blade," she shouted with all the indignation she could muster.

"Save your breath, Dani," Blade muttered, "it won't do any good."

"Maybe not, but at least I'll go down knowing I told this piece of crap exactly what I think of him." She eyed Doug. "Blade's got more talent in his pinky finger than you have in your whole body. And he's a pressure player. He was the only one who kept his cool when the boat went down." Emotion clogged her throat. "I may've helped Blade, but he saved me. He's the real hero."

"How sweet," Doug drawled, clapping fast at first then slowing down to a single clap. He chuckled in amusement as he looked at Blade. "Your lap dog has teeth."

Dani turned her wrath on Rena. "Do you think you can just shoot us and ride off into the sunset? The police will know it was you. They know Doug's accomplice is a blonde." The bite in her voice increased when she saw the alarm on Rena's face. "Someone saw you and Doug lurking around the house the night you broke in." She leaned

forward, shooting Rena a death glare. "The man's willing to testify."
Checkmate.

"She's bluffing," Doug said.

"No, brother, she's not," Blade added.

Rena started laughing, a high-pitched grating sound that peeled down Dani's skin. "That's the beauty of this whole thing. We'll shoot you, and after all is said and done, the police will think it's you."

Dani realized Rena was looking at her. She pointed to herself. "Me?" She huffed. "Yeah, right."

Rena sighed, outlining everything in slow speech like she was talking to a third grader. "The stalker, Dani, has one final gift for Blade, which she will leave next to Blade's lifeless body before she shoots herself. A rose in a gold box with a note explaining why she did it." She sniffed. "Sounds like something out of a Greek tragedy."

Dani felt the fingers of hysteria gripping the edges of her mind. She scoffed, trying to hide her terror. "You're crazy!"

"Am I?" A smug look came over Rena. "The rose and box have your fingerprints all over them."

Dani was about to say she didn't understand, but then it all came together in a hard blow. "The night we made candy, you were wearing gloves. I picked up the boxes off the floor after you knocked them off the counter and arranged the flowers for you." This whole thing was madness. But how could Dani have known Rena was setting a trap for her? And to think, she'd gone over there because she wanted to help a friend. *No good deed goes unpunished.*

A cruel smile twisted over Rena's lips. "Bingo."

"Get on with it," Doug said in a bored tone, like he was done with the whole thing.

Time seemed suspended as Blade barreled into Doug, knocking him back. Rena screamed, pointing the gun at Blade who was on the floor, trading blows with Doug. Before she could fire, Dani saw a blur of movement as Tal lunged at Rena and hit her with such force that it knocked her unconscious. Dani would later describe it as a bull playing kickball with a turkey.

Dani scrambled to get the gun. Just as she grasped it, the police pounded on the door and rushed in. The officers had to manhandle Blade who was on top of Doug, pounding his face over and over.

"Ma'am, I need you to put down the gun," the officer said. It took Dani's mind a second to register that she was holding it. "Oh, yeah." A shaky laugh escaped her throat as she let the gun fall noisily to the floor.

Tal stood, holding up his hands. "I'm a bodyguard," he explained in a calm, professional tone. "I'm going to pull out my wallet to show you my credentials."

"Easy," the officer warned, tightening his hold on his gun.

"Call Detectives Kalama and Ripley," Blade said flicking his wrists and rubbing his lacerated knuckles. An ugly bruise was spreading down the side of Blade's jaw, his right eye swollen. Not too bad, considering the situation. Doug, on the other hand, looked like he'd been bludgeoned with a sledge hammer.

One quick phone call to the detectives had Doug and Rena in cuffs, hauling them to jail. Blade stood in a battle stance, his jaw set in stone as he glared at Doug who wouldn't make eye contact with him.

Shakes rattled through Dani's entire body as she moved to the couch and slumped down. Blade sat down beside her. She reached for his hands, pulling them into her lap as she carefully placed her hands over his, being careful not to hurt his wounds. Then she realized he was also trembling.

"I knew Doug was mean and spiteful, but I didn't realize he was crazy ... or a murderer." Tears gathered in his eyes. The raw anguish in his voice sliced through Dani. She wished she could say something to take away the sting, but there were no words. His jaw started working as he cleared his throat. Then he pulled his hands out from beneath hers and wiped at the tears. She was surprised when a tiny smile touched his lips. The fierce look in his compelling eyes pierced her to the core. "I love you so much."

"I love you too," she uttered.

"What you said, about me being a hero..."

She touched a strand of hair that had fallen over his eye. "It was true. Every word of it," she added firmly.

"It's my fault we were put in that position to begin with."

The remorse in his eyes nearly moved her to tears. "No, it's not your fault." She squared her jaw. "You're the best thing that's ever happened to me. As for everything we've been through ..." A rueful chuckle tickled her throat. "Samantha always says I have a knack for finding trouble. I guess she's right." She sighed. "And to think I've tried so hard to be responsible."

A full smile broke over his lips, dispelling his former gloom. He slipped his arms around her. "You're a fighter, Dani Fairchild, my beautiful warrior. Don't ever change."

She chuckled. "Don't worry. For better or worse, I'm here to stay."

"I'm counting on that," he said, leaning in to kiss her.

EPILOGUE

Butterflies fanned Dani's stomach as the limousine pulled up to the curb. Her eye caught on the long, red carpet with herds of paparazzi crowded on each side. Dani sucked in a deep breath before adjusting the straps on her red evening gown. She hoped her designer dress would cut the mustard. It had certainly cost enough! She turned to Blade who looked like a million bucks in his tux. His dark hair was messy, just the way she liked it. A wicked grin tugged at his lips as his eyes roved over her in that leisurely way that melted her bones. He leaned in, his warm breath tickling her ear. "Maybe we should stay in the limousine." He nipped at her ear.

She giggled. "Don't mess up my hair."

"I can't wait to take it down later," he murmured.

Tal was sitting directly across from them. He grimaced. "Hey, don't forget I'm right here, hearing every word."

Dani chuckled. "You'd think you'd be used to us by now, Tal."

He waved a hand, rolling his eyes. "Yeah, yeah," he huffed, but Dani caught his subtle smile, knew their open affection didn't bother him one iota. Blade had brought Tal on as his permanent bodyguard. The more time they spent around him, the more they really did feel like he was family. For Dani, he was the big brother she'd never had.

Her thoughts flitted over the past few months. On the official closing day of filming for the Jase Scott movie—just as Dani was celebrating the fact that Eden Howard would be officially out of their lives and onto another movie—Blade got down on one knee and whipped out a diamond so large it could've lit up the Waikiki skyline. Then he asked Dani to marry him. She yelled out, "Yes" so fast he had to tell her to wait so he could get the whole proposal out.

Unwilling to leave her beloved Hawaii, they reached a compromise. Dani would go with him on location while he was filming, and they'd live in Hawaii the rest of the time. The good news was that Dani could operate her blog from anywhere, providing she had Internet and a good kitchen. Now that news had leaked of Dani and Blade's engagement, her blog was getting tons of attention. Of course, it didn't hurt that Everly had been guest blogging with her. It irked Dani that it took having Hollywood connections for her blog to take off, but there wasn't much she could do about that—except simply smile and enjoy it. And count it as a blessing. Dani had even gotten a call from Chef Ray a week prior, asking if she wanted to do some co-op blog posts with him. While she was tempted to tell the little man to take a flying leap, she held her tongue and politely told him that she'd consider it, and get back to him. Samantha was pleased with how responsibly Dani had handled the situation.

The only dark spots on the horizon were Doug and Rena. Both were awaiting trial. When the trials commenced, Dani feared the media would turn it into a circus. It would be hard on Blade, but they'd get through it together.

"You look incredible." Blade touched a lock of hair, trailing from her messy bun. "I love your hair up." He frowned. "There's only one problem."

She quirked an eyebrow, getting the feeling she was waiting for a punch line. "Oh, yeah?"

"This is supposed to be my movie premiere, and everyone will be watching you."

She touched his jaw, giving it a pat as she winked. "You are charming, blue eyes. No wonder all the girls love you."

Lightly, he touched the tip of her nose. "I only have eyes for you."

"And I, for you."

A crooked grin slid over his lips, his eyes sparkling with adventure. "You ready?"

She stilled the butterflies in her stomach, flashing a radiant smile. "Bring it on."

When they stepped out of the limousine, Blade linked his fingers through hers. As they smiled and waved at the cameras, Dani knew that so long as they were together, there was nothing in this world they couldn't accomplish.

GET the entire series of Hawaii Billionaire Romance in one collection HERE.

GET YOUR FREE BOOK

Hey there, thanks for taking the time to read *Loving the Movie Star* from the Hawaii Billionaire Romance Series. If you enjoyed it, please take a minute to give me a review on Amazon. I really appreciate your feedback, as I depend largely on word of mouth to promote my books.

Loving the Movie Star is a stand-alone novel, but you'll also enjoy reading the other books in the Hawaii Billionaire Romance Series.

Love on the Rocks

Love on the Rebound

Love at the Ocean Breeze

Love Changes Everything

Love Him or Lose Him

Loving the Movie Star

If you sign up for our newsletter, we will give you one of our books, Beastly Charm: A contemporary retelling of beauty & the beast, for FREE. Plus, you'll get information on discounts and other freebies. For more information, visit:

http://bit.ly/freebookjenniferyoungblood

BONUS EXCERPT OF LOVE UNDER FIRE (A COMPANION BOOK TO THE HAWAII BILLIONAIRE SERIES)

Peyton couldn't help but feel like Cinderella as her gaze took in the opulent surroundings of the courtyard at the Webster Mansion. Twinkling white lights and thin strips of gauzy fabric adorned the gazebo and trellis, adding a dreamlike quality to the warm evening. A live orchestra played soft music in the background, and the tender scent of fresh flowers filled the night air. Stars shimmered brilliantly above, applauding the happy occasion of her upcoming wedding.

Peyton looked down at her exquisite mango-colored dress and couldn't resist swishing discreetly from side to side, loving how the wind whooshed underneath the silk fabric. She felt as buoyant as a balloon, soaring high and free, where nothing bad could touch her. It was still hard to believe she was marrying Carter tomorrow.

His mother, Kathryn, had been vehemently opposed to the union, but was starting to come around. This party at Kathryn's sprawling mansion was her gift to Carter and Peyton. It meant the world to Peyton that Kathryn was finally accepting her.

Peyton straightened her shoulders as she nodded and smiled at the mayor and his high-society wife. She straightened her back. A part of her wondered if she'd ever feel completely at home in Carter's glitzy world of mansions, expensive cars, and spontaneous trips to

Europe. It boggled Peyton's mind that Carter could just up and go anywhere he wanted when it had taken six months of planning, scrimping, and saving for her family to drive nine hours to Disneyland.

Peyton was sure there would be battles to fight when it came to the differences in their upbringing, but she was confident her and Carter's love was strong enough to see them through the rough spots. They'd weathered their fair share of storms already. She scanned the sea of faces, relieved when her eyes found a familiar face, Mr. Labrum. Her high school English teacher smiled and waved as he walked over and gave her a one-armed hug.

"Good evening," he said stiffly. "You look lovely as always." He pushed his inch-thick glasses back up on his nose and cleared his throat like he was about to deliver an important speech.

"Beauty, sweet Love, is like the morning dew,

Whose short refresh upon the tender green

Cheers for a time, but till the sun doth show,

And straight 'tis gone as it had never been."

Peyton laughed. "Thanks ... I think."

"A sonnet by Samuel Daniel, born in 1562."

"Oh, I haven't heard that one," said Payton. A self-confirmed, life-long bachelor, Art Labrum spent his life buried in a book. Socially awkward, with a ruler-straight part in his oiled hair, he reminded Peyton of George McFly from the movie *Back to the Future*. Mr. Labrum's eccentricities made him an easy target for the meaner kids in high school, but Peyton had always liked him. She found his quirks endearing, and he was kind and helpful to his students.

"You know, Peyton, I had a feeling you and Carter would end up together the first time I caught you locking lips in the supply cabinet." He wagged a finger, a smile creeping over his lips.

Peyton chuckled. "Yeah, you weren't too happy about that. Made us do two rounds of detention, if I remember correctly."

He snorted. "Oh, the foibles of youth. To be—" He stopped mid-sentence, looking thoughtful. "You know, the two of you remind me a little of Mr. Darcy and Elizabeth Bennett. You have my sincerest congratulations. It's not often that people have the fortitude to defy convention and follow their hearts."

"There she is ... the lady of the hour," a female voice squealed.

Peyton turned to see two girls about her age approaching.

"How sweet you look tonight," the pretty blonde bubbled. Her dress was poured on—so tight Peyton doubted she could sit down.

"I'm sorry. Do we know each other?"

The girl touched Peyton's arm. "I'm Claire and this is Mindy."

Mr. Labrum shrank into himself. "Well, I must be going," he said in a formal tone. He gave Peyton a slight bow before shuffling away.

Peyton turned her attention to the two girls, her mood dampening slightly. She'd rather endure Mr. Labrum's long quotes a hundred times over than be forced into making small talk with strangers. Then again, maybe she was missing out on a friendship. They were part of Carter's world, and she was about to marry into it. She'd better start developing her own contacts. "It's nice to meet you," she said, in a voice that sounded falsely cheerful to her own ears. "Are you friends of Carter's?"

Claire smirked. "You could say that. Carter and I used to date."

Peyton tensed. "Really? He never mentioned you."

An easy laugh escaped Claire's lips. "You know how Carter is. He probably didn't want to upset you." She waved a hand. "Anyway, it was a thousand years ago. Water under the bridge."

Peyton lifted an eyebrow. And yet she chose to mention it now. *Interesting.*

"You're so lucky," Claire chirped, turning to Mindy. "Doesn't she look darling?" She zeroed in on Peyton. "I'll bet you look good in any old thing. I saw your same dress on the clearance rack at Dillard's last season. Only a short girl like you could pull off wearing it. I had to have something specially made by my designer to fit my tiny waist."

Mindy sniggered while Claire fluffed her curls, her lips forming a sultry pout. "I always wondered what kind of girl had enough torque to lasso Carter Webster." She looked Peyton up and down. "Huh," she mused softly. "Just goes to show, you never can tell what's going to make love click."

Mindy giggled and lurched forward. "Funny!" she gasped, wiping at her eyes.

Peyton's cheeks warmed. *All right—I'm done playing nice.* She looked Claire in the eye and smiled brightly as if she were in a toothpaste commercial. "And sometimes, dresses are like clunker cars—no matter how much money you pour into them, they'll never be a classic."

Claire's face turned scarlet like she might have a heat stroke.

Peyton was about to excuse herself when strong arms encircled her waist from behind. She looked back as Carter leaned in, tickling her ear with his warm breath.

"Hey, I've been looking for you. We're about ready to do the toast."

"Oh, I've just been getting acquainted with your old girlfriend."

He jerked. "My what?"

Peyton motioned. "Claire. According to her, the two of you were thick as thieves."

Carter's eyes went large, and Claire suddenly took interest in someone across the way as she caught hold of Mindy's arm. "Oh, look, there's Steven." With a sniff, she cut her eyes at Peyton and Carter. "Well, it was great to see you both. Congratulations again," she quipped, as she and Mindy scattered.

Peyton chuckled dryly. "Yeah, just as I thought."

Carter shook his head, amusement twinkling in his gray eyes. "Peyton," he hummed in a low tone, "what've you been up to?"

She laughed. "She started it."

He pulled her close, gazing into her eyes. "I have no doubt. Poor Claire got more than she bargained for when she tangled with you."

The corners of her lips turned down. "Poor Claire, my eye!" She spiked an eyebrow. "So you did date her?"

"We might've gone out once or twice." A devilish glint lit his eyes. "Not jealous, are you?"

She scowled. "Hardly."

"Don't worry. I only have eyes for you." He leaned in, his voice going husky. "You are so beautiful. I can't wait to get you to myself."

She laughed, a tingle of anticipation circling down her spine. "The minute we say *I do*, I'm all yours."

"I'm counting on it." Carter pulled her closer, swaying to the beat of the music, his eyes locking with hers. "I love you, Peyton Kelly. I always have, and I always will."

"I love you too." Peyton felt her heart swell to the point of exploding. She'd never been this happy. He was so handsome she could hardly breathe when running her fingers through his thick mane of dark blond hair. She loved his strong jaw, with just enough stubble to give him a rough-and-tumble charm, and his kind eyes lit up and flowed warmth when he smiled. He was smart, attentive, witty, and—miracle of miracles—he loved her!

"Ladies and gentlemen, I'd like to make a toast."

Peyton and Carter looked toward the portable stage where Carter's mother, Kathryn, stood, looking regal in a sleek black dress, hair twisted in a chignon. She held a glass of wine in one hand and a microphone in the other.

A waiter offered Peyton and Carter a glass. Peyton was about to decline when Carter whispered in her ear, "It's sparkling water." He winked. "I got your back." Carter knew how much Peyton detested alcohol on account of her alcoholic stepfather.

"Thank you," she mouthed.

"I so appreciate all of you joining us this evening to celebrate the union of my son Carter and the lovely Peyton Kelly." Kathryn paused as if collecting her thoughts. "I'm not ashamed to admit that at first I wasn't sure how Carter and Peyton's relationship would work."

Peyton stiffened, not sure where this was going. She saw Carter's jaw clench and his arm tightened protectively around her waist.

A magnanimous smile stretched over Kathryn's lips. "But seeing them together, it's obvious the two of you love each other very much."

Her eyes went misty. "And I suppose that's what it's all about—true love." She lifted her glass. "May you have a lifetime of happiness and joy."

Applause broke out around them. "Speech!" a man bellowed from behind.

"Speech!" another man repeated, and then the crowd started chanting it.

Carter held up a hand to quiet the crowd. "Okay, a speech it is." He clasped Peyton's hand and pulled her to the stage, where Kathryn handed him the microphone.

Carter peered over the crowd. "Is someone here getting married?" he asked dubiously, eliciting ripples of laughter.

Peyton gave him a playful shove.

"Seriously, I'm the luckiest man alive. Tomorrow, I'm marrying the woman of my dreams." His voice caught as he turned to Peyton, sincerity shining in his gray eyes. "Thank you for taking a chance on me. I promise I won't let you down."

Peyton's eyes teared up as she nodded.

Carter handed Peyton the microphone. "Your turn."

A commotion went through the crowd. Peyton looked toward the back to see what was happening. Her heart lurched when she saw Harold, her stepfather, staggering through the guests. He mumbled incoherently and pointed toward the stage.

For a second, Peyton was paralyzed with humiliation. Her fairy-tale evening had suddenly turned into a nightmare as she thrust the microphone at Carter and rushed down the steps of the stage to Harold's side. The crowd parted, equal looks of horror and disgust carpeting her way.

"What're you doing?" she seethed. "You need to leave!"

Check and *courtyard* were the only two words Peyton could make out of his garbled speech. She tried to take his arm, but he jerked out of her grasp. Pushing her away, he sent her sprawling backwards, where she landed on her rear end, her beautiful mango dress bunched around her legs.

"Hey!" Carter jumped off the stage and put Harold in a chokehold. Harold tried to resist, but his efforts were futile. Two security guards ran in, took Harold from Carter, and dragged him off the grounds.

"Are you all right?" Carter asked, helping Peyton to her feet.

Tears stung her eyes as she nodded. The twinkling lights, so romantic earlier, now blared. The place was spinning, menacing faces closing in around her. She caught sight of Claire and Mindy's triumphant sneers. Peyton could only imagine what they must be thinking. "I need to go to the bathroom," she hiccupped.

Carter took her arm. "Okay, I'll go with you."

The overseer of the wineries, a silver-haired man with hard eyes, stepped up to Carter. "I'm sorry to interrupt, but can I talk to you for a moment ..." He lowered his voice. "About the incident."

Carter looked like he might protest until Peyton put a hand on his arm. "It's okay," she said quickly. "I'll be right back." She needed a little space to pull herself together.

Carter searched her face. "You sure?"

She offered a tight smile. "Yeah."

"Okay," Carter said reluctantly. "I'll be right here."

Peyton attempted to go to the guest bathroom off the foyer, but it was occupied. A maid directed her to another, more private bathroom in the back section of the mansion.

After Peyton composed herself, she had to fight the temptation to head home. Instinctively, she knew if she didn't go back out and show her face tonight, she'd never be able to look these people in the eye again. There'd never been any love lost between Peyton and Harold, even though she'd never outright hated him. But at this moment, she did.

And she was super ticked at her mother. Her mom refused to come to tonight's party because she detested Kathryn Webster. The last Peyton heard, Harold was staying home, too. Why did he have to pick tonight, of all nights, to show up here? Had Peyton's mother come to the party, she might've been able to keep Harold in check before he made a buffoon of himself.

When Peyton left the bathroom, she heard voices coming from the nearby study. She almost walked on by when she heard her name. She halted in her tracks, easing toward the door.

Carter was sitting in the overstuffed chair, his back towards Peyton. Kathryn was standing over him, her expression livid. A catering cart was parked just outside the double French doors, preventing Peyton from getting closer. She attempted to push it aside, but it wouldn't budge. Peyton craned her neck to see inside, without being seen.

Kathryn's voice was harsh, her face pinched. "I've never been so humiliated in my entire life. I told you, it's never going to work with Peyton. She's not like us. You come from two different worlds. I know you feel obligated to her." She held up a finger. "Don't try to deny it, because I can see it in your eyes. That's the problem with you, Carter: you're too good-hearted. You feel sorry for Peyton, but this can't continue. Otherwise, you'll end up resenting her in the end."

Heat stung Peyton's face as she waited for Carter to respond.

What Peyton saw and heard next would be branded in her mind forever as her world shattered to pieces. A tremor started in her hands and rippled through her body. Tears sprang to her eyes as she gulped down a sob and ran the other direction. Her only thought was to get as far away from Carter Webster as possible.

Continue reading HERE.

BOOKS BY JENNIFER YOUNGBLOOD

Check out Jennifer's Amazon Page:
http://bit.ly/jenniferyoungblood

Georgia Patriots Romance
The Hot Headed Patriot
The Twelfth Hour Patriot

O'Brien Family Romance
The Impossible Groom (Chas O'Brien)
The Twelfth Hour Patriot (McKenna O'Brien)
Rewriting Christmas (A Novella)
Yours By Christmas (Park City Firefighter Romance)
Her Crazy Rich Fake Fiancé

Navy SEAL Romance
The Resolved Warrior
The Reckless Warrior
The Diehard Warrior

The Jane Austen Pact

Seeking Mr. Perfect

Texas Titan Romances
The Hometown Groom
The Persistent Groom
The Ghost Groom
The Jilted Billionaire Groom
The Impossible Groom
The Perfect Catch (Last Play Series)

Hawaii Billionaire Series
Love Him or Lose Him
Love on the Rocks
Love on the Rebound
Love at the Ocean Breeze
Love Changes Everything
Loving the Movie Star
Love Under Fire (A Companion book to the Hawaii Billionaire Series)

Kisses and Commitment Series
How to See With Your Heart

Angel Matchmaker Series
Kisses Over Candlelight
The Cowboy and the Billionaire's Daughter

Romantic Thrillers
False Identity
False Trust
Promise Me Love
Burned

Contemporary Romance
Beastly Charm

Fairytale Retellings (The Grimm Laws Series)
    Banish My Heart **(This book is FREE)**
    The Magic in Me
    Under Your Spell
    A Love So True

Southern Romance
    Livin' in High Cotton
    Recipe for Love

The Second Chance Series
    Forgive Me (Book 1)
    Love Me (Book 2)

Short Stories
    The Southern Fried Fix

ABOUT JENNIFER YOUNGBLOOD

Jennifer loves reading and writing clean romance. She believes that happily ever after is not just for stories. Jennifer enjoys interior design, rollerblading, clogging, jogging, and chocolate. In Jennifer's opinion there are few ills that can't be solved with a warm brownie and scoop of vanilla-bean ice cream.

Jennifer grew up in rural Alabama and loved living in a town where "everybody knows everybody." Her love for writing began as a young teenager when she wrote stories for her high school English teacher to critique.

Jennifer has BA in English and Social Sciences from Brigham Young University where she served as Miss BYU Hawaii in 1989. Before becoming an author, she worked as the owner and editor of a monthly newspaper named *The Senior Times*.

She now lives in the Rocky Mountains with her family and spends her time writing and doing all of the wonderful things that make up the life of a busy wife and mother.

facebook.com/authorjenniferyoungblood

twitter.com/authorjenn1

instagram.com/authorjenniferyoungblood